IT WAS ALWAYS YOU

ALEXA RIVERS

*To all the little girls out there who'd rather
play with test tubes than lipstick.*

Dr. Avery Brown strode down the long, white corridor toward her laboratory at the far end of the building—located to better keep her samples separate from any sources of contamination. She arrived at a heavy glass door and frowned. In the intermediary room between the corridor and the laboratory, the cleaning equipment had been knocked over and the mop lay on the floor.

How odd.

A strict protocol managed entry into, and egress from, her laboratory, and only three people were authorized to use it—two, if you excluded Avery. Each of those people knew better than to leave a mess behind. Cautiously, she pushed open the door, reached for a pair of sterile booties, slipped them onto her feet and stepped inside. The door clicked shut behind her. She selected nitrile gloves from the floor and donned them—better than nothing—then shimmied into full-body coveralls, careful not to touch the exterior of the fabric. Finally, she tied a face mask at the back of her head and pulled a second pair of gloves over the first, spraying her hands with ethanol to disinfect them.

Then she opened the door and stopped dead. Oh. My. *God.*

Now she could see what she hadn't before: her entire laboratory was in absolute chaos. Her precious instruments, spectrometers, and separation devices had been knocked over, materials thrown off shelves, and all of her glassware smashed. The air flew out of her lungs as if she'd entered a vacuum.

"Shit," she gasped, dropping to her knees, heedless of the transfer of contaminants from the floor to her coveralls. She felt a tightness in her chest and reminded herself to breathe. With difficulty, she hauled in a lungful of air through the face mask.

Vandals. It had to be. They'd left nothing untouched. If there had been an accident or natural event, *something* would have remained intact, but looking around, her heart lodged in her throat at the sheer extent of the damage. Hell and damnation. Whoever had done this either hated *her,* hated *science,* or had a very specific reason for their actions and wanted to make sure they left no stone unturned.

She stilled, her hand at her chest. *A specific reason.* Like avoiding a murder conviction. Realization dawned. Stumbling to her feet, she raced over to the chiller where she kept the library of soil samples she'd gathered from around New Zealand—two years' worth of work. A cry tore from her throat. The chiller door was ajar and every tray of samples had been upended, the glass vials either broken or open, their integrity hopelessly compromised.

No. This could not be happening. The culmination of years of planning and hard work, destroyed, in one night. How was it possible? Her brain whirred, going a million miles an hour. Every vial of soil she'd collected for her groundbreaking mapping system was in this laboratory, amidst the mess of dirt on the floor and shelves. Every carefully catalogued sample, some from the most remote and difficult-to-access locations in the country. Places she'd gone to herself, to ensure everything was done exactly as it should be, because her work was nationally critical and she couldn't afford any errors.

It was all ruined. Tears burned the backs of her eyes. No, she couldn't think like that. She blinked them away, knelt and sifted through the soil scattered on the floor until she located the vial from the Christchurch Police Department. It had been smashed to smithereens like the rest, the precious soil forming part of a homogenous layer. Fury coursed through her. That sample had been the police's best hope of finding Millie Grant, a young backpacker who'd vanished, presumed dead, and nailing the man suspected of her murder. It had been Avery's job to use the soil, taken from a spade found in the suspect's car, to find the burial site. Without a body, the police had squat.

She sucked in a breath. They must have another sample saved somewhere, and she'd get her hands on it. She could still help the girl's family get closure. Even if there wasn't another sample, she'd done enough preliminary testing to know the general area the soil had originated from. Nothing specific enough to find the body, but if a body was found by other means, she could speak to the likelihood of the spade having been used at the burial site.

She wouldn't let this beat her. She'd get justice for Millie Grant.

But not for the dozens of other victims her work would have helped. Her program had been heralded as the tool that could help revolutionize law enforcement by people at the very top of the legal system. And now this. Squeezing her eyes shut, Avery fisted her hands. Regardless of what had happened to her meticulously curated collection of soil samples, she still had the online database of results she'd gathered. The physical and chemical characteristics of the soil samples and the locations they'd come from.

But would her program still stand up to scientific and legal scrutiny if no one could verify it by peer-reviewing the results using the original soil samples? She swore. It was unlikely. She'd have to obtain more funding and start over.

Years of painstaking research, wasted. Had the vandal considered how much manual labor had been required to gather samples, transport them safely back to her laboratory without corrupting them, refine them by sieving, and carry out dozens of testing procedures? For months, her hands and feet had been blistered from the hiking and sieving. All for nothing. Despair threatened to overwhelm her.

It won't be for nothing. She'd make sure of it.

Picking herself up, Avery stepped around the remains of her sample library and crossed to the isotope ratio mass spectrometer, the most precious instrument in her lab. It looked like someone had taken a cricket bat to it. She swallowed, her tongue uncomfortably thick in her mouth.

"Not Old Faithful," she rasped, trying not to cry. Crying would serve no purpose. Instead, she mentally cataloged the damage. The instrument would need to be replaced, as would the High Performance Liquid Chromatograph connected to a computer on the next counter. While Old Faithful allowed Avery to determine the breakdown of isotopes in soil samples, her High Performance Liquid Chromatograph, affectionately referred to as The Beast, showed which organic molecules were present.

She'd need new glassware. And a new computer monitor, she added, noticing a metal pipe had been rammed through the screen. Then, with a heavy sense of dread, she opened the cabinet beneath the monitor. Her knees went weak with relief. Her first bit of good luck. She'd hardly dared to hope for it. The computer brain hadn't been touched, which meant she could disconnect it and attach it to a new monitor to retrieve any saved information. Her primary electronic database was intact. Hallelujah.

Buoyed a little, she moved on, edging around the shards of broken glassware strewn on the floor. She noted the personal protective equipment and basic gear—tweezers, syringes, mortar and pestles, test tube racks—hadn't been damaged, just thrown about. Her acid supply, in a cabinet labeled "dangerous goods" was also untouched. A pity. For one ferocious moment, she wished the vandal had been stupid enough to open the cabinet and smash the bottles within. The searing burn of ultra-concentrated sulfuric acid on skin might have given him a taste of the visceral pain she felt at the sight of her life's work in pieces, and her orderly lab in total disarray.

Avery wanted to yank her hair out and scream with frustration, or alternatively, make an inventory of what needed replacing so she could get back in business. But neither of those things was what she *needed* to do. Given the circumstances, she needed to alert her contact in the police force and let them do their thing. This laboratory was no longer her workplace, it was a crime scene.

An angry burn started in her chest at the thought of allowing a bunch of clumsy cops, who didn't know the correct protocols and precautions, into her lab, but she needed to accept the facts: whoever else had been in here hadn't observed protocol. Everything was hopelessly compromised already. She would just have to make the call and undertake a full cleaning, sterilizing, and decontamination procedure once they'd completed their investigation.

She pushed back the hood of her coveralls and unzipped the front. Then she peeled off her gloves—god, it felt so wrong to do that without leaving the lab—and reached for her phone. She found Inspector Adaline Rata's number and pressed call.

"Inspector Rata," the woman snapped, answering on the second ring.

"Inspector," Avery said. "It's Dr. Brown here. There's been

an incident at my laboratory." She swallowed the lump in her throat. "Someone vandalized it."

She didn't say more, allowing Rata the time to think.

"Extent of damage?" Rata asked, getting straight to the point. This was why Avery liked the inspector. She didn't ask for extraneous detail and didn't beat around the bush. All she needed was logic and facts.

"Severe. The sample from the Grant case is compromised, and so is my entire library of samples. My instruments will need to be replaced, but I still have the soil database safe on the computer storage system."

Avery waited a moment for Rata to process that. While Avery's laboratory was owned by a private company, the government had funded her recent research, so the loss of her samples affected Rata as well as Avery.

"At least you have the data. I assume you've come to the conclusion that this is related to the Grant case?"

"It wouldn't surprise me, but it's best not to assume these things." A scientist should approach everything from a strictly unbiased viewpoint. Of course, the suspect in the Grant case, Dwayne Broderick, faced a murder conviction if the trial run of Avery's mapping program was successful, so he had the most to gain by ruining her work.

"I agree, Dr. Brown, on both points. I'll send a unit to you immediately to see if the perp left any evidence behind. Have you moved or touched anything?"

"I entered the lab wearing PPE—that's personal protective equipment—and circled the room to determine how much damage had been done, but I haven't touched anything except a cabinet door and the floor. I was wearing gloves."

"Good." Rata's tone was approving.

The two women shared a mutual respect. Being women in male-dominated fields could be difficult, but they'd both found their way—Rata through her determination and take-no-shit attitude, and Avery through her sharp mind, sharper tongue, and the fact she often came across as one of the guys.

"Stay put. You can expect a unit to arrive in five minutes. Meet them at the door and be sure to cooperate, but remember, your work for us is confidential. You don't tell any of those uniforms anything that could be sensitive without checking in with me first. Got it?"

She resisted the urge to salute. "Yes, Inspector."

"Thank you." A moment of silence, then Rata added, "I'm sorry this has happened."

"Don't be sorry," Avery said. "Just catch the bastard."

"I'll do everything in my power to make that happen."

They hung up. Avery pocketed her phone, zipped the coveralls, and waited.

Sergeant Gareth Wayland slowed his police cruiser to a stop beside the picnic area adjoining Lake Itirangi, an expanse of glacial blue water that formed the boundary of the township by the same name. It translated to "Little Sky" in Te Reo, the language of New Zealand's Maori people. He wound down the window and leaned out.

"Mrs. Dodds," he called. The frail white-haired lady trying to coax her feisty feline Milo down from a tree didn't turn. "Mrs. Dodds!" he called again, more loudly.

She looked over her shoulder, then smiled. "Sergeant," she said. "How lovely. You have the best timing. Do you think you could rescue my Milo for me? He's gotten stuck again, and I do worry he might fall and hurt himself. He's terrified, poor dear."

Gareth wondered if Mrs. Dodds' vision was failing as well as her hearing. Milo was decidedly *not* terrified. The ginger tomcat hissed and spat as though he'd gladly tear Gareth limb from limb. But Mrs. Dodds tilted her face up hopefully and the thick glasses that sat askew on her nose magnified her pleading eyes to twice their normal size. He sighed. Once again, he'd be going up a tree after her damn cat.

"Sure thing, Mrs. Dodds," he said, getting out of the car and taking a deep breath to fortify himself. Being a cop in a small town meant, first and foremost, taking the residents' problems seriously. "I'll have Milo down in just a moment."

Wrapping his palm around a branch above his head, he hefted himself up the trunk and wedged his foot into the split between the trunk and the first branch. Slowly, he ascended another two branches, arriving at the one Milo clung to. His left foot slipped and a nerve twinged in his bad knee. He grimaced.

You knew this was going to happen, he reminded himself. *As soon as you stopped the car, you knew you'd end up here.*

And yet, there he was. Like a masochist. Or the lone policeman of a practically crime-free town, whom the locals viewed as their personal errand boy. Tugging the ends of his uniform shirt over his palms to protect them as much as possible from Milo's claws, Gareth inched along the branch and reached for the cat, who yowled the instant they touched.

"Be careful with him," Mrs. Dodds called, her voice warbling. "He's very fragile."

He studied the furious kitty, with his fluffy coat and squishy belly. "Fragile, my ass," he muttered. Then he grabbed the cat.

Though he expected it, nothing could have prepared him for the pain of four sharply-clawed feet digging into his arms as Milo struggled to break free. He switched hands, holding Milo up by the scruff of his neck, and the cat quieted. *That's more like it.* It had taken a year to learn this trick. Twelve months, during which he'd spilled more blood than he rightly should have.

Holding the cat far away from his body, Gareth backtracked down the tree and jumped, landing on the ground with a thud, the vibrations causing a dull ache in his left knee.

"Here you are," he said to Mrs. Dodds, handing the hateful creature over. "Safe and sound."

Of course, Milo immediately curled into her arms and purred happily. Little demon.

"Thank you, dear," she replied. "You know how much I appreciate it." She smoothed a hand over the cat's head and ruffled his fur. "Say, my great-niece is visiting this weekend. Lovely girl. Wish I saw her more often. Why don't you come and have dinner with us?"

"Gee, thanks for the offer," Gareth began, "but I'm on duty this weekend." He shrugged as if to say, "what can you do?". "Someone needs to keep this place safe."

Her lips firmed into a line. "Oh, but can't someone else cover your shift for just one night? I promise you'll like my Camille."

He shook his head sorrowfully. "Afraid they can't, Mrs. Dodds. I'm sure I'll be able to meet Camille some other time." He tipped his hat to her. "You have a good day, now."

Spinning on his heel, he strode back to the cruiser. He had, in fact, met Camille Dodds before, and she was a lovely girl. Lovely, but not for him. Just like all of the other pretty young relatives the local biddies tried to set him up with. The fact was, he was happy single. Or if not happy, then at least, not unhappy.

Static crackled on his radio and he paused to listen.

"Attention all. A break-in has been reported at Sandiford's Laboratory on Walsh Street. Nothing missing so far, but part of the property has been vandalized. Unit seven, please respond. Repeat, unit seven, please report to the site immediately."

Gareth frowned. Sandiford's Laboratory was where his ex-girlfriend, Avery Brown, worked.

Avery.

Even thinking her name brought a wave of complicated emotions washing over him. Tenderness and concern, because she was the only girl he'd ever connected with on a soul-deep level. Confusion and frustration, because he'd always thought they'd reunite one day, but she treated him as nothing more than a distant acquaintance.

The call repeated. Unit seven being requested to cease any other activities and respond immediately. Interesting. Unit seven was the highest ranked unit in the district and boasted a pair of top-notch cops, one of whom was forensically trained. Their being assigned made no sense, in the circumstances. Why would two highly decorated officers be sent to handle a simple case of breaking, entering, and vandalism?

Unless it wasn't so simple.

Against his better judgment, he found himself doing a U-turn and heading toward Sandiford's Laboratory. He wasn't nearby, but if Avery was in trouble, he needed to be there. Switching the sirens on, he increased speed and raced toward the nearby town of Timaru, and Avery.

When he arrived, unit seven were already on the scene. He parked outside and hurried into the building, flashing his badge to the recruit on the door. He entered a long corridor with clinically white walls and sighted a uniformed officer at the far end. The officer stood beside a door that was ajar. Even from a distance, he could see that the laboratory had been trashed. Someone had done a number on it with a blunt object and a whole lot of rage.

Senior Constable Nathan Lang hovered inside, wearing his usual unflappable expression, but Gareth spotted something different in his eyes. Something fascinating. *Nerves.* But why would a veteran officer be nervous?

As he passed through the doorway, he began to understand. Facing Lang, hands balled in fists at her sides, jaw clenched, speaking through gritted teeth, was his high school sweetheart.

Yeah, so maybe "sweetheart" wasn't the right word. She was a dynamo.

"I know you have an investigation to complete," Avery Brown ground out, oblivious to his presence. "All I'm saying is, perhaps you could be a little more careful around my terribly expensive, world-class equipment."

"With all due respect, ma'am—"

"Ma'am?" she interrupted, clearly mad enough to spit tacks, her blue eyes like icy beams of fury. "Ma'am? I'm a doctor. I call you by your title, because I know how hard you worked to earn it, and I'd appreciate it if you did the same."

Lang glanced up at the roof, his lips moving silently as though whispering a prayer for patience. "My apologies, *Doctor*," he said, and though Avery had pushed his buttons, Gareth could tell she'd also earned his grudging respect. "But as you can see, your world-class equipment is already damaged beyond repair."

His tone wasn't unsympathetic, but Avery's laser-beam eyes narrowed. "Don't make anything worse," she snapped. "Your partner over there," she gestured vaguely behind herself, "is competent. How about you leave handling the equipment to him?"

Lang nodded shortly. "I can do that, ma'am—uh, Doctor."

Finally, her gaze ventured away from Lang's face and swept to the side, focusing on Gareth. As usual, she momentarily stole his ability to speak. Even dressed in a full-body suit with her long brown hair tucked inside a hairnet, she was stunning. Though that couldn't be attributed only to the way she looked, but also to the gleam of intelligence in her eyes and the way she held herself like she'd never experienced a moment of self-doubt in her life.

"Sergeant Wayland," she said, crossing her arms over her chest, her expression going from cold to downright arctic.

He didn't like it, the way she tended to clam up around him. He had no clue why she felt the need to.

"Wayland," Lang said with a nod.

"Lang," he replied.

"Didn't realize you were coming," Lang remarked.

"I was in the area."

Neither of them acknowledged the fact that if that had been the case, he wouldn't have taken twenty minutes to arrive.

"You know *Dr.* Brown?" Lang asked, emphasizing Avery's title.

"I do. We grew up together."

"Ah." A shrewd light entered his eyes. "I see. Perhaps you can encourage her to be a little more forthcoming about the work she carries out here."

Gareth glanced at Avery and her chin jutted out defiantly. He was surprised to realize he didn't actually know what she did, beyond it being some kind of chemistry. Somehow, despite all the events they'd attended that had been hosted by mutual friends, she'd never shared details and he'd never asked.

"What are you working on, A-Bee?" he asked, the old nickname slipping out by mistake. When she scowled, he wished he could take it back. He'd undermined her authority in front of Lang.

"Like I told your buddy here, it's classified." Her eyebrows clashed over the bridge of her nose in a familiar stubborn expression. They weren't getting any information out of her. "If you want answers, ask your boss."

"Rata?" Lang asked, visibly startled. "You're doing work for us?"

Her expression didn't change. "As I said, I can't tell you."

A movement drew Gareth's gaze down and he noticed her hands were trembling. Likewise, her skin was pale and the freckles splashed across her nose stood out starkly.

"You're going into shock," he told her. "Sit down. I'll get you a hot drink."

"You'll do no such thing, Gareth," she said. "I'm perfectly fine. If it weren't for this—"

The buzz of his personal radio interrupted her. He lifted it to his mouth. "Wayland here."

"Sergeant, I've had a report of a suspicious fire at 6 Ruataniwha Drive," the dispatcher said. "I repeat, a suspicious fire at 6 Ruataniwha Drive. The fire brigade are already on their way."

He didn't think it was possible, but Avery went even whiter.

"That's my house," she whispered.

Oh, *shit*. Gareth stared at the destruction around them and felt sick. This violence wasn't directed at the laboratory, it was targeted at Avery. Someone had it in for her.

"Copy," he said into the radio. "I'll be there soon."

2

*A*very flicked her cheek with her forefinger. "Snap out of it," she said to herself. "This is all a big misunderstanding. Everything will be fine."

But as Gareth's police car drew nearer to Itirangi, sirens blaring, an ominous cloud of black smoke blossomed on the horizon and an awful feeling settled in the pit of her stomach.

"It's just a terrible coincidence," she muttered. But Avery didn't believe in coincidences. At least, not ones like this. To do so would be scientifically flawed.

Gareth glanced over at her, his strong jaw working as he chewed gum, a habit her friends told her he'd picked up since he quit smoking. She'd never seen him smoke, but apparently he had for a couple of years after he joined the force.

"You need to brace yourself," he warned. "I doubt it's a coincidence, and seeing the fire for yourself may be quite upsetting." He paused and tilted his head as if weighing his next words carefully. "You don't share the house with anyone, do you?" he asked. "Roommate? Pets? Boyfriend?"

"No," she replied. "It's just me."

14

"Good. At least we don't need to worry about anyone else being in there."

As they drew nearer, the smoke cloud seemed to grow larger. Logically, she knew it was proximity that made it appear so, but that didn't prevent her intestines from knotting or her stomach from threatening to hurl back the oatmeal she'd eaten for breakfast.

To distract herself from the uncomfortable sensations in her gut, she turned over this latest development. Assuming the laboratory had been vandalized by Dwayne Broderick, or someone working on his behalf, it was likely her house had been targeted by the same person, for the same reason. They didn't want her locating the missing girl's body so they destroyed her equipment to ensure she couldn't undertake any more tests. Then, on the off-chance she'd already conducted all the tests she needed, or stored anything important at home, they'd gone there too. But it would have been more difficult to search or trash the inside of a house than it was a single-room lab, so they'd opted for a more efficient means of disposing of the evidence: burning everything.

Sensible. And the fact was, she did keep hard drives at home with backups of all her research, databases and systems, as well as a copy of the textbook she'd begun writing with Dr. Jesse Stone from the University of Otago, an introduction to soil chemistry for undergraduate students.

The textbook. The calmness she'd fought for evaporated. If the hard drive melted or burned, so did all of her work on the book because she foolishly hadn't backed it up online.

When they turned onto Ruataniwha Drive, any hope she may have harbored vanished and an uncomfortable pressure settled in her chest. She watched smoke billow through the windows of her compact timber-frame house and flames lick at the windows and doorways. Everything she had was in that house. Her clothing, books, mementos from school, university, and travel. The threadbare blanket her mother had given her. *Everything.*

A fire engine was parked on the road, connected to the nearest fire hydrant. Firefighters occupied her front lawn, two men aiming a massive hose at the house, another around the side wielding the garden hose and trampling the flower bed. She winced. Her poor flowers would never be the same again.

While smoke still poured from inside, it seemed to her that the firefighters had the situation largely under control. *Thank god.*

Gareth pulled over, but before he had time to park, she threw the passenger door open and sprinted for the open front door. Her feet pounded on the pavement. One of the firefighters saw her and called out. Another reached for her, but she dodged around him and flew up the steps, then she was inside.

Heat beat at her from every angle. Smoke obscured her vision, stinging her eyes and burning the back of her throat, but Avery knew the layout of this house by heart. She turned into the bedroom, took one step and an arm fastened around her waist. She lashed out, striking something with the back of her elbow and heard a man grunt. Then she was lifted off her feet. She kicked and yelled and writhed but couldn't break free of his hold. She saw a flash of blue uniform. *Gareth.* He hauled her outside, stumbled off the porch onto the lawn and dumped her unceremoniously on the ground, pinning her there with his body.

"What the hell were you thinking?" he demanded, chest heaving as he fought to catch his breath.

Avery didn't answer. She made the mistake of looking up and was caught by his angry golden gaze. His pupils were pinpricks. Distractedly, she realized she hadn't seen any emotion in Gareth's eyes for a long, long time. They were always polite. Disinterested.

"Were you trying to kill us both?" he growled, drawing her attention back to the situation at hand.

"Don't be ridiculous. The fire is under control. I need to save my work. It's important." She tried to roll out from under him, but he held her down.

"I'm not letting you go until I'm sure you won't endanger anyone," he told her.

Obviously, she needed to make this really simple. "I won't endanger anyone," she said. "If you hadn't chased me inside, you would never have been in any danger. As far as I'm concerned, that was your choice, not mine. Now, let me go. You know I can fight dirty."

He didn't budge. "I'm a cop. It's my duty to protect you. I can't let you go back in there. But if you feel like you have to try, then let me have it."

He was right, damn it. That didn't stop the band tightening around her chest at the thought of losing *everything*. All of her hard work, all of the things she'd accumulated over a lifetime, the home she'd only been able to call hers after years of saving.

"Please, just let me go," she whispered. "Don't follow me. I need…" She trailed off, already reading the answer in the firm line of his mouth. Her shoulders slumped against the ground and she closed her eyes. She didn't want to see his pity. "Just tell me when it's over. I want to see if anything survived."

She listened to the sound of water rushing, men calling to each other, and smelled the bitterness of smoke in the air. Her eyes stung behind closed eyelids, whether from emotion or the intense heat she'd been exposed to, she didn't know. But she refused to cry. Tears wouldn't make her home stop burning, un-smash her workplace, or lift Gareth's big frame from on top of her. So instead, she lay quietly and waited.

~

Gareth watched Avery's lips tremble as a heavy lump seared its way through his insides. When she'd disappeared into the smoke, she'd taken five years off his life. Thank god he'd been able to grab her before she made it any further. But now she was suffering, no doubt feeling overwhelmed and powerless. She'd collapsed into a sad little heap beneath him and he longed to let her up—he didn't enjoy bullying her into submission—but he couldn't. Not until the fire was well and truly out. It was his duty to protect her, and it was also basic instinct. As long as he had control over his faculties, he'd always do what it took to keep Avery from harm.

"How's it looking?" he called to one of the firemen, Eugene Pou.

"Think the fire is out," Eugene replied. "But we'll give it a few more minutes, then a couple of the boys will head inside to see."

Gareth nodded and took the opportunity to study Avery's face. He hadn't been this close to her since before they'd broken up, and he noticed subtle differences. Faint crinkles at the corners of her eyes, either from smiling or squinting as she worked. The freckles across her nose had faded, so the darker ones remained but the lighter ones had vanished. Perhaps most telling of all was the way she held herself, as though she wanted to distance herself from him even when he was right on top of her.

"What were you trying to get to that was so important?" he asked softly.

Her lips tightened. "It hardly matters now."

"It matters to me," he told her. "You were willing to kill both of us to save it."

She met his eyes, her blue-gray irises turbulent. "I'm sorry," she said, taking him by surprise. "I didn't intend for you to follow me."

"So, what—"

"All clear!" Eugene called. "Miss, if you'd like to go inside now, someone can escort you."

She shoved Gareth's shoulders and he scrambled off her, pain zinging through his knee at the sudden movement. "Great," she replied to Eugene. "Show me the way."

Gareth started to follow her, but his phone rang with his boss's ring tone. "Wayland," he answered, stopping a few yards from the blackened porch.

"Sergeant," Inspector Rata said in her typical clipped fashion. "You're at Dr. Brown's home?"

"Yes, sir."

"She's with you?"

"Affirmative. The fire has been subdued and she's entering the building with one of the firemen to assess the damage."

"Good." The next words out of Rata's mouth gave him pause. "Don't let that woman out of your sight, Sergeant."

"Why not?" he demanded. "What's going on?"

"Has she explained to you what she's working on?"

"No. She told Lang it was confidential."

"It is," Rata confirmed. "What I'm about to tell you, you can't discuss with anyone other than Dr. Brown. Is that understood?"

"Yes, sir."

"For the past two years, the government has been funding her work to create a detailed map of soils from around New Zealand. Thousands of samples have been collected, processed, and analyzed, and Dr. Brown has collated the results into a mapping program. The intention is to use the program when trace soil is found at a crime scene to determine the approximate location from which it originated."

Gareth's eyes widened and he whistled. *Wow.* If he interpreted that correctly, Avery had been working on a system that could revolutionize crime fighting in New Zealand, and he'd been completely in the dark. So far as he knew, *everyone* had. Except Rata, and presumably the higher-ups.

"I know you can understand the importance of this work," she continued. "The difference it could make to some of our major cases. A few days ago, we decided to trial the system for the Millie Grant case. As you know, as long as we don't have the girl's body, we can't make an arrest because we can't prove murder. We asked Dr. Brown to test the soil from a spade found in the back of the suspect's car to help locate the body. If we find the body, it's a slam dunk."

With this context and the way the inspector had ordered Gareth to watch Avery, he surmised that she suspected someone was trying to sabotage those tests, or perhaps even the entire program.

"Do you know whether the perp succeeded in destroying the case work?"

Rata sighed, the sound carrying down the phone line. "He made a good effort, and the results from the initial analysis were destroyed, but he missed the hardware that Dr. Brown stores her database on. Even if he hadn't, we keep a second back-up in a secure location. The program is too important to risk losing. So while it's not ideal that her samples and equipment were destroyed, the case can go forward for two reasons. Firstly, if we can get another sample for Dr. Brown to test, the program will work as effectively as before. And secondly, she already carried out a high-level test. She knows the approximate location of the body, down to a fifty-kilometer radius, and can speak to that in a court of law. It's not a small enough area to search, but if we find the body—"

"She can tie it to Broderick," Gareth said, a chill coursing through him. If Avery could testify against a murderer, then a target had been painted on her back.

"Exactly, Sergeant," she replied, her voice devoid of emotion. "If the perp finds out that vandalizing the lab and burning down the doctor's house didn't destroy the database, that Dr. Brown knows enough to damn him already *and* has everything she needs to conduct more tests, he'll come after her."

Fuck. Gareth's vision swam before his eyes and his head spun dizzyingly.

"She's not safe," he said, as much to himself as to his superior.

"No, she's not. And losing Dr. Brown would be a far greater tragedy than anything that's happened so far. There's no one else who's been involved in her project the entire way through. No one else who has all the background knowledge and expertise required to do the testing. And then there's the preliminary results, which only exist in her mind now that the results were destroyed. Not to mention," Rata cleared her throat, "she's a damn fine woman and I don't want her suffering any more misfortunes on the country's behalf. Take her into protective custody, Sergeant, get her out of the public eye, and keep her safe. That's an order."

"Yes, sir." Gareth nodded sharply, though Rata couldn't see him. "I'll report back once I have her somewhere safe."

He hung up and started toward the house, his movements jerky, feeling detached, as though watching himself from a distance. Fear churned in his stomach and adrenaline was the only thing that pushed him inside. It was of the utmost importance that he get Avery out of here immediately. He could scarcely believe he'd been on the perimeter of her life for years and had no idea what she'd been doing.

Did he even know her at all?

The foul scent of smoke and charred materials crept up his nose as he passed through what had been the hall, with four rooms attached that looked wholly burned out. He found Avery with Eugene, standing in what he guessed to be the kitchen based on the long stainless steel counter along one wall.

"We need to leave," he said. "Now."

Avery glanced over at him and blinked. "No, we don't," she replied. "The fire is out. We're safe."

"You're *not* safe," he insisted. "I'll explain everything if you just come with me."

She crossed her arms. "You'll explain it *now*."

He stalked toward her and grabbed her by the shoulders. Not firmly enough to hurt, but enough to jar some sense into her. "I need you to listen to me, A-Bee. I have a very good reason to believe that you're not safe and that we need to get away from here. I know you want to know the reason why." She always did. "But I also know you're smart enough to hear what I'm saying and use that logical brain of yours to figure out that the faster you do as I say, the faster you'll get the answers you want."

"Okay." She might be stubborn and infuriating, but she was also practical and wouldn't put up a fight simply for the sake of it. Or at least, that's the way she'd been back when he knew her better than he knew himself.

"If there's anything you can salvage, you've got two minutes to grab it, then we're leaving. Take anything you can find. You might not be able to come back for a few days."

Her brows mushed together but she hurried into an adjoining room. He heard a door open and shut, then she emerged a moment later with a basket of damp laundry.

"It was on the clothesline in the yard," she explained.

He followed her back down the hall to one of the burned-out rooms. An office perhaps. The aroma of melted plastic permeated the air. Avery laid down the basket and strode to the remains of a wooden desk.

She looked over at Gareth. "You got any heat-proof gloves?"

He shook his head. "One of the firefighters will. Give me a moment."

He headed outside, crossed the lawn to the firefighter manning the fire engine, and requested heat-resistant gloves.

The man searched the cab and returned with a thick pair. Gareth thanked him and jogged back to the office. Avery took the gloves when he offered them and sifted through the remnants of the desk. Then her eyes lit up and she extracted a small metal box, perhaps some kind of lock box. She dumped it on top of her damp clothing and flinched when it made a hissing sound, steam curling up from the clothes. Apparently the metal box had retained a lot of heat.

"All set?" he asked.

"For now."

He followed her from the house, his eyes on her feet to make sure she didn't trip or hurt herself. Once at his car, he opened the trunk for her to load the basket into it and ushered her into the passenger seat.

"Where are we going?" she asked as soon as he sat and turned the key in the ignition.

He considered their options. He couldn't take her to his place; someone may expect that. Similarly, staying with any of their friends or family was out of the question. Frankly, anywhere in town was dangerous. They needed to get away. Needed to be far from anyone.

The hut. Gareth's friend Ram owned a cabin near the lake, thirty minutes out of Itirangi, which he'd inherited from his grandfather. It was hidden from the road and completely off the grid. Perfect.

"Ram's cabin by the lake," he said. "But we've got a couple of stops before that."

The first place he pulled up outside of was his sister Caroline's home, a pretty white stone house on a quarter-acre lot with a lawn decorated with children's toys.

"Wait here," he instructed, getting out and locking the door behind him. He jogged up the concrete path and knocked on the door. Heels clacked across tiles and then it opened. Caroline smiled at him. She stood nearly six feet tall in heels, so they looked each other in the eye.

"Gaz!" she exclaimed, leaning forward to kiss his cheek. "Good to see you. The girls have already left for school and Glenn has gone to work, so it's just me here."

Caroline was a one-woman public relations and communications firm. Even though she worked from home and likely wouldn't see anyone face-to-face today, she wore tidy business-wear and jewelry, with her blonde hair pinned neatly atop her head and her makeup just so.

"Hi, Caro," he replied. "I'm glad to hear that. I need a favor, and you can't mention it to anyone." Given free reign, Caroline would gossip until the cows came home, but if asked to keep a secret, she buttoned up tighter than Fort Knox.

"Anything you need," she said.

"Can I borrow a few changes of your clothes?"

She tilted her head to the side. "Don't suppose you want to tell me why."

He lowered his voice. "I can't. I'd like to, but I really can't."

He looked at her meaningfully, and after a moment, she nodded. "Work stuff, right?"

"Yes."

"Any outfits in particular?"

"Warm, comfy clothes. Socks, too. A pair of pajamas."

Her eyebrows rose. "You're going to explain all this to me later."

"Maybe," he said noncommittally.

"Not maybe. Definitely. You know I can keep a secret. But I won't push you now."

"Appreciate it."

He stayed in the doorway while she left to retrieve a bag of clothes. He didn't want to let Avery out of his sight, or assume she was safe in his car. He still couldn't believe that in all of the parties, barbecues, and get-togethers they'd both attended, they hadn't spoken enough for him to have some idea of what she was doing. He wondered if that was a coincidence or by her design. He didn't want to believe she'd been avoiding him, but when he thought about it, it was strange that they'd never had a decent conversation in all that time. Certainly *he* hadn't been avoiding *her*. But what reason would she have to avoid him? Their relationship was well and truly in the past, it had ended amicably, and they were both adults. He must be imagining things.

"Here you go," Caroline said, reappearing in front of him with a duffel bag. "I expect you to return them in good condition."

"I will. Thanks, Caro." He took the bag, gave her a one-armed hug and waved goodbye.

Back at the car, he tossed the bag into the back seat, hopped in and set a course for his house. Avery seemed to have withdrawn into herself, perhaps working through the emotional trauma of the morning. He didn't say anything, letting her take whatever time she needed. She'd talk to him when she was ready.

When he parked outside his own place, Snookie barked from behind the tall wooden fence. Gareth left the car, flicked the latch on the gate to let himself onto the property, and greeted her with a scratch behind the ear. A retired police dog, she followed on his heels as he opened the front door, her shaggy black and tan body brushing against his leg. Two minutes was all it took to throw some of his own clothes in a bag along with a laptop, toiletries case, and dog lead. He rummaged through the pantry and packed a selection of food—both human and dog—into another bag. Enough for a few days, just in case. He grabbed the emergency kit he kept on the bottom shelf and stowed it in with the food. Then he called Snookie to heel and headed out, locking both the door and gate behind them. He let Snookie into the rear of his cruiser.

Avery turned at the sound, visibly startled. "Who's this?" she asked.

Oh, yeah. He'd forgotten that she wasn't the biggest fan of animals. "This is my main girl, Snookie. She'll be joining us."

"Fantastic."

Despite himself, he chuckled. "Same old A-Bee."

She rolled her eyes as he got in and started the engine. "Hardly. So, now will you tell me what's going on?"

3

*A*very waited for Gareth's reply, feeling as though they were in a different universe as he gunned the engine and drove toward the road leading out of Itirangi. Her laboratory—her pride and joy—had suffered tens, if not hundreds, of thousands of dollars' worth of damage. Not to mention the setback to her groundbreaking research. Her life's work had been vandalized as effectively as the lab, and dozens of criminals might avoid sentencing as a result. On top of that, her home had been obliterated.

She hadn't fully processed what the loss of her home meant, hadn't cataloged all of the things that had been ruined. Instead, she felt dazed and disoriented, as though this was all a nightmare she needed to wake up from. The murky slowness of her thoughts supported that theory. Usually, she was quick-smart, not sluggish and foggy-headed.

"Well?" she challenged Gareth, vaguely aware he hadn't answered her question—which had been what, exactly?

He swallowed, his throat working. Her gaze skimmed from his even-featured face down his broad chest encased by a pale blue uniform shirt and navy protective vest then further down to his lean hips and strong thighs. With a certain detachment, she noted that he was as sexy as ever. Damn, she sure had been disappointed when she'd moved back to Itirangi and found him hotter than when she'd left. It would have satisfied her vindictive streak if he'd gone to seed since they'd broken up.

"You're in danger," he said. "That's why we're going out of town. We need to get you out of harm's way."

"I'm in danger?" she asked. "Don't you think you're being a bit overdramatic? If someone wanted to hurt me, they would have trashed the lab or burned down my house *while I was inside it*. But they didn't. Ergo, no one wants to hurt me."

She'd already followed the chain of logic in her head. The arsonist could have set a fire while she slept, but they'd waited for her to leave, so there was no sense in panicking now.

"The inspector told me what you're working on," he said quietly.

She sucked in a breath and released it slowly. That made him the first of her social circle to know about it. Oddly, it was a relief to have it out in the open. "Then you can under-stand why I need to be at my lab, doing whatever I can to get the situation under control." Not that she could stomach the thought of seeing the devastation there again yet. "The sooner I can replace or repair my equipment, get my hands on another sample of the soil—if one exists—and run more tests on it, the sooner I can narrow down where it came from, and the sooner we can put all of this behind us. I need to be *working*." She fairly itched for something useful to occupy her hands and brain so she wouldn't keep recalling the acrid smell of her life as it went up in smoke. "This has put me a few days behind in terms of finishing my analysis for the police, and then there's an overwhelming amount of work I need to do to get my research back on track. I can't afford to waste any time worrying about what may or may not happen."

She'd also rather be hard at work than in the middle of nowhere, with nothing to do but dwell on everything that had gone wrong on this hellish day. For crying out loud, she didn't have anywhere to *live*. Where would she sleep tonight? What clothing would she wear tomorrow? What would she use to brush her teeth, and what could she snuggle up with for comfort in the evening? She flicked the soft skin on the inside of her left forearm with her right forefinger, telling herself to snap out of it. Worrying wouldn't do her any good.

"Thing is," he said, "assuming the perp wanted to mess with the Millie Grant investigation, it won't be long before one of two things happens. Option one, he realizes that your system is backed up and that the tests can still be done, in which case he'll have another go at destroying them. Or, option two, he realizes that the preliminary results are in *your* head and that you'll be a valuable witness if a body is found and it goes to court." She opened her mouth to counter his argument, but he barreled on. "Come to think of it, there's a third option. The perp realizes that your system can be fixed *and* that you're the only person who is capable of using it. Then he comes after you."

"Someone else could use my system," she broke in. "Many other scientists are capable of using the technology. It's just that, well, no one else has had oversight over the entire project and I haven't written any standard operating procedures yet. Without those, they'd be fumbling along blindly." A situation she should rectify as soon as possible.

He raised an eyebrow. "So my argument stands. In two out of three possible scenarios, the perp decides you're worth getting rid of."

Avery shook her head, dismissing the notion. "I think you're overreacting. This isn't an episode of *CSI* or something. People don't just go around killing scientists in real life."

"Maybe not in Itirangi, but it does happen, and you need to take the threat to your safety seriously."

She thrust her chin forward. "I will when you take me seriously. I'm not some silly child."

He muttered something under his breath. Just like old times.

"Relax, G," she said. "There's no need for name-calling."

He glanced over guiltily. "Didn't call you any names."

"Uh-huh."

He gripped the steering wheel so tightly his knuckles were white. Snookie whimpered in the back seat, as if sensing her master's tension.

"As it happens, my boss gave me orders to protect you. So whether or not you think it's warranted, I'm going to do just that. And yes, I have no doubt that you're smarter than me, but when it comes to criminals, I'm the expert."

She could hear the conviction in his voice, so she didn't push the issue, certain she'd get another opportunity to say her piece later. They drove along the road that bordered the lake, but as they went deeper into the countryside, it became separated from the water by a narrow strip of forest. She remembered that Ram's cabin was located within that strip of forest, out of sight from the road, and only a short walk from the shore.

She also remembered it was where she and Gareth had lost their virginity to each other. It was the first thing she'd thought of when he told her their destination. They'd spent dozens of long summer days paddling together on the lake, hiking the trails through the forest on the other side of the road where it was deeper and thicker, and making out on the narrow bunk bed. Then, one night, they'd gone further.

But that had been a lifetime ago.

"How long have you been working on the soil map?" he asked, breaking the silence that had descended.

"Since I moved back," she replied. "Two, maybe three,

years. I did the initial planning while I was studying and pitched it to the right people so I could get started as soon as I graduated. I haven't done all of the grunt work by myself, I've had help along the way, but it's still my baby."

He nodded. "I get that."

Avery watched him navigate the road as the hard seal ended and a stretch of gravel began. There was such concentration in his expression that she knew it wasn't wholly focused on the terrain—he'd driven this road dozens of times. Gareth was thinking, hard. And damned if she didn't find his intensity sexy.

It's the effects of adrenaline, she told herself. *Adrenaline increases levels of arousal and attraction to the opposite sex.*

Knowing that didn't stop it, but it gave her the motivation to turn away and watch the trees fly by. Another ten minutes passed, then he slowed and veered down a narrow driveway that wound into the forest. The cabin came into view. Timber-framed, rustic, with a rainwater tank to the side, and a lean-to stacked with firewood nailed to one of the external walls. A pair of kayaks lay upside down in the small clearing beside a trail that led to the water.

Avery's stomach tightened. She tried, and failed, not to remember that blissful summer with Gareth. Something wet touched her ear and she jerked in surprise, turning to see Snookie's nose inches from her face.

"Leave me alone," she muttered. "I'm not a dog person."

"She'll take that as a personal challenge," Gareth told her.

Great. She threw the car door open and stepped out. A cold breeze stirred her hair and goosebumps rose on her skin. She'd planned to spend the day inside at work, so the jeans and t-shirt she wore weren't suited to the outside temperature.

"Let's go inside," he said. "Get comfy. Then we can talk about what to do next and you can take a little time to process things. I'll text Ram and let him know we're here."

"Will it be a problem?"

He shook his head. "Doubt it. He hardly ever comes here during winter."

Avery could understand why. Though the forest was beautiful, it was also soggy, the ground muddy, and from what she could remember, the cabin had no insulation.

She waited until Gareth had let Snookie out of the back seat and slung his bags over his shoulders before she retrieved her damp clothes from the trunk and lugged them to the door. He collected the spare key from the woodshed and unlocked the door. Stale air met them.

She coughed. "You should've mentioned no one's been here since the dark ages, G. I would have stood back a little more."

She expected him to chuckle, but instead he said, "Don't be overdramatic. I'm sure it hasn't been more than a few weeks, tops."

"Not sure I'm buying that."

She dumped her basket on the wooden bench just inside the door, walked across the room, and opened the window to freshen the place up. Then, with mechanical movements, she started to hang each item from the laundry basket on the clothesline that crossed the cabin at head height. She'd made it halfway through when she realized she'd put her bras and panties on display in front of her ex-boyfriend. Suddenly, the space felt too small. She wanted to snatch them back, but forced herself to continue like she hadn't noticed, as though it didn't bother her.

Gareth sat on the bottom bunk, forearms resting on his thighs, and watched her. She could sense that he wanted to talk, but didn't know what to say. Strange, the boy she'd known had never been at a loss for words around her. Sure, he'd been a little awkward at times, but never lost.

"Cat got your tongue?" she asked, hoping to provoke him into losing that expression. She didn't like it, not one bit.

"I'm surprised you're so calm about this," he replied. "Most people would be in hysterics by now."

Calm. He thought she was *calm.* She certainly didn't feel it. Thoughts whirred busily through her mind, circling away before she could grasp them, but provided she kept moving, kept doing things, she could ward off the feeling of powerlessness that threatened to descend.

"No point in hysterics. We need to figure out what we're going to do next."

~

"WHAT WE'RE GOING to do next," Gareth began, "is hide out here and keep you safe while the inspector catches whoever is behind the attacks on your home and work." As he'd thought, she didn't appear to like that answer.

"Whoever is behind those attacks is probably the person who's responsible for Millie Grant's death," she said. "So the smart thing to do would be to find the body and put the killer away. Then there's no more reason for anyone to target me."

There it was. Right on cue. Avery thinking she knew better than anyone else.

"Not gonna happen. At least, not today. It's my job to protect you and at the moment, that means keeping you here."

She rolled her eyes and scoffed. "Are you going to hold me down to stop me leaving?"

His back teeth ground together. "If I have to."

Her posture stiffened. Finally, he'd surprised her. *Good.* It was important she know that he wasn't the same easygoing kid he'd been. He wouldn't let her get her way all the time. She didn't have him wrapped around her talented pinky finger anymore. Moreover, he damn sure was going to keep her safe. He'd seen what happened when policemen didn't take threats against women seriously, and he wouldn't allow that to happen to her. Intellectually, she was leagues ahead of him, but physically, he had the advantage and he wasn't afraid to use it.

"Okay," she acknowledged. "Not today. But you should call Rata and ask her to arrange for another soil sample to be sent in, if there is one. I can find another lab to do the tests. Shouldn't be a big hassle. When do you think I might be free of my bossy bodyguard?"

"I'll stop protecting you when you're no longer in danger," he said. "Forget about the case. Think of the long-range implications of your work. It's important you stay safe so you can take it where it needs to go."

She huffed out a breath. Took a step back. Nodded. "That makes sense. But I need to *do* something."

She started to pace with restless energy, the old wooden floorboards creaking beneath her feet. He had seen this before. When someone was victimized, they needed to feel in control. He should assign her a task. Something that wouldn't get her in trouble, and which she could do from here.

"Give me a minute," he said. "I'll cut some timber and you can get the fire going." He didn't want to risk her going outside unless absolutely necessary. He paused before he left and held out his palm. She stared at it blankly. "Give me your phone," he said.

She reflexively covered the pocket where her phone was with her hands. "Why?"

"Because there's a chance someone's tracking it. You can't use it, and we should take the battery out, just to be safe."

She rolled her eyes. "No one will be tracking it."

"You don't know that. These guys go to big lengths to keep themselves out of prison."

She extracted her phone from her pocket but didn't seem willing to hand it over. "What if I need to use it?"

"You can use mine." He handed her the encrypted satellite phone that had been issued to him earlier in the year. "It should be safe from any tracking devices or programs and it actually has coverage out here."

He thought he glimpsed irritation cross her features, but it vanished so quickly he wasn't certain. "Guess that'll have to do." The words were reluctant but at least she'd moved on from being openly antagonistic. She slapped her phone into his palm and he cracked the back cover off it, pulled the battery out and pocketed it.

"Sit." He gestured to one of the old camp chairs in the corner, beside a rickety two-person table. She glared at him and remained standing. God save him from difficult women. "I'll be outside," he told her. "Keep Snookie with you. I'll be back soon. Sit, or don't sit. Suit yourself."

"I'm going to call the insurance company," she told him. "Try to make a start on the paperwork for the lab and," she sighed, "my house and contents."

Gareth patted her shoulder, then cringed at his own awkwardness. "Go ahead, as long as you use my phone. I'm right outside if you need me."

4

---

*A*very hung up from her insurance company and set about balling old newspaper in the fireplace, and piling the kindling Gareth had brought atop it. She held a match to the paper, and as black smoke curled upward and the paper caught alight, she jolted and dropped it. She thrust the door closed and opened the flue. Damn. For a moment, staring into the glowing orange, she'd been right back there, watching as the last flickering flames in her home were extinguished.

She couldn't dwell on that. Gareth's phone rang and she answered without thinking. He looked up from where he sat at the table, Snookie resting her head on the side of his thigh, and raised an eyebrow.

"Hi, this is Avery."

"*Avery!*" a voice screeched so loudly she held the phone away from her ear for a moment. Snookie grumbled, and Avery glared at her. "Thank god! I've been calling every two minutes for the last twenty minutes. Why haven't you answered? Are you okay? I've been so *worried* about you!"

"I'm okay, Soph," Avery said to her friend. "How did you know to call me on Gareth's cell?"

"Your next-door neighbor, Mrs. Chen, said she saw you leave with a handsome police officer. What happened? Your house is destroyed. Was there an accident? Did you leave the oven on or something? I'm *so* sorry. Are you sure you're okay?"

Avery barked out a laugh and felt some of the tension in her shoulders melt away. Trust Sophie to make her feel better, just by virtue of being more panicked than Avery was.

"Slow down. I'm not hurt, I promise, but I can't tell you anything at the moment other than that I'm with Gareth, and I'm safe."

Something in the tone of her voice or her choice of words must have alerted Sophie to the fact that there was more going on than a freak accident.

"Uh-oh," she said. "What's up? And don't tell me nothing, I won't believe you. Is Gareth protecting you from something? Are you in danger?"

"*Sophie.*" Avery sighed, exasperated. "I really can't tell you, but trust me that I'll let you know if I need anything."

From her friend's unhappy grunt, she knew Sophie didn't like her answer, but she also knew she wouldn't push.

"Where will you stay tonight?" she asked. "You're welcome at my place anytime. I'm used to having someone else around. It's quiet with Mum gone. It would be nice to have your company, and you could stay for as long as you wanted."

"Thank you." Avery's chest constricted, both at the reminder that she no longer had a bed of her own and at the sweetness of Sophie's invitation. Avery knew she'd taken to sleeping at her boyfriend Cooper's house since her mother had been checked into a mental health facility for treatment, and Avery appreciated that she was willing to sacrifice her time with him for her. "I might take you up on that eventually, but I'm not sure exactly when that will be."

"Just promise you'll call me if you need help, or even just someone to talk to. I'm here anytime you need, babe."

Just when she'd thought the possibility of crying had ended, there Sophie went, making her eyes prickle like a sentimental wimp. "I appreciate that, Soph. I'll call you later."

"Love you," Sophie said. "And hey, maybe there's an upside to this. You can take some time to explore all that chemistry you still have with Gaz."

There she was. Cheeky, romantic Sophie. Never missing an opportunity to set up one of her friends.

"There's nothing to explore," Avery replied.

"Mm-hmm. You keep telling yourself that, honey. But we have eyes, and we're watching. Bye for now."

Avery wondered exactly who "we" was. Sophie and Cooper? Sophie and their friend Aria? Everyone? "Bye."

She rolled her shoulders back, then cracked a kink out of her neck.

"You okay?" Gareth asked.

"Yeah." She returned his phone. "I'm hanging in there."

"Good. Let me know if you need anything. I'm going to scout around outside. I'll be within hearing range."

Avery nodded, added a log to the fire, kicked up her feet and lay back as he left, taking his clingy mutt with him. The inside of the cabin was beginning to warm. Her stomach grumbled, and she wondered whether he'd thought to pack food for lunch, dinner, breakfast—however many meals they needed. Somehow, she doubted it. Gareth may take his duties seriously, as evidenced by his willingness to wrestle her into submission and his determination to treat her like a damsel in distress, but the bag he'd brought from his home had been far too small for everything necessary for an extended stay.

Despite the situation—or perhaps *because* of it, and her subsequent need for a distraction—she was curious to learn more about how he'd changed since high school. She'd intentionally stayed away from him since she'd been back in town. Not because she disliked him, but because she feared if she took the time to get to know him again, she'd like him too much. Back when they were kids, he'd been her kryptonite, and while they'd had a relatively friendly breakup, each going separate ways to pursue their chosen careers, she would have toughed out a long-distance relationship if he'd wanted it. But he hadn't, and she'd had too much pride to argue.

God, it still stung now. Not because she still felt about Gareth the way she had back then, but because that was the first time she'd wondered if things would have been different if she'd been more feminine, daintier, or less capable. But he'd had no compunction about waving her off into the big, wide world by herself because he knew she could handle anything it threw at her. And so she had.

It worked out for the best, she reminded herself, because she'd been places and seen things she never would have if he'd been waiting at home for her. She was grateful for those experiences. They'd molded her into the person she was today. But still, she wondered.

Her limbs twitched, her body as restless as her mind. She needed to move, to burn off energy. Immediately.

GARETH WAS PACING a circuit around the clearing, the dog on his heels, checking to see if anything had been disturbed or whether anybody seemed to be nearby, when Avery jogged out of the hut, wearing Caroline's jacket. She looked remarkably composed. She had gumption, he'd give her that. No panicked meltdowns on the cards for her.

"I need to burn off some energy," she said, without any preamble. "I'm going to take a kayak onto the lake."

So much for that.

"No," he replied slowly. "You're not. You're going to go back inside and lie low for the rest of the day."

"Don't be ridiculous. No one knows where we are, and even if they did, how would anyone do me any damage out on the lake?"

He didn't point out that someone could easily shoot her from the lake shore. She didn't need to hear that.

"Come on," she continued. "I'm jittery as hell. You can't keep me cooped up with this sort of shit going on."

He straightened and crossed his arms over his chest. "With all due respect, yes I can. You're a sensible woman. You know that staying inside for a single day isn't a big ask, under the circumstances."

She scowled, as if she resented him for appealing to her good sense. Too bad. He'd play whatever angle he needed to in order to keep her safe. An image flashed into the back of his mind. A woman, sprawled on the floor of a dingy hotel, her limbs at awkward angles, the side of her face purple with bruising, and blood pooling beneath her.

I won't let that happen.

"Don't push me on this, Avery. If you need something to do, why don't you start by making a list of all the tests you need to run and the equipment you need to do them?"

She jabbed him in the chest with a pointed finger. "Quit playing dirty and trying to be smart about this. That's my job."

He let out a sharp bark of laughter. She'd taken him by surprise. "Oh honey, I'm not playing dirty yet. Trust me, you'd know if I were playing dirty."

Damn. The flirtatious words were out before he could prevent them from escaping, his candor a spontaneous reaction to her own. *Not smart, G. Not smart at all.* Especially given the way awareness flared in her gray eyes and her gaze flitted down his body before returning to his face.

"There he is," she murmured.

What?

He must have spoken out loud, because she held eye contact and said, "The real Gareth. The one you hide behind this rigid cop routine."

He slammed the lid on the fizz of emotion she evoked. This wasn't the time to be disturbed that she could see through him as well as ever, or annoyed by her dismissive attitude toward his profession.

"Get back inside," he said. "I'll be there in two."

Shaking her head, her upper lip curled, and she spun on her heel and strode back inside. She might not be happy, but so be it. It wasn't his job to make her happy.

He popped a piece of gum into his mouth and chewed, patting Snookie's head as he took a moment to collect himself. Hell, but she was beautiful when she was pissed. Eyes sparking, cheeks pink, expressive mouth twisted into a smirk or pout.

Get a hold of yourself.

He traced her footsteps, closing the door with a soft click behind the dog. Avery sat at the table, scribbling on an old notepad—the one the boys used to keep track of the score when they played card games. Taking the seat opposite, he watched her dark eyelashes fan out when she blinked. They were thick and black without the aid of mascara. Her pointed chin dipped down toward her chest and she paused to tap the pen against it as she thought.

Gareth considered her. They moved in the same circles, but rarely talked. He'd often wondered whether she'd accomplished everything she'd wanted to when she left for university. She'd had such big dreams, and he hadn't wanted to hold her back, so he'd let her go, believing in the old adage that if it were meant to be, she'd come back to him one day. Besides, who was he to lock down a woman like her? He'd had aspirations, but his ambitions were nothing like hers, which probably explained why he was a small-town cop and she was a world-class scientist.

He supposed he shouldn't be surprised that she hadn't held onto the memory of their relationship the way he had. According to their mutual friend, Aria —the nosiest person in Itirangi—Avery had traveled to Africa, Antarctica, and the United States to study. She may have settled in Itirangi for now, but what was to stop her from moving on when a new adventure came along? By the sound of it, her work on this project was nearly complete. Or at least, it had been. What would she do next? Where would she go?

He watched her reach up absentmindedly to rub the back of her neck, then wince.

"Hey, you okay?" he asked gruffly.

"Neck's a bit tender," she said. "It's fine though. I must have bent it at a funny angle sometime today."

Probably when he tossed her over his shoulder and pinned her to the ground. He felt a twinge of guilt. Her day had been difficult enough without him manhandling her. Standing, he made his way behind her, swept her hair over one shoulder, and smoothed the pads of his thumbs over her delicate skin. Initially, her shoulders stiffened, but then she relaxed into his ministrations.

"Not too hard?" he asked.

"No, it's good." She hummed contentedly, sending a bolt of lust straight to his groin.

He snatched his hands away from her and covered poorly by muttering, "That should be enough for now. Don't want to overdo it."

She looked at him oddly. He gazed over her shoulder, willing the rapid thumping in his chest to subside. He should never have touched her in the first place. *This is what happens when you ignore the rules.* He had a professional reputation to uphold, and an important job to do. Laying his hands on a distressed, emotionally fatigued woman didn't figure into that. Especially when that woman already saw far too much, and especially when he couldn't afford to be distracted.

"Don't suppose you brought anything for lunch?" she asked.

Thank god. A question he could answer. "As a matter of fact, I did."

~

A WHILE AFTER LUNCH, by which time Avery had exhausted her list of work-related tasks and was playing solitaire, Gareth's phone rang. Snookie's ears perked up and Avery laid down a card and paid attention as Gareth answered. Hopefully the caller was bringing good news. But then he raised a brow and handed the phone to her, mouthing something she couldn't understand.

"Hello?" she asked tentatively.

"Avery!" Aria exclaimed. "I'm so glad to hear your voice. Sophie said you were all right and that I should give you some space, but I needed to hear it for myself. You're okay?"

Yet more evidence that gossip diffused through Itirangi rapidly. Between the locals, at least. "As much as I can be," she said. "I'm not hurt, but I'm pissed the hell off."

"Do you know who was behind the arson and the vandalism? Was it the same person?" Aria muttered under her breath, "Don't be silly, of course it was. No such thing as a coincidence, right?"

The back of Avery's neck prickled. "Are you asking as a friend, or as a reporter?"

"Both?" The word emerged as a squeak. "Obviously as a friend, first and foremost. But if there's anything you could tell me for a story, it wouldn't go astray. This will be front-page news tomorrow."

While Avery didn't doubt her friend's good intentions, she'd rather not go through the details *again*. "I can't share any details with you, Ri, but when it comes out, I promise I'll talk to you first. It'll be a big story."

"Okay." Aria sounded disappointed, but unsurprised. She didn't push the matter. No doubt she knew that doing so wouldn't accomplish anything. Avery could rival a clam when she wanted to. "Seriously though. How are you holding up?"

Avery rested her forehead on the table, messing up the card game, but she didn't care. "Been better." She tried to figure out how to put words to the confusing tangle of emotions inside of her. "You know, when I woke up this morning, it never occurred to me that I'd be homeless by noon. That sort of thing just doesn't cross your mind. You know these things happen, but you don't expect them to happen to *you*."

"Why would you?" Aria asked. "You had no reason to think anything might happen to take that away from you. It's illogical, and I know how much you hate anything that doesn't make sense."

Actually, it was perfectly logical, and the possibility of something like this happening should have crossed her mind, but she didn't admit that to her friend. "Thanks for checking up on me. I'd better go. Don't know how much charge Gareth's phone has."

"All right, but can you put Gaz back on before you hang up?"

"Sure. Bye, Ri."

"Bye, sweetie. Take care of yourself."

Avery passed the phone to Gareth. "She wants to talk to you."

He raised it to his ear and listened, then said, "You can confirm the location of the house and the person who owned it, but no other details at this point. No, don't link the vandalism to the arson. I'd prefer it if you didn't report the vandalism at all. No, we have no suspects to make public." He nodded, hummed in the back of his throat, made a sound of agreement, then said, "Sounds good. Can you tell the other girls not to call? I know you want to support Avery, but the best way you can do that right now is by keeping your distance for a while. See you." He hung up. Then he smiled, twin dimples appearing in his cheeks. Avery turned gooey inside. She was such a sucker for his dimples. "She's special," he said. "Told me to look after you, or I'd answer to her."

Avery shook her head. "You must be quaking in your boots."

Short, sweet, and pregnant, Aria wasn't the type to frighten anyone. Her fiancée, on the other hand… well, to be honest, Avery wasn't one hundred percent convinced she should trust him, but Aria did and as long as she was happy, Avery would support her. Then she'd help bury the body if that day ever came.

"I'm petrified," he said drily.

"What was that part about them not calling me?" She was a bit miffed he seemed to have assumed control over her communications with the outside world. "I thought you said your phone is safe."

"It *should* be," he confirmed, "but the fewer people you talk to, the better. All of this is on a strict need-to-know basis, and your friends *don't* need to know."

She pursed her lips. She wasn't swayed by his certainty that she was in danger, but she'd pick the fight when the time came. No sense in rocking the boat yet.

5

s time passed, and the morning's events became more distant, Gareth kept a careful eye on Avery, watching to see if the symptoms of shock worsened. She seemed to have rallied from earlier, but then as the afternoon wore on, her hands started trembling, a telltale sign. When she couldn't deal cards anymore, he laid a hand over hers and took the pack from her.

"You'll get through this," he said, then squeezed her hand once and stood. "Rest your eyes for a moment."

He offered her an old shirt from his bag. She looked knackered. "Here, change into this. You should get some sleep."

"But it's only partway through the day."

"What else were you planning to do?"

She shrugged and took the shirt with a wry smile. "Nothing, I guess."

He turned his back until she gave the all clear. When he looked around, her shoulders were stooped, and he was struck by the urge to track down the bastard who'd torched her house and administer some good, old-fashioned justice. The unfamiliar desire disturbed him more than he'd care to admit. Gareth was a stickler for the rules. The cop who lectured his colleagues on protocol. He'd hardly ever wished to take matters into his own hands before.

Except that once.

"We'll find this guy," he told Avery softly, hovering beside her while she made her way to the bunk bed. "I have total faith that you'll find whatever you need to make sure he's locked away for as long as he deserves."

"Damn right, I will."

She lay down and he covered her with a blanket. "And in the meantime, I've got your back."

He thought she might have flinched, but perhaps he'd imagined it. He started toward the chair by the table. She lifted her head from the pillow. "You won't leave, will you?"

Something in his gut twisted. For all she might act like a tough nut to crack, she was only human, and she'd had the day from hell. Now she wanted him with her, and that meant something. He shook his head at that thought. If he didn't get himself under control, he'd be tied in knots over the only girl he'd ever loved.

"I'm not going anywhere," he promised. As far as he was concerned, until this guy—or girl—was behind bars, Avery wouldn't be able to move without stepping on him. "You're safe, A-Bee. I've got you."

She gave him a strange look, but then rolled over, presenting him with her back. He longed to lie in the space beside her and curl around her, to share his warmth and be a shield between her and whoever wanted to do her harm. It was both his duty and personal mission to protect the people of Itirangi, but he'd never experienced an impulse quite like this one, and it had him wondering about the remark Aria had made at the end of their conversation. One he hadn't shared with Avery.

Hold onto her this time. Don't push her away again.

He'd wanted to tell Aria she was being ridiculous. That

their breakup after high school had been mutual and the best thing for both of them. But he couldn't say that with Avery in the room, so he'd muttered an incomprehensible response and hung up. But now he couldn't get the thought out of his head.

~

AN OBNOXIOUS RINGING pierced the fog of Gareth's sleep, followed by Snookie's low whine. He fumbled for his phone, pressed a number of buttons, and held it to his ear.

"Yes?"

"Sergeant," Inspector Rata said. "Report."

Sitting up, he blinked sleepily and gazed around. He'd fallen asleep on the top bunk the previous night after settling Snookie on a rug in front of the fire, eating a sandwich from his bag and firmly deciding that he wouldn't be sleeping, not until Avery's tormentor was behind bars. Apparently, his body had decided differently.

He leaned forward and peered beneath him, checking that she was still sound asleep on the bottom bunk. She breathed evenly, her hair forming a silken curtain over one cheek and the pillow. Closing his eyes, he listened for a moment. Not a sound to be heard, except for the chirping of birds and the quiet thump of Snookie's tail against the floorboards.

"Everything is good here," he replied. "Dr. Brown is sleeping and we haven't had any problems."

"Excellent. I know this isn't your typical work. Are you happy to stay there and watch over her, or would you like me to send a replacement so you can resume your usual duties?"

"No," Gareth snapped, coming fully awake as abruptly as if he'd been doused with cold water from the lake. He took a deep breath to calm his stuttering heart before he continued. "What I mean is, I know Avery, sir. She's stubborn and determined and she'll walk all over anyone else you assign to her.

I'll stay here, provided someone else covers the station in Itirangi."

Rata was silent for a moment, then asked, "Exactly how well do you know *Avery?*"

The palms of his hands sweated. He knew with utter certainty that this question was a trap. If he answered incorrectly, he'd probably be removed from the case and someone else assigned to protect Avery. That couldn't be allowed to happen. He respected his colleagues, but none of them would have the same drive to keep her from harm as he did. None of them would adhere to protocol so strictly.

"There was a time I knew her very well," he replied hesitantly. "But that was a long time ago. There's nothing to worry about now. Nothing at all."

"You're quite sure about that?" Rata sounded suspicious, but that was par for the course.

He ran a hand through his close-cropped hair and rubbed the back of his neck. "Yes, sir."

"Good. Stay where you are. I expect to hear from you later today."

"You will. Can you keep me informed if there are any developments in the case or if anything is found at either of the crime scenes?"

"That depends on if I think it's in your best interest to know."

While disappointed, he hadn't expected anything else. Rata kept her cards notoriously close to her chest. "Okay. Before you go, Avery wants to know how soon we can arrange for another sample to come so she can get busy."

"Tell her I've already put in a call to the team up north. They're couriering a package down. It should arrive tomorrow."

So quickly? Rata was efficient as hell, but this was a level beyond what he was used to. He weighed this latest development, wondering if she had pushed forward quickly because she was worried the person targeting Avery would make another move sooner rather than later. Prickles of concern danced up his spine.

"Is there a problem, Sergeant?"

He snapped to attention. "No, sir." At least, there wouldn't be if he had anything to do with it. Avery wouldn't be more than fifty yards from him until they had this perp in handcuffs. "Permission for Dr. Brown to arrange an alternative laboratory for testing?"

"Permission granted." Rata paused, then added in a more conversational tone, "Dr. Brown is a woman I respect and admire greatly, but I know this can't be easy for her. My guess is she'll try to distract herself by channeling her energy toward nailing the bastard who did it, and I can certainly sympathize with that. She's not a reckless person by nature, but what she's been through could push her that way. Keep an eye on her, and keep her safe."

"I will. You have my word." Gareth took his promises very seriously, just like he took his duties as a policeman seriously. If he didn't, how could he ever expect to keep innocent people safe? "I'll check in later."

He hung up, stretched, and emitted a low groan at the way his muscles protested. He was a big guy. Tiny beds didn't agree with him. Slinging his legs over the edge, he lowered himself until his feet touched a rung on the ladder then climbed to the ground. Glancing into the bottom bunk to check on Avery, he looked directly into her clear cobalt gaze and found himself caught. He couldn't look away. So many emotions flickered through her eyes. It was like he could see straight into her soul, but what he saw there confused the hell out of him. Pain, loss, determination—none of which were surprising—but also…distrust? What had he done to earn that? He ran back through his conversation with the inspector. He hadn't said anything to warrant her suspicion.

"Good morning," he said, breaking the taut silence. "How are you feeling today?"

"I'm fine," she said. A blatant lie. No one could be fine after the day she'd had yesterday, but if she didn't trust him enough to be honest, that was her prerogative. Though he felt the sting of her doubt.

"Did you sleep all right?" he asked.

She pulled a face. "I guess so. I was pretty out of it, but I still feel exhausted."

They were back on familiar ground. This, he could deal with. "That's usual. After an adrenaline dump like the one you had yesterday, it could take several days or even a couple of weeks to come right. Don't rush it."

She nodded and wiped the corners of her eyes. "I've experienced adrenaline crashes once or twice before. Not much fun, but they don't last forever." Coming upright, she shook her hair out of her face and gestured at the top bunk. "Was that Rata you were talking to?"

"That's right. She called to check in."

Avery ducked out from the bunk, ignored the dog, who nosed at her legs, and crossed the small space to the clothesline. She grabbed a fistful of one of her T-shirts. Apparently dissatisfied, she tested another.

"Have they made much progress with the investigation?" she asked, pulling the shirt off the line, along with a beige bra and a pair of cotton panties he'd been trying not to notice. "I'm keen to get back to work this morning. It's bad enough missing one day, let alone two. Especially when I'm working on something so important."

He stared at her in disbelief. "You do remember your house burned down yesterday? I think that justifies a few days off work."

She shrugged one shoulder and didn't look him in the eye. "The sooner I nail this guy, the sooner I can start fixing what needs to be fixed."

Rata's words echoed in his mind. He needed to make sure she didn't do anything reckless. She needed to slow down and take care of herself. It was no good him protecting her from criminals if he couldn't protect her from herself.

"You won't like to hear this," he began cautiously, "but we might be here for a while. My colleagues are still investigating. They didn't find any evidence at your house except for the gasoline that was used as an accelerant." One of his colleagues had messaged with that detail late last night. "They found a partial print at the lab but not enough to match to anyone conclusively. The soil sample hasn't arrived yet, although Rata says it should be here tomorrow so you can go ahead and arrange for an alternative lab to test in. Besides that, there's not much you can do this morning."

As soon as the last phrase left his mouth, he winced. Poor choice of words. Never tell the victim of a crime that there's nothing they can do. Particularly not in the case of a clever, stubborn woman like Avery.

She scowled mutinously. "There is, actually. If I had my computer or the copy of my program that Rata keeps somewhere safe, I could start doing prep work so then all I need to do once I have the laboratory test results is plug the numbers in."

"Oh." Well, damn. He hadn't known that, but he shouldn't have made assumptions, either. Time to try a different tack. "I don't like being stuck out here anymore than you do. I'd much rather be part of the action, doing my part to get justice for you and that poor girl, but my boss assigned me this job so we have to make the most of it." He gestured to the clothing she held. "Why don't you get dressed and I'll see if I can find us something for breakfast."

She didn't agree with him, but nor did she argue, so he took that as a win and started searching the cupboards, listening to the rustle of clothes being removed and resisting the urge to peek. He wanted to know how Avery's body had changed over the past years, but spying on her would be disrespectful and unprofessional.

In the cupboard beneath the sink he found a box of cereal and a bag of powdered milk. *Success*. He grabbed a couple of chipped pottery bowls, poured cereal into them—ignoring the fact that it appeared to be stale—and reconstituted the milk powder using water from the tank. Thankfully it was winter, so rainwater was plentiful. He grabbed a handful of dog biscuits from a bag and placed them outside for Snookie, leaving the door ajar so she could come back in, then set both cereal bowls on the table and found two spoons, which he wiped clean. Keeping his attention strictly on his side of the room, he began to eat. Stale, as he'd thought, but edible.

After a moment, Avery joined him, wearing a new t-shirt and her jeans. He needed to change as well, but at least he'd stripped out of his uniform and donned a pair of track pants and a t-shirt before he'd fallen asleep.

"So," she said after she swallowed the first mouthful of her breakfast, not making a fuss over its lack of freshness. "If you want to be in town, working the investigation, and I want to be in town, preparing to do the tests, what's stopping us? It seems to me like there's no reason to stay here. I could do my work at the police station and I'd be as safe there as I am out here. Probably safer, since I'd be surrounded by police officers."

He couldn't deny that she spoke the truth. Most likely, she'd be safe in the police station, and he could ease his frustration by digging into some meaty investigative work, but his orders were to keep her out of town, and keep her safe. Gareth followed orders. Always. When cops didn't do as they were told, bad things happened, and others paid the price.

"I'm sorry, A-Bee," he said. "I wish I could do that, but I have my orders. We're not leaving this cabin. At least, not today. Is there anything I can do to make you more comfortable?"

If looks could kill.

"Your orders make no sense," she snapped. "I have no problem with you doing your duty but there's no point in following orders just for the sake of it. I'm sure if you spoke to Rata, she'd agree."

Gareth's hackles rose, the way they always did when someone suggested he bend the rules or be lenient on them. Broken rules led to broken bodies.

"I'm a *cop*, it's my job to follow orders, whether I like them or not. I'll speak to Rata later and see whether anything has changed, but I won't disrespect her by behaving as though her orders are optional. She's my superior officer, and I respect her position more than I sympathize with your desire not to be stuck here."

Her shoulders slumped and he felt like a jerk.

"I don't want you to disrespect Rata," she muttered. "I just hate feeling so useless."

"You're not useless," he assured her. "You're going to be the one who brings this guy down. You're the brains here. Me and the guys, we're just foot soldiers. You'll get your chance, I promise." She almost smiled. He took that as encouragement. "Why don't you tell me a bit more about your work and how you got into it?"

*a*very swallowed her frustration and shoveled more cereal into her mouth. This inactivity was killing her. Yes, she'd been awake for less than twenty minutes, but usually by this point she'd be well on her way to work. Instead, she was facing down the prospect of a day sitting around with nothing to do except call a friend about a lab and think about the mess that awaited her at home. Could she even call it "home" if there was no longer a house there? Probably not. That's right, she was homeless.

Gareth watched her expectantly. Had he asked something? "Can you repeat that?"

"This work you're doing for the government," he said. "How'd you get into it?"

Chewing the last of the cereal, she pushed the bowl aside. "Do you know what I studied at university?"

"Soil science," he replied, offering her an encouraging nod.

"That's right." He must have paid some attention to her over the years. "Specifically, I studied isotopes in the soil and whether the composition of isotopes varied depending on climate."

"Fascinating."

Briefly, it occurred to her that he might be mocking her, but he looked enthralled. *Don't doubt him without any evidence.* Besides, even if he'd found her postgraduate study utterly dull, of course he'd be interested in her answer because it had brought her to where she was now: using her knowledge and skills to advance law enforcement.

"Remind me what an isotope is," he said.

"Isotopes are the different forms of chemical elements. Oxygen, carbon, nitrogen, metals... many of them exist in different forms which have slightly different characteristics."

"Right, I remember now." He looked pleased with himself. "We learned about them in high school chemistry."

"That's right!" She grinned. "I spent a couple of years travelling around to some of the hottest and coldest places in the world to get samples of soils from places with extreme climates. I spent a few weeks each in Antarctica, Alaska, Russia, California, Libya and Mali."

He whistled through his teeth. "Wow, what an interesting group of places. I can't believe you visited Antarctica. That's incredible. What was it like?" His gold-brown eyes were alive with curiosity.

She summoned the memory of Antarctica to the forefront of her mind, so vivid she could almost feel the bitingly cold wind whispering across her cheeks. "Just like what you'd imagine. Snow and ice as far as you can see in every direction. Like a frozen desert. Bitterly cold, but completely beautiful. Distance gets distorted there. An ice shelf might look like you could walk to it in five minutes when it's actually a day's walk away. On clear days, you can see for miles, but then the fog rolls in and if you're not careful, you can get trapped outside, unable to see more than a couple of meters ahead, walking in circles for hours."

"Amazing," he breathed.

"Yes, but terrifying too."

"I can see how it would be. What about the other places? Some of them don't sound very safe."

She laughed at his concern. "I survived."

His expression darkened, and she thought she'd ruined the easy conversation between them, but then he asked, "Which place was your favorite?"

She thought for a moment. "They were all so different, and while I tried to have a look around while I was there, I didn't always have much free time. Still, I'd have to say I enjoyed Antarctica the most. It's just breathtaking."

"I'm proud of you, Avery." He spoke quietly, his expression—when she glanced up at him—soft but intense. "You've done things no one else from Itirangi ever has. I don't know if you realize it, but the whole town is proud of you."

Her chest felt like it might bubble over with emotion, but at the same time, she wanted to duck her head and shrug off his compliments. She wasn't a great adventurer or anything, just a girl with a lot of unanswered questions and the motivation to chase the answers. "Thank you. That's sweet of you to say."

"It's true," he insisted. "For years, the gossips couldn't stop gabbing about your latest adventure."

Strangely, she had no desire to rub his face in the fact she'd made something of herself after they broke up, though she'd always believed she would, given the chance. Instead, she found herself hoping he didn't have any regrets over how his life had turned out. Ridiculous, but there you had it.

He must have seen something in the way her nose crinkled or her mouth slanted, because he said, "I'm happy with how things have gone for me. Coming back to Itirangi wasn't what I expected, but there's nowhere I'd rather be. Sometimes life has plans for you that don't mirror your own."

At that moment, the door creaked open. They both stiffened, but it was only Snookie returning. She curled up on the rug and wagged her tail.

"Very wise of you," Avery said. He'd always had a good head on his shoulders. Even if he wasn't an academic, he had common sense and understood people.

"If there was one thing I could change…" He trailed off. "Never mind."

She didn't push him, too afraid of what he might say. She remembered what she'd overheard earlier. Gareth assuring Rata that there was nothing at all to worry about when it came to keeping the relationship between them professional. She wasn't hung up on him, but hearing him say what amounted to having no regrets over ending their relation-ship… it hurt. She'd like to think he'd doubted his choice once or twice over the years. Certainly, she'd doubted her decision not to fight for him. He'd been her lover and her best friend rolled into one; how could she not have mourned his loss?

Gathering their bowls, she carried them to the outside tap to rinse them off. Then she put them upside down on the countertop to dry and sat cross-legged on the bottom bunk. There was nothing else she could do, and she hated it.

"So tell me," she said to Gareth. "What have you gotten up to since high school?"

He sat at the other end of the bed, his legs extended before him, ankles crossed. He'd changed back into his blue uniform shirt and pants, but his vest was draped over a chair. "Nothing as exciting as what you've done. It's a boring story. Sure you want to hear it?"

She gestured around them. "We're in a cabin in the middle of nowhere. I haven't got anything better to do."

He huffed a laugh. "True. After school, I went away to police academy in Porirua," he said. "You already know that. Then I spent a year as a rookie in Wellington and another year in Christchurch before I moved home."

"Really?" She'd never asked about him, never looked him up. Had, in fact, preferred to pretend he didn't exist until she encountered him again at a social function. She'd always known there was a reason she didn't go out much, and that day had reinforced it. Seeing his face had been like receiving a kick in the gut. But she'd gotten over it.

"You were still at university then," he continued.

She studied her palms. He'd given her an easy out. An excuse for not showing a polite level of interest in him. She wasn't sure if she deserved it.

"I worked out of the Timaru office for three years before I was given the senior position at Itirangi," he continued, oblivious to her discomfort with talk of the past, and she had no one to blame but herself. She *had* asked. "No one else particularly wanted to work here, so they were all relieved when I had enough experience under my belt to take over."

"I bet they were." Many people loved to vacation in Itirangi, but few would choose to live or work there. It was too small, and too far from any large cities.

"During those first five years of my police career, I studied psychology part-time through the University of Canterbury."

Avery's head jerked back and her lips parted. "What?"

He shrugged, like it was no big deal, but she knew how much work it must have taken to fit in study, assignments, and exams while learning the ropes of a new job. His cheeks turned pink under her scrutiny and he cleared his throat. "I was always attracted to the science of the mind, and it's relevant to my work."

"How come you never told me?" And how had she not known? Itirangi was a hive of gossip. Everyone knew everything about everyone else. One of her friends should have filled her in if this was common knowledge. "Wait." She leaned toward him and continued in a softer voice, "Does anyone know? Your parents?"

He laughed and it felt like a knot loosened inside her

chest. "Of course they do. It's not a secret. It's just not something I talk about a lot."

"But why not?" She grabbed his arm, feeling his bicep flex beneath her palm. "Earning a degree while you're working full time is difficult. You should be proud of yourself."

"I am." He smiled and it warmed his eyes, which twinkled as they met hers. She licked her lips self-consciously. His breath caught. Her heart hammered as they locked eyes. She had to break this moment, before she said or did something she'd regret.

"Underwear," she said, then mentally slapped herself as his brows tugged down into a befuddled frown. Of all the things she could have said.

"Underwear?" he asked, confused.

Well, she'd dug herself into this hole, she'd have to get herself out of it. "I need more," she told him. "Other supplies, too. We should go into town and pick a few things up."

"No." His expression closed off instantly, giving her the distance she'd needed, but she wasn't as relieved as she thought she'd be. "We're not leaving here," he said. "End of story. If you need things, make a list and I'll arrange for someone to drop them off."

"Fine," she grumbled, frustrated she'd failed to convince him to leave, but not surprised. "I'll do that."

When a car engine hummed up to the cabin, Snookie barked and Gareth ordered Avery to lie flat on the ground while he checked to see who it was. A gray four-wheel-drive vehicle had parked outside. His shoulders relaxed as he recognized the driver and he motioned for Avery to get up.

"It's Mum," he told her. "With supplies."

She grinned. She and his mum had always gotten along like a house on fire. Poor choice of words.

The point was, she adored his mum, and the feeling was mutual. Sharon Wayland had cried nearly as much as he had when they broke up, if not more so. She'd said he was being thick-headed, and as far as he knew, her opinion hadn't changed. She'd never approved of any other woman he'd brought home, though she'd never been openly hostile. During the last few years, she'd suggested several times that he should get his head out of his ass and ask Avery out before someone else did.

To be fair, if Avery had shown the least bit of interest, he probably would have.

The door swung open.

"Sharon!" Avery cried, rushing forward to hug her, Snookie following close behind, also a fan of his mother. "It's so good to see you. It's been ages."

Sharon's eyes widened. He hadn't mentioned that her favorite past-prospective daughter-in-law would be here.

"Avery!" Sharon exclaimed, recovering quickly and wrapping her arms around the younger woman. "Hi, honey." Releasing Avery, she stepped back, dropped to one knee to cuddle Snookie, then looked from Avery to Gareth. "Does one of you want to explain what's going on?"

Gareth hadn't told her anything on the phone, other than that he was at Ram's cabin and needed supplies—and *yes*, it was work related. As if he'd have his mother running personal errands just so he could have some downtime.

Sharon caught his eye. "You said you were here for work."

There was an accusation in her voice. She thought she'd been misled. The smile hovering at the corners of her mouth proved she wasn't too upset—if he'd actually gotten back together with Avery, he suspected she'd be excited enough to throw a party—but nonetheless, she didn't like being deceived.

"I did," he confirmed. "Did you read the newspaper this morning, Mum?"

"No." She looked puzzled. "Never do. If there's anything worth knowing, someone will tell me."

"Apparently you missed the news," Avery said wryly. "My house burned down yesterday."

"Oh my god!" Sharon gasped, her hand flying to her mouth. "That's awful. I'm so sorry. I saw the smoke, but I assumed it was a burn-off gone wrong. What happened?" She glanced between the two of them and her brows lowered. "Was it arson?" she whispered, finally reaching the inevitable conclusion.

"Yes," Avery said, at the same time as Gareth replied in a more circumspect way, "We believe so."

Sharon pulled Avery back into a hug and squeezed her tightly. Avery buried her face in her hair.

"I'm so sorry, baby girl," Sharon murmured. "I can't believe anyone would do that. You've always got a home with me if you want one."

"Thank you." Avery's voice was thick, almost as though she were crying, but when she extricated herself from Sharon's grasp, her eyes were dry, her complexion white.

"Tell me everything," his mum ordered, dragging a chair over and dropping into it. "Was it random, or did someone target our girl?" Her questions were directed at her son.

"I can't share any details," he said, repeating the comment he'd been making non-stop for the past twenty-four hours. "It's an ongoing investigation."

She harrumphed. "I don't give a shit about your politically correct answers, Gaz. I'm your mother, and I deserve to know the details."

Gareth's lips firmed. She knew better than anyone not to push him on this. He wouldn't budge an inch. Not only for the sake of his job, but also for her own safety. The fewer people who knew about the connection with the Grant case, the better.

But Avery had no such compunction. She brought the

other chair over to join Sharon. "I'm working on a forensic tool for the police," she explained. "And someone doesn't want me to use it."

He leveled her with his darkest glare but her chin lifted in a challenge, letting him know he didn't intimidate her. He sighed. At least she'd kept the particulars to herself.

"So this person burned your house down?" Sharon asked, shocked. "Why? Wouldn't this tool be at your work?"

Gareth and Avery exchanged looks. He nodded, giving her permission to go on. Now she'd shared half of the story, they'd never get rid of his mum until she knew the rest.

"My lab was vandalized, too," Avery explained. "Everything was destroyed. Well, nearly everything."

"How horrible," Sharon said. "You poor thing." She turned to Gareth. "I hope you've got everyone out looking for this monster."

"We do."

She nodded. "Good. Is there anything I can do?"

He motioned to the bags she'd set on the floor when Avery hugged her. "You've been a great help by bringing that over. We need to keep Avery out of town until my colleagues track the perp down."

"Is she in danger?" she demanded, the color leaching from her cheeks.

"We don't know. But we're taking precautions, just in case."

"Good." She jammed her hands in her armpits, arms across her chest as though she were hugging herself. "I guess I'd better get going. I don't want to distract you when you've got such important work to do." She jerked her head toward the door. "Gaz, can I talk to you outside for a minute?"

Gareth nodded and waited while Sharon forced a smile—which came out as more of a grimace—then followed her outside.

"What is it?" he asked when the door clicked shut behind

them. He was curious about what she felt she couldn't say in front of Avery.

His mum unhooked her hands, grabbed his elbow and tugged him toward her car. She spoke in a low voice. "You take care of that girl," she hissed. "You hear me? Nothing happens to her on your watch. *Nothing*."

He swallowed around the lump in his throat. "I'm well ahead of you on that one. Trust me, I'll keep her in one piece."

"You'd better." Her eyes narrowed. "She's too stubborn for her own good sometimes." Then she hesitated, glanced away, and hunched her shoulders the way she did when she needed to say something uncomfortable.

"Out with it," he demanded. "Whatever it is, get it off your chest."

Sharon craned her neck to meet his eyes. "This is your chance," she whispered. "Reel her back in. Don't let her go again. Promise me you won't blow this."

"Mum—"

"No." She shook her head forcefully. "Don't deny it. I can see there's still something between you. I stood by and let you make mistakes in the past, but I won't do it again. I want to see you happy."

He hadn't planned on denying it. Fact was, he did want to see whether he and Avery could have a future. But that couldn't happen until this case was wrapped up. He couldn't be distracted from his duty, or take advantage of her during a difficult time. There was a thin line between good cops and bad cops. A line that was easy to cross.

Running a hand through his hair, he muttered, "You didn't exactly 'stand by' last time. I remember you calling me a brainless nitwit, or something along those lines."

She snorted. "Well, you were."

Ouch. Her jab landed like a well-placed fist in his diaphragm. His darling mum didn't pull any punches.

"The breakup was mutual," he said. "We made the decision together. It was the best thing for both of us. Anyway, I can't make a move on Avery while I'm working her case, but I promise you I will when everything is finished. Okay?"

She pursed her lips. "I suppose that will have to do. Now, give your old ma a kiss and I'll be off."

He kissed the cheek she offered and waved as the vehicle rumbled back toward the road.

7

By the time evening fell, Avery had read the James Patterson novel she'd found tucked inside one of the cupboards, and played what seemed like fifty games of solitaire. She'd tried to entice Gareth to join her, but Sharon had brought him some paperwork from the station and he'd filled in his day catching up on work.

Lucky for some.

She'd even tried playing with the dog to pass the time, but the German shepherd seemed disinterested in tug of war and Gareth wouldn't let them go outside to play fetch. Lying on her back on the top bunk, staring at the wooden slats above her head, Avery counted down the minutes until it was time to prepare dinner. At least then she'd have *something* to do. An electronic noise sounded, so abrupt in the quiet cabin that she flinched.

"That's mine," Gareth said, as if there were any doubt. He fished it from his breast pocket, touched the screen and raised it to his ear. "Wayland." He listened for a moment, then extended his arm toward her, holding the phone out. "It's for you."

She grabbed it from him, too relieved by the distraction

to care who it might be, and said cheerily, "Avery here. Please, whoever this is, tell me I can go somewhere or do something."

A woman chuckled, and she recognized the raspy laugh as belonging to Adaline Rata. "Good news, Dr. Brown. You can go somewhere *and* do something."

Avery's heart lightened. "Oh, thank god. I've got to tell you, I'm not built for waiting."

"I suspected that might be the case." Rata sounded amused. "We've received a second soil sample. If you and Sergeant Wayland collect it tomorrow, you can run your tests as soon as you've organized somewhere to do so."

"I'll sort that right now," Avery replied, grinning. "It won't be a problem."

"I'm glad to hear that. I'm sure you're as eager as I am to see this case closed."

"Absolutely." The sooner the police arrested this guy, the sooner he could pay for what he'd done to that young girl, and to Avery. He needed to be *made* to pay. But still, she couldn't help thinking that once her involvement in the case ceased, she'd have to figure out what to do and where to live. *And how to move on.*

"Avery..." Rata began slowly, as though turning over a thought in her wonderfully organized brain. "Can I call you that?"

"I'd like it if you did."

"I hate to ask you this," she continued, "but how are things with the sergeant? He told me the two of you have a past, and I want to make sure you're comfortable with the situation. He was frank about it and didn't seem concerned, but I'd kick myself if I left you with a man who made you uncomfortable for whatever reason." She paused, allowing her words to sink in. "You're going through enough at the moment without having anything else to worry about."

The question had Avery scowling at the unpleasant recollection of the conversation she'd overheard, but she shook off her doldrums. Knowing that Rata cared for her well-being was nice. She didn't make female friends easily. Most of the friends she had, she'd known all of her life.

"Thank you for worrying," she said, meaning it. "But I'm okay. The sooner this is over, the better, but I'm not going to have a breakdown."

She certainly wouldn't have one just because Gareth didn't see her in a romantic light. She had more self-respect than that.

"That's a relief," Rata said brusquely. "Go ahead and confirm the use of a laboratory, and I may see you tomorrow when you come by for the sample."

"It's a plan." She hung up and handed the phone back to Gareth, who hadn't stopped watching her for the duration of the call.

"They have the soil sample?" he guessed.

"They do. We can pick it up tomorrow."

His brow furrowed in a familiar expression of caution. "The inspector is okay with you leaving the cabin?"

Avery held up a finger and clucked. "Oh, no. Don't you give me that look. I'm taking this damn sample to a lab and testing the shit out of it. Rata isn't worried about me braving the world beyond the cabin, so there's no reason for you to worry. You can get any thoughts about stopping me out of that thick skull of yours. Come with me if you must, but I'm going either way."

He folded his arms across his chest, his shirt straining over well-developed pecs. "You about done?"

She didn't dignify that with a reply.

"We'll go to whatever lab you can arrange," he said, as though it was ever in doubt. "But we're taking my cruiser and you don't leave my sight at any time."

She shrugged. She'd expected more of an argument. "Okay."

To be honest, she would have accepted a number of other conditions if it meant getting out of here. Being cooped up inside with Gareth and his sexy broad shoulders and the alluring pepperminty smell from the gum he chewed was more than she could stand for much longer. If he wanted to watch over her like a glorified bodyguard, so be it. At least she could interact with other people and do something productive with her time.

"We'll need to stay elsewhere for a night, maybe two," she told him. "I won't get through all of the lab work in one day."

His jaw worked, and he obviously didn't like it, but he tilted his head in acknowledgement. "I pick the hotel."

"Sure." Their accommodation didn't bother her in the slightest. She'd overnighted in a tent in Antarctica, spent three weeks in an open-sided shelter with one of the indigenous tribes of Mali, and lived for years in sub-par student housing. She could sleep anywhere. "Can I borrow your phone to call my friend Jesse to see if I can use his lab tomorrow?"

"Where is Jesse's lab?"

"Dunedin."

He nodded and passed the phone back to her. "Make sure he understands that it needs to be empty except for the people who absolutely have to be there."

"I will." Jesse's lab was too small for more than two people, anyway. "Am I allowed to turn my phone back on to find his number?"

"No."

"Fine, then." She was too excited to let his inflexibility bother her. She googled the University of Otago's chemistry department, called reception, and asked to be put through to Dr. Stone.

"Hi, Jesse," she exclaimed, far too brightly. "It's been ages! How are you?"

"It's great to hear from you, Avery," her friend replied. "What's up?"

"I have some tests I need to run, time sensitive, and I've had some problems with my equipment. Any chance I can come down there tomorrow and borrow your lab?" She crossed her fingers. Often laboratories were booked out days or weeks in advance. She heard him check the booking diary.

"It's just me in here tomorrow," he said. "None of the work I need to do is on a tight deadline, so I can shuffle it back a couple of days."

A triumphant grin stretched her lips.

"I wouldn't do it for just anyone," he continued, "but it's not often the famous Dr. Brown deigns to visit my humble space. Say, I don't suppose you'd be available for a guest lecture next month?"

"If you pull this off for me, I'll be available for an entire week, if that's what you want."

"Done."

"Thank you so much. I owe you one."

"I'm going to hold you to that." She heard the smile in his voice. Pictured his attractive, symmetrical features and the glasses that were always perched on the tip of his nose. He'd made it clear several times during the years that he was interested in her as more than a colleague, and she wished, not for the first time, that she felt the same way. Alas, while she had more in common with academic men, she was typically attracted to athletes and outdoorsy types. Probably her cavewoman instincts telling her they'd make a better provider, which was, in this modern day, frankly ridiculous. But she couldn't control her biological reactions. Go figure.

"Bye, Jesse," she said warmly. Perhaps she didn't want to jump his bones, but she genuinely liked him. "I'll see you tomorrow."

"See you later, Brainiac," he replied, ending the call.

"All set," she said, putting the phone in front of Gareth,

who sat at the table scrawling on a piece of paper. He added the paper to a pile then shifted the pile to a cardboard folder, which was labeled with a bunch of numbers and hyphens that presumably related to some type of filing system.

"What did Mum bring to eat?" he asked as he packed the folder into his duffel bag. Snookie roused herself from the corner and wandered over, nosing his leg, seeking attention. He stroked her head absentmindedly as Avery checked the other bags.

"There's a vegetable stir fry, dehydrated mashed potato, and a ready-to-eat bag of rice. Or if you'd rather, there's cheese, crackers, and a jar of Marmite." She licked her lips. "Mama Sharon's got good taste."

"She did *not* pack Marmite," Gareth muttered, brushing past Snookie to look for himself. "Well, I'll be."

His disgruntled expression drew a laugh from Avery. He'd preferred Vegemite to Marmite growing up, but no one in his family, or indeed, in their circle of friends, shared his preference. Marmite was a Kiwi staple. Vegemite was a second-rate Aussie substitute. Simple as that.

"Stir fry and rice for dinner," he announced. "You fire up the cooker and I'll clean out the pan."

They set to work, and before long they were sitting opposite each other at the table, each with a bowl of vegetables that were charred on the outside and hard on the inside. Neither of them had mastered the art of stir-fry. Avery tossed the rice through her veggies and ripped open a sachet of soy sauce, mixing it through. She was all about salty food, something they had in common. They ate in silence, then washed their bowls and each lay on a bunk, while Snookie curled on her rug.

Avery's stomach was full, she was warm, and tomorrow she could make herself useful. For the first time in forty-eight hours, she felt okay. Not wonderful, by any stretch, but it felt like she'd been precariously balanced on a tightrope above a fifty-foot drop for the past two days, and finally there was a net beneath her to catch her if she fell.

"Can I ask you something?" Gareth's voice came from above, because he'd been relegated to the top bunk again.

"Fire away."

She expected him to query their course of action for tomorrow, or perhaps make generic small talk.

"Why did we never get back together? I always thought we would one day, but instead we grew apart."

The question made her insides lurch as if she were on a rollercoaster. It felt like someone had stolen the net from beneath her tightrope. Squeezing her eyes shut, her breath whooshed from her chest and her hands fisted at her sides.

"Y-you never said," she stammered, caught off guard.

Suddenly, everything tipped on its head. All of her assumptions that he'd taken the easy way out and broken up with her ostensibly because of the difficulty of a long-distance relationship when in actuality, he'd wanted someone else. Someone more feminine, shorter and curvier, less apt to act like one of the guys.

She swallowed. If he'd thought they'd get back together, then her assumptions had been flawed. She was floundering, trying to swim in water over her head, but no one had taught her how.

"I didn't know you felt that way." Avery never shied away from difficult conversations. Her friends would say she wielded her tongue like a blunt instrument, but that was only when she involved herself in other people's problems. When it came to her personal life, she'd rather slam the door on all those old, unwanted emotions and pretend they didn't exist. She didn't want to admit the embarrassing truth.

"I didn't think I had to say it," he replied, oblivious to her distress. He couldn't see her, so he didn't know that she was praying for someone to set fire to the cabin right this minute so she could run out, throw herself into the lake and head for the opposite shore. Anything to avoid this goddamned awful conversation.

"We were so good together, I figured we'd settle down once we were both back in Itirangi. Assuming you ever came back," he added as an afterthought.

"You thought…" She trailed off, stubbornly refusing to open her eyes, hoping by some miracle she'd fall asleep so she didn't have to piece together the words that would form an appropriate response. With an effort, she corralled her thoughts, sat upright and rubbed her temples.

"People grow apart," she muttered, not really knowing where she was going with this, but if she didn't say something, he'd prolong the conversation. "We're different now than we were in high school. I guess we don't fit as well as we did back then."

That sounded half reasonable. Somewhat distant, perhaps, but she'd rather he think her a cold bitch than know that he'd hurt her back then, far more than she'd ever let on, and she wasn't prepared to let herself be vulnerable to him so he could take another shot.

"Maybe," he said, noncommittally. "But I don't think that's it."

When a minute ticked by in silence, she hoped he didn't have anything further to say and relaxed, rolling onto her side and slipping her hand beneath her cheek.

"I've often wondered if you were the one who got away," he mused, so softly that perhaps she'd misheard him. Shit. She could not be having this conversation. Just thinking of the promises he'd made back then had her breaking out in a cold sweat. All the pretty words about "forever" and "always" that she'd fallen for hook, line, and sinker, only to have the ground buckle beneath her. She uttered a snuffling sound, like a snore, then exhaled slowly and deeply, as if she were asleep.

He laughed quietly to himself. "Of course. I finally come clean, and you're asleep. Sweet dreams, A-Bee."

Curling tightly into herself, she tried not to feel deceptive or cowardly. This would be best for both of them, in the long run.

8

In stealth mode, Avery slipped from the bottom bunk and tiptoed across the wooden floor to grab her phone and its battery, which were tucked into the pocket of Gareth's jacket, hung over the back of a chair. She carefully jiggled the device free, so as not to wake him, then stepped into her shoes to go outside. She shivered as the cold morning air swept along her bare arms, leaving goosebumps in its wake. Snookie tried to follow. Glancing at Gareth's slumbering form, she let the dog out, and Snookie ran to the edge of the trees, happily sniffing the base of one.

Keeping an eye on the dog, not trusting her to stay silent, she slotted the battery into its compartment, started the phone up, and suppressed a twinge of guilt. Sending one or two texts couldn't hurt, and she desperately needed her best friend's advice. Besides, Gareth was probably being paranoid. She scrolled through her contacts and selected Clarissa's number, then tapped out a message.

Hey, Riss. Need your perspective, and also a reality check. I've spent the past couple of days with Gareth. Struggling to keep a level head. Help!

She hit send, and watched the icon whir round and

round, searching for a signal and eventually finding enough of one to send. A thought occurred to her and she quickly added, *P.S. Don't call.*

She extracted the battery and shoved both parts of the phone into her pocket, then stuck two fingers between her lips and whistled. The noise pierced the silence around them and Snookie's ears perked up. She turned and trotted back to Avery, tail wagging. She stopped at Avery's feet and sat, looking up as though waiting for praise.

"Good mutt," she mumbled grudgingly.

The door opened behind her. Presumably her whistle had woken Gareth.

"Get back inside," he snapped, and she rolled her eyes—not that he could see. "It's not safe out here."

"Yes, sir, Mr. Warden, sir." She turned on her heel and squeezed past him through the doorway when he didn't move out of her way. Sheesh, you'd think if he wanted her inside that badly, he'd make it easier. "Your dog needed to pee."

"Oh." The grim lines around his mouth softened. "Well, thanks, then."

She didn't feel bad for the lie. Not at all. Besides, Snookie *had* answered the call of nature while they'd been outdoors. "No problem."

He was at a disadvantage and she wanted to keep him there so she stripped off her shirt, ignoring the choking sound he made, and turned her back to replace her bra with one from the bag his Mum had brought. When he hurried to avert his eyes, it gave her the opportunity to return her phone to his jacket pocket.

Inside, she buzzed with something like satisfaction. The stoic sergeant wasn't immune to her nudity. Good to know.

"You going to get a move on?" she demanded, not looking around. "We planned to be out of here first thing, remember?"

"Hold onto your britches," he said, "It'll take me two minutes to change my shirt and brush my teeth, then I'm good to go."

She didn't hear any movement. She turned to face him again, and realized he'd been waiting for her to do just that. He raised his eyes and, completely expressionless, grabbed the hem of his shirt and tugged it over his head. At the sight of his bare torso, saliva filled her mouth. He had hard abdominal muscles, tapered hips and firm shoulders she longed to grasp. She swallowed, unable to look away, like a starving woman before a buffet. He lifted one arm and deodorized, the oblique muscles along his side pulling tight.

Hell and damnation, he was one sexy-ass package of alpha cop who was giving as good as he got. This was punishment for stripping in front of him—she knew that, and she should be annoyed, but if he never covered himself up again, she'd die a happy woman.

Then he did, yanking a plain black t-shirt on over all of that hot, muscled goodness. She squelched her disappointment and struggled to get a hold of herself. At least she hadn't gaped with an open mouth, or drooled. He met her gaze, his expression neutral, but something sparkled in his eyes. Amusement. He was enjoying this. Oddly enough, she was, too.

Damn, she really did need Clarissa to slap some sense into her.

"You about done?" she croaked, exactly like someone who'd just been fantasizing about running her tongue down the groove in the middle of his six-pack.

He shoved a few items into his duffel bag, zipped it and slung it over his shoulder. "Yep. Lead on, sweetheart."

She bit her tongue so she didn't cuss him out and tell him not to call her sweetheart. That was what he wanted. He may be putting up a professional front for the most part, but the flush on his cheeks told her he liked riling her up. Even though she didn't say a word, he gave her a sidelong glance and a smirk. The smart-ass thought he had her all figured out.

Two could play at that game.

She dumped the stuff she'd packed into the trunk of his car and opened the back door so Snookie could jump in, then slid into the passenger seat and buckled up.

"So, we'll be sharing a hotel room tonight?" she asked as he fastened his seat belt beside her. "Just the two of us? Did you make sure the room we're staying in has two beds, or do we both have to squeeze into one? I'm all for sharing heat—Dunedin is damn cold this time of year—only, I don't have any pajamas."

His Adam's apple bobbed.

"The room has two beds," he grated out. "This is *work*, not a romantic getaway."

She shrugged. "Hey, you don't have to tell me twice. I'm the one who's homeless because of this case."

The words came out before she thought to censor them, and his entire body stiffened. His knuckles became white where he gripped the steering wheel and he clenched his teeth. Uh, oh. Should have stopped while she was ahead. She hadn't seen this version of Gareth before. He'd been prone to being too serious when they dated, but he'd never been particularly moody. He'd never radiated dark intensity the way he did now. She edged away from him. When he turned to her, his golden irises were the same shade of caramel as his hair. Deep and fierce.

"I won't let anything else happen to you," he said fervently, releasing the wheel with one hand to clench hers. "I'm sorry for the fire and the vandalism, but I promise, I'll take care of you now."

Avery's lips parted. "I believe you," she whispered.

In that moment, she didn't know the man looking at her. He was a stranger, inhabiting the body of someone she'd thought she knew. Had this fire always blazed within him, hidden away? Or had it grown as he changed from a boy into a man?

"Good," he said, dropping her hand and breaking eye contact. He turned the key in the ignition and put the car into gear. "We'll drop Snookie off at Justin's place, then stop by the station in Timaru to collect the sample and carry on to Dunedin. We should be there before lunchtime. Does that work for you?"

Nodding, Avery said nothing. Her tongue refused to work She needed a moment to process things.

They drove to Itirangi and stopped at Justin's house, where she waited in the car while Gareth unloaded Snookie and left instructions for her care. When they were halfway to Timaru, she remembered her text to Clarissa.

"Can I use my phone while we're at the police station?" she asked.

"No."

"Come on. I'll turn it off as soon as we leave, and what does it matter if someone tracks us there?" Not that she believed anyone would. "We'd be surrounded by police. Totally safe."

"I said no."

"But…" Desperation stole over her. She needed her friend's advice. Suddenly, she felt isolated. Alone, with no one to talk to. Ridiculous, and if any of her friends asked, she'd deny ever having such a melodramatic thought, but she couldn't help it. She pressed her lips together and swallowed. "Please, G. Just for five minutes."

He glanced over. "I'm sorry, but you can't. If someone tracks you to the station, they could follow us from there to Dunedin. It's not safe."

She deflated. She'd thought she had a solid argument, and hadn't really expected him to deny her. She peeked at his jacket, which he'd donned before they left the cabin. She had no hope of swiping the phone from his pocket without him noticing. She hunched her shoulders and tried to think of what Clarissa would say to her in this situation.

Be smart, honey. Remember what he did to you. How you felt afterward. He can't be trusted. You know that. Don't buy into his tricks.

She tried to draw comfort from this imagined response. She and Clarissa shared many world views, including the trustworthiness of certain members of the male gender. Clarissa had more reason for her opinion than Avery, although no one knew that except for the two of them. During senior year, Clarissa had learned a tough lesson from a man—technically, two—and subsequently moved out of home, onto Avery's sofa. No one ever asked why. Certainly they wondered, but they never asked.

It may have seemed strange for one of the prettiest, most sought-after girls in school to partner up with the local tomboy, but their shared secrets had formed an unbreakable bond, and each would happily go to war with anybody who upset the other. Hell, after Gareth and Avery had broken up, Clarissa had delivered him a stinging slap that was heard all around the world. No explanation, no apology. As far as Avery knew, they'd never spoken since.

"It's for your own good," Gareth said now. "Who is it you want to talk to?"

"Clarissa," she replied, wondering whether she'd imagined his flinch. Her lips curved up.

"We won't be able to visit her while we're in Dunedin," he said stiffly.

"Oh, I know. I just...wanted to talk to her. She's my best friend, after all." That time, she definitely didn't imagine the flinch. Oh, yeah. Big bad Gareth was scared of soft-spoken Clarissa, who was half his size and two hundred kilometers away.

"What's she doing these days?" The question came as he swerved into a car park behind the police station in Timaru.

"Running a bridal boutique in Dunedin. Designing dresses. Making everyone's happy-ever-after come true." The fact that Clarissa had gone into the wedding industry mystified Avery, since she was so wary of men herself, but to each their own.

"Ah. Right." He shoved the door open and almost stumbled in his haste to escape the conversation. Avery made to follow him, but he held up a hand. "No, you wait here. Stay low, and keep the doors locked. We want to get out of here quickly. If you come inside, you'll be answering questions for the next hour."

While she hated his high-handed approach, he had a point. "Fine," she agreed. "But be quick."

LUSH GREEN PADDOCKS flew by as they drove south toward Dunedin. Gareth had tucked the metal box that contained the soil sample beneath the seat, and was careful to keep his driving steady so the box didn't move around too much. Beside him, Avery sat in silence, still sulking about being unable to call Clarissa, one of the girls they'd gone to school with. He'd heard from his mother that Avery and Clarissa had lived together from the end of senior year, right through until Clarissa finished studying. They were as close as two emotionally shy, overly logical women could be.

There'd been a time when he and Clarissa had got on well enough, but after he'd separated from Avery, Clarissa had delivered a nasty slap to his left cheek and stomped on his toe so hard his nail had turned black and fallen off. Back then, he hadn't known why she'd assaulted him, and the intervening years hadn't brought any clarity.

"Tell me about the lab we're going to," he said, to distract himself from the mystery of women. "I need to get an idea of the terrain. How's it set up? Where is the lab within the building? Does it have many exits and entrances? How many people will be around?"

Avery gazed out the side window. Beyond the profile of her face, the paddocks had given way to views of the coast, with just a narrow strip of green between the road and the sand. "It's an old building," she said. "Five stories high. The clean room—where we'll be working—is on ground level. The corridor is split off from the foyer by a door that you need a key card to get through."

"Do you have one?"

"No, but Jesse will let us in. There's a fire exit at the other end of the corridor. Only one way into and out of the clean room, and you need a key."

He nodded, picturing it. "I guess Jesse has that key, too?"

"He does."

"Do many other people have access to the corridor or a key to the clean room?" He wanted to know what kind of crowd he could be dealing with.

She turned toward him and cocked her head. "Pretty much every chemistry student and staff member will have a key card. That could mean a couple of hundred people. Only a handful will have a key to the clean room, though, and the first floor is usually fairly deserted. The teaching labs are all on the higher floors."

"Good." The fewer people around, the lower the potential interference. "Fill me in on your buddy, Jesse."

She blinked. "Why?"

"Because we're giving him access to the biggest criminal case in New Zealand, and I want to know if he's trustworthy."

"One hundred percent," she answered firmly. "Jesse is a good man and a great scientist. I've known him for nearly ten years. We studied together during my first year of university, and we worked closely in our postgraduate years."

A dark suspicion flared within Gareth. He'd assumed, for some reason, that this Jesse fellow was a white-haired professor type, but if he'd studied with Avery, that made him a good thirty years younger than Gareth had assumed, and cast a different light on things.

"Is your relationship strictly professional?" he asked through gritted teeth, justifying the question by telling himself it was relevant to the case.

She shrugged. "We're friends. We have a professional relationship, but we also have a social relationship. At the moment, we're actually collaborating on a textbook for undergraduate students interested in soil science." Her lips slanted wryly. "You can imagine the nerdy conversations we have."

He could. Unfortunately, that only worsened the creeping feeling of unease. Because he hadn't seen Avery date, and because she didn't have a live-in partner, he'd thought that there was no man in her life. A miscalculation. These days, people engaged in long-distance relationships all the time. Just because they'd once opted not to do it didn't mean she wouldn't try with another man. Video calling, social media and cell phones meant distance wasn't the death knell for romances it once was.

Not trusting himself to sound calm, he didn't reply. Instead, he dwelt on the fact that they would be sharing a hotel room tonight. No Jesse, no Snookie, or any other third party to break the tension. He both longed for it and dreaded it in equal measure. He was beginning to realize that he wanted to be with Avery, but it wouldn't be appropriate to pursue her until the case was complete. He didn't mix business with pleasure. Ever. So while he welcomed the opportunity to spend time with her, just the two of them, it would be torture knowing he couldn't give in to her teasing again as he had this morning.

They crested a hill and Dunedin came into view, sprawled before them in a basin, bordered by the ocean on one side and hills on the others. He slowed the car, and Avery directed him to the university campus, which covered a large portion of the northern part of the city. Dunedin had a population of approximately one hundred and twenty thousand, but a quarter of those were students who attended the university or polytechnic and often didn't live locally year-round. As a result, certain parts of the city were largely empty during the semester breaks and summer holidays.

He parked and fed a meter while Avery retrieved the metal box. She led him toward a chunky concrete block building with glass doors that opened as they approached. Inside, two vending machines—one full of soft drinks and the other full of chocolate bars—dominated the foyer. Avery made for a door to the left, but Gareth held up a hand to stop her.

"Wait, I need to look around."

Rolling her eyes, she rested her hands on her hips and tapped her heel impatiently as he studied the interior of the foyer. He resisted the urge to snap at her. His job may not be single-handedly improving the law enforcement system like hers was, but it was important and he'd do it to the best of his ability.

Four doors opened onto the foyer, as well as a lift to the upper floors that appeared to require a key card to operate it. There were two heavy wooden doors to their left and one to their right, which also had key card entry. Through an internal set of glass doors, a surprisingly modern reception area was visible, and needed no key card for access.

He looked up. The roof was high above their heads, as was the popular fashion in the era the building was constructed. A breeze whistled through, presumably a result of poor insulation. Or good ventilation, he supposed. Ventilation must be important in a place where chemicals could accumulate in the air and be breathed in by visitors.

Nothing appeared out of place, or inherently dangerous. The foyer was empty of people, although he noted two women sitting behind the reception desk and a man in a white coat talking to them.

"Okay," he said. "Continue."

Avery took off, pressing a button beside one of the doors and murmuring a few words into a speaker that he couldn't hear. Then she stood back and waited. Thirty seconds later, the door opened inward and a man hurried out and hugged her. He had curly brown hair and deeply tanned skin, a fact which seemed incongruous considering his job, but Gareth couldn't make out any other details, as the man promptly buried his face in Avery's shoulder. Gareth dug his fingernails into his palms and battled the urge to tear the two of them apart.

"Hey," he barked, and the man flinched and drew back. "How about we take this behind the locked door."

The man—Jesse, he presumed—had curious sea-green eyes that were magnified by a pair of small, round spectacles, and they seemed to beam out from the olive skin of his face. They alighted on Gareth, then flicked back to Avery.

"Who's this?" he asked. "A bodyguard or something? Are you in trouble, Ave?"

Unconsciously, Gareth puffed his chest up. He stuck out a hand. "Sergeant Gareth Wayland. Avery's protective detail. Unfortunately, we can't share any other details with you at the present time." He shot Avery a warning look to make sure she understood, and caught the tail end of another eyeroll. She didn't take the danger to herself seriously. Damned if he knew why. The perp had already wreaked havoc on her life.

"Dr. Jesse Stone," the scientist replied, and they shook

hands, Gareth squeezing a little harder than strictly necessary.

He surveyed Dr. Jesse Stone from head to toe. Although he wore a knitted sweater with a number of holes, and jeans with tears in the knees, he was a handsome guy, if you liked the absent-minded academic type. Smaller than Gareth, he'd pose no physical threat if he tried anything to hurt Avery—not that he would, judging by the softening of his expression when he smiled at her.

Jesse wiped his palms on his jeans. "Come on in," he said to Avery. "I set everything up the way you asked."

They started down the hall and Gareth treaded behind them, glancing through the glass pane of each door they passed, noting the people he saw. Halfway down the corridor, Jesse pushed a door open and stepped through, pausing inside to don a white coat that was liberally streaked with yellow and brown smudges, and a pair of thick goggles. Avery also shrugged into a lab coat and chose a pair of the geeky safety glasses.

"You'll need a lab coat," Jesse told him. "They're compulsory for everyone in the lab. You'll find an XXL right at the back of the rack."

Gareth peered at them to see if they were teasing. Deciding they weren't, he muttered, "Fine." He garbed himself in a hideous knee-length coat, which smelled musty, then focused his attention on the lab. All manner of equipment and glassware lined the wooden benches attached to the external walls, while five solid benches occupied the center of the laboratory, running from one end to the other, with industrial-sized metal sinks at the end. Next to the whiteboard at the front of the room was a door labeled "Clean Room," and to the right of that, a circular glass portal was set into the wall, through which the interior of the clean room could be viewed.

"That's where you're going?" he asked.

"Yes," Avery replied. "But you'll have to stay out here. You haven't been through the proper training protocol and testing regime to enter the clean room. Having you in there would risk the integrity of the sample."

Lifting the hem of the coat, he reached into his pocket, extracted a strip of gum, and popped it into his mouth. "I have to stay out here?"

The laboratory was hardly inviting. The only seats were wooden stools without backs, but he'd been in less comfortable circumstances during stakeouts in his rookie years. Working in the relative comfort of Itirangi had made him soft. He raked a hand through the bristly ends of his hair. "How many—"

"There's only one entrance to the clean room," Avery said, anticipating his question. "No one will be able to get inside without going past you."

That soothed his aggravation a little.

Jesse looked from Avery to Gareth. "I-I think I need to know exactly what's going on here. I don't like the sound of it."

Gareth glowered at him. "Then don't listen."

Jesse's chin drew back and he frowned, then turned to Avery. "Is this Neanderthal for real?"

Gareth expected her to join in mocking him or to make light of the question, but she raised one sardonic eyebrow and said calmly, "That *man* is actually rather intelligent and can speak for himself."

Score one for the cop.

"Go do what you need to," he said to Avery. "I'll be out here." She nodded.

"Jesse," he couldn't bring himself to call the guy *Dr. Stone*, "is it a problem if I do some work on a tablet while I'm here?"

The scientist shook his head. "Not at all. Just keep it away from any chemicals and don't touch anything that looks wet. It may not be water."

Jerk-off. "Thanks for the warning."

Dragging a stool to a position near the clean room door, he watched as Avery and Jesse stepped inside, one at a time, and left him alone. A machine whirred and beeped in the corner. He eyed it cautiously. Damn, he was so far out of his element.

"Just don't blow up," he pleaded. It wouldn't do to prove the smarmy scientist right.

9

"What's that guy's deal?" Jesse asked once the door clicked shut behind them, sealing them in the transitional chamber between the laboratory and the clean room. "I get weird vibes from him. You sure you're safe with him?"

Avery balanced on one foot, sliding into the full-body coveralls without touching the exterior. Men and their egos. They'd been like a pair of dogs sizing each other up, each prepared to piss on her to mark their territory. She'd expected better from the both of them. Gareth may not be the academic type, but he'd never been a stupid jock either, and Jesse should be advanced enough not to engage in such silly posturing.

"I've known G for years and years," she said, unrolling the hood over her head and edging the zip up. "He might have a stick up his ass sometimes, but he's a good guy."

"Oh." Jesse was chagrined. He sprayed his gloved hands with ethanol and rubbed them together to disperse it. Then he deftly tied a surgical-style mask over his mouth and nose so that only his vivid aquamarine eyes were visible over the top. When he spoke, his voice was muffled. "I assumed you'd just met."

"Well, you know what they say about assumptions."

He didn't answer, so she waited for him to finish dressing and then used her knuckle to push the button that opened the door.

Inside the clean room, time passed quickly. They processed samples, operated the testing instruments, and did what they could to prepare for the analyses that needed to be done tomorrow. Avery jotted columns of data on a book kept in the clean room. At the end of the day, she'd tear out the page and take it with her. She wouldn't risk leaving it here overnight, even though none of the numbers would mean the slightest thing until she ran them through her program to search for locations with matching soil characteristics. Without her program, the test results were nothing more than chemical parameters that did not paint a meaningful picture.

At different times, she and Jesse exited the clean room to eat at a café on campus, and answer the call of nature, but never for long. Gareth accompanied her, like a hulking shadow, making sure she returned safely to the lab each time she left.

It felt good to be doing this again. In a laboratory, every-thing made sense. Each action had a purpose and they were all familiar to her. Soothing. She'd done this hundreds of times, if not thousands, and could easily get into a groove. For the first time since she'd arrived at work two days ago, her heart rate was normal, her muscles were loose, and she could pretend this was a day like any other; that this dirt she was working with didn't matter any more than the other samples she'd worked with. She could forget the pressure she and Jesse were under to prove that soil chemistry had more far-reaching applications that anyone had thought.

By the end of the day, when they'd done all they could,

her back, legs and feet ached from standing hunched over, but she wore a smile as she left the clean room, shucked off her coveralls in the transitional chamber, ripped off the face mask and stretched the kinks out of her body. Then she and Jesse made their way out into the main lab, where Gareth stood sentry by the door.

"Thanks for all your help," she said to Jesse, giving him a one-armed hug. "I really appreciate it."

"No worries," he replied with a gleaming smile. He glanced over at the clock on the wall. It was after eight and everything outside was black. "Say, it's gotten awfully late. Why don't we go out for dinner? Catch up a bit?"

Just as Avery opened her mouth to politely decline, Gareth said shortly, "No. Avery can't go out for dinner with you, sorry."

He didn't look sorry. Her eyes narrowed. Suddenly, it didn't matter that she'd been about to turn the offer down herself, having decided it would be better to stay in tonight. She didn't like being bossed around.

"Why the hell not? I'm hungry, he's hungry, and I'm sure you need to eat, too. Not to mention, Jesse has done us a massive favor."

"Then I'd be happy to buy Jesse dinner," Gareth replied, with exaggerated patience. "But that doesn't change the fact that you can't go out in public yet."

Jesse's arms crossed over his chest and he adopted a wide stance. "You're not Avery's keeper," he said. "If she wants to come out to dinner with me, she can. You can, too, if you'd like. Unless, of course, you don't require normal human necessities, like food, to function."

Here they go again. Avery's jaw clenched. Was it too much to ask for two grown-ass men to behave like adults?

"I'm sorry, Jesse," she said, swallowing her pride. "Much as I hate to admit it, G is right. I'd better lie low tonight. But

I'll see you again tomorrow, and we can plan another visit, when I'm free from Big Brother."

He relaxed. "Okay. See you tomorrow, Ave." Then he meandered off into his office with a backward wave.

"I don't like that guy," Gareth muttered.

She chuckled. "The feeling is mutual."

Together, they walked back through the building and out via the fire escape, since the main exit had been locked hours ago.

"Did you do what you needed to?" Gareth asked, hovering near her left shoulder, close enough that they bumped against each other frequently and she could feel the heat radiating from him. He'd always been naturally hotter than anyone else.

"Everything we could get through today, but it'll take another day to finish."

"Right."

They lapsed into silence. When they arrived at the car, her stomach grumbled loudly.

"Did we really have to say no to dinner?" she asked. "We do need to eat, and I haven't had anything decent in hours."

GARETH CLICKED his seat belt into place and steeled himself. He needed to make her take this seriously, and he owed her an explanation for his own rigid behavior. He could only think of one way to do both of those things. He needed to be straight up with her.

"Here's the thing," he said, turning to face her. He could barely see her in the dark, but the whites of her eyes were gleaming. Somehow, the dark made it easier to dig deep and open up. "I'm not just being an overbearing asshole for no reason."

"Your job," she said. "I know—"

"No," he interrupted. "Hear me out." If he dithered, it would only get harder. "It's not just my job either. Well, I suppose it is, kind of. There's a story behind it. Back when I was a rookie, I was assigned to protective detail for a battered wife who was hiding out from her husband until she could get out of town."

He paused, trying to read her expression, wishing she'd give some indication about whether she saw where this was going, but she remained silent, waiting for him to go on. "When I arrived to take over, the cop who'd been on duty before me had already left. Apparently he'd had to pick up his sick kid from a sleepover, or something like that. Anyway, he'd thought it wouldn't matter if he took off ten minutes early, because he knew I'd be along soon enough."

He took a deep breath. This was the nasty part. "I knew something was wrong immediately. The window had been smashed and the door was open. The woman's husband had beaten me there." He heard her inhale sharply. "All it had taken were those ten minutes. He'd smashed the window to get in because she'd barricaded the door with a dresser."

"Was she okay?" Avery whispered.

"No." He swallowed, fighting back the rising wave of emotion that always threatened to overwhelm him when he thought of what he'd found in that hotel room. "He'd beaten her with a golf club. She was unconscious, bleeding, and her face was so swollen I could hardly recognize her."

"But she was alive."

He nodded. "She survived, but she'd suffered enormous brain damage. She was in a coma for weeks, and when she woke, the trauma had reduced her mental capacity to that of a child. She's in an assisted living facility now, because she isn't capable of taking care of herself anymore."

"That's awful." Avery's hand landed on his knee and she squeezed gently. "I'm so sorry that happened. I know how awful it feels to see someone get hurt and not be able to do anything about it."

He covered her hand with his own and leaned closer. "The worst part is, it could have been avoided. If that cop had asked me to come a little earlier, or done the job by the book and waited an extra ten minutes before he went to pick up his kid, she'd be living a full life, free of that abusive sonofabitch, by now."

"And that's why you're being obsessively protective."

With his free hand, he gripped her chin and smoothed his thumb along her cheekbone. "I couldn't bear it if that were to happen to you, so I can't let myself slip, even a little bit." He released her, and put his hands on the steering wheel before he did something he'd regret, like kiss her. "Do you understand?"

"I think so." She removed her hand from his thigh, and despite himself, he mourned the loss of her touch. She tucked a loose strand of hair behind her ear. "For what it's worth, I'm sorry if I've been a pain in the ass. I'm not trying to be difficult, it's just not in my nature to sit still while others control the action."

He laughed, and it released some of the tension from his muscles. "Don't I know it."

"Thank you for sharing that with me."

He nodded, not knowing what to say.

"So," she said, businesslike. "What do we do for dinner?"

"Order take-out pizza," he suggested, grabbing the lifeline she'd thrown him. "Get it delivered to the hotel."

She nodded. "Okay, but we're doing this right. Pay them extra to bring popcorn and pretzels, too. We can watch one of those corny old horror movies and binge."

"Like we used to?" The words were out of his mouth before he thought them through and they hung between them, the tension tight enough to be plucked like a violin string. He shouldn't have asked. Shouldn't have reminded her of the long winter evenings they'd spent curled around each other, deteriorating into fits of laughter as the movies they watched became increasingly awful. No doubt she'd back off faster than—

"Yeah," she said, leaving him gaping like a stunned mullet. "I'd like that."

She smiled over at him. An unfamiliar smile that had nothing to do with irony or amusement, or even sympathy for the story he'd told her. It was a hopeful smile. Shy. The beauty of it hit him like a cricket bat in the gut, knocking all of the air from his body. As quickly as it had appeared, the smile morphed into her too-familiar smirk, which he was beginning to think was a defense mechanism.

"Don't make me regret it," she added.

"I'll do everything in my power to make sure you don't." Passion colored his voice and he winced, realizing he'd been a bit more intense than the situation warranted. Luckily, she didn't mention it. His throat constricted and he gripped the steering wheel more tightly. It had taken that beautiful smile for the truth to hit home. He wanted Avery Brown back in his life with everything he had in him, and he'd do his damnedest to make sure it happened, as soon as they finished this case.

AVERY'S EMOTIONS were storming so furiously she couldn't pick the dominant one. The precariousness of her current situation had really sunk in since Gareth told her about the woman who'd been assaulted when he was a rookie. This shit was serious. She could *actually* be in danger. A murderer may *actually* want to do her harm. Her skin prickled with goosebumps despite the warmth in the car. For the first time since this entire debacle started, she was afraid.

Until this point, she'd felt untouchable. Obviously not

invincible, because someone had accessed her lab and destroyed her home, but she'd never felt like her personal safety was at risk. Well, she did now. Was this what he had been trying to tell her since they left the ashes of her house two days ago? Had she truly been conceited enough to think she knew better than him?

Shame burned in her gut. She was a fool.

Not only was she a fool, she was a fool who was having feelings for her ex. She should be smarter than that. She buried her face in her palms. Their conversation had reminded her of the way things used to be between them, of the secrets they'd shared and the low-key fun they'd had. She'd started wondering whether it would really be so bad to try to get to know him again.

Now, every neuron in her brain was sending messages to abort the mission. Years of self-flagellation had taught them to recognize situations that were dangerous to her well-being and warn her off. She should heed the warning, but some traitorous part of her brain was sending another message: that she should investigate the new Gareth. The man who was determined to keep her safe. Who was haunted by a woman he hadn't been able to save. A man who was far too intriguing for her peace of mind.

Five minutes later, they checked into the motel, which was situated near the university, at the bottom of the hill at the city entrance. The main room contained a sofa, a TV, a coffee table, and an open loft with two single beds side by side. Doors off the main room led to a kitchen and a bathroom. Gareth motioned for her to wait while he checked the other rooms for intruders. She humored him, surprised to note that she actually felt better when he gave the all clear. To tell the truth, it was sexy thinking that he was prepared to fight to protect her.

She tugged at her collar, overly warm. Beer. She needed beer. Unfortunately, they didn't have any, and she doubted he'd leave her alone to dash to the liquor store across the street, or agree to her accompanying him over there. She sighed. Water would have to do.

The doorbell rang and Gareth answered. She heard him exchange words with the pizza delivery person as she went to the kitchen and snagged a couple of plates from the cupboard. She grabbed a bowl for pretzels, stacked it on top of the plates, and headed back to the main room.

The delicious scent of melted cheese and doughy pizza emanated from the boxes. Gareth had already opened them. Her mouth watered. She laid down the plates, opened the bag of pretzels and poured them into the bowl.

"Catch," Gareth said, and she reacted instinctively, catching the can of Sprite he tossed to her. She popped the tab open, took a mouthful and enjoyed the refreshing coolness.

"All the fixings," Gareth said appreciatively, helping himself to a pretzel.

"Except beer." She grabbed a piece of pizza and did her best not to notice when he licked the salt from his fingers.

I wonder what he tastes like. She tamped down the errant thought. *That's none of your business, Brown.*

"Do you have a movie preference?" she asked.

He swallowed and assessed her with eyes that, in this light, seemed almost bronze. "How about Hobgoblins?"

She didn't bat an eyelid. So what if he remembered her favorite bad horror movie?

"Sure, sounds good." She shrugged one shoulder, intentionally casual. "I'll just set the TV up."

~

GARETH RECLINED ON THE COUCH, arm outstretched across the top, fingertips brushing Avery's shoulder. A heater purred in the corner, keeping the room toasty warm. She had cocooned herself in a blanket from the loft, and was near enough that if he shifted even a fraction, his side would touch hers. Her laughter rang through the air, husky and rich, as the closing credits rolled. He smiled in appreciation, keeping his eyes open though he longed to close them and bask in the sound of her laugh. He couldn't get enough of looking at her. Her strong chin that tilted upward, the indent that gave her a stubborn countenance, the lips that parted as the breath left her in little puffs, and deep-set eyes that shone with humor.

This was the Avery he'd missed—the woman who expressed her happiness openly, but could flay you with a sharp tongue if you deserved it. Warmth grew in his chest and diffused through his body, making his limbs languid, his soul content. He couldn't recall the last time he'd experienced such a perfect evening.

"I've really enjoyed this," he told her, hoping she felt the same way and wouldn't clam up.

"So have I," she agreed, lips still twitching with mirth. "It's been nice."

Nice. He could think of many better words, but hey, he'd take it. "Nice" meant she might give him the chance to have a repeat.

"Very nice," she amended.

He realized she'd gone still, her face angled toward him. The gray of her eyes had darkened to the color of gunmetal and he almost couldn't tell where the irises ended and the pupils began. She sucked her lower lip into her mouth, then released it. Blood rushed away from his head, leaving him giddy. She looked like a woman who wanted to be kissed. All the reasons why he shouldn't fled from his mind and his heart sang as he claimed her lips. He kept the kiss chaste, enjoying the sensation of his mouth sliding over hers, like silk against skin. She tasted like the coconut lip balm she'd always favored.

It was Avery who deepened the kiss, swiping her tongue across the seam of his lips as her hands came up to rest on his shoulders. His heart hammered against his rib cage almost painfully and he reminded himself to go slowly and not frighten her. He stroked her tongue with his, pleased at the breathy sound that escaped her. She dug her fingers into his shoulders and her fingertips could have been hot pokers for all that they scalded him to the core of his being.

He grabbed her by the hips and lifted her onto his lap. She shook free of the blanket and growled in frustration when their lips separated, but kissed him with renewed vigor once her bottom was cushioned against his crotch. In hindsight, perhaps this position wasn't such a great idea. She was nestled against him in such a way that she couldn't possibly mistake his arousal. She wriggled, and he moaned. She stiffened.

"Oh, god," she groaned, and not in a good way. More like someone who just decided they'd made a mistake. Gareth's stomach sank to his feet. They *had* made a mistake. Or at least, *he* had. He was *working*. Regardless of how pleasant the evening had been, he couldn't kiss Avery while he was on the job. Especially when that job was to keep a professional distance and protect her at all costs.

"We shouldn't have—" she muttered, at the same time that he cursed. They exchanged wry glances. "That was a bad idea," Avery said. "Been there, done that, you know." She swung herself off his lap.

Ouch. He grunted, annoyed by her attitude, especially since she'd instigated the kiss. Just when he was becoming optimistic about the future, too.

"You started that, A-Bee, not me."

"I know." She rubbed her eyes. "I'm sorry, G. Believe me, I don't want to lead you on or freak you out. This evening has been intense. It brought back old memories and I guess I got carried away."

"That's not such a bad thing," he replied. "This isn't the best time for it, but you don't have to act like you're made of stone. It's been a tough few days. You're allowed to let loose a little. I'll be here for you, I promise." He only hoped she didn't crush him while she was figuring out how she felt.

"I—" The noise came out choked. "I can't let loose. If I do, I might never pull it together again."

She sounded miserable, and so unlike herself that he grew concerned. He stood and dropped a kiss on her forehead, frustrated when she remained wary.

"Go brush your teeth," he said. "We both need a good night's sleep."

AVERY LOCKED herself in the bathroom and slumped on the floor, her emotions a whirlwind that wouldn't stop long enough for her to figure them out. Sometime while they'd been chatting, laughing, and snuggling on the sofa, she'd started having fluttery sensations in her stomach. She hadn't fluttered in years and it made her feel like a teenager again.

Gareth's minty scent had set her pulse skittering madly and she'd wanted to close her eyes and pretend they'd just met and that tonight had been an exceptionally good first date. So she had, for a moment, and then they'd kissed and… wow. He didn't kiss like he had back in high school. She could have been kissing a stranger. The taste of gum was new, as was the restraint he'd shown initially—he'd always been full steam ahead when they were younger.

Then he'd physically picked her up, and for some reason that only turned her on more. He was so *strong*. She fanned herself, then staggered over to the vanity and splashed cold water on her face. *No harm done*, she reminded herself. Imagine if she'd let him go further. Wincing, she acknowledged that he probably would have stopped it before they got to that point. He seemed able to exercise more self-control than she could.

"Bloody men," she muttered. She needed someone to talk to, and there was only one girl for a situation like this. She ventured back into the main room. "Can I please borrow your phone? I really need to talk to Rissa. I promise I won't be long, and I won't even tell her I'm in Dunedin."

Gareth hesitated, looking torn. "I don't know if that's such a great idea."

"Please," she begged. "I won't do anything to jeopardize your job or my safety. I just need my friend."

Her voice cracked on the last word, and his expression softened. He handed her his phone. She retreated back to the bathroom and dialed Clarissa's number, crossing her fingers that her friend would answer.

"Hi, Clarissa Mitchell speaking." Clarissa's sweet voice came through the speaker on her phone.

"Hey, Riss. It's Avery. Are you free to talk?"

She heard rustling down the other end of the line. No doubt Clarissa had been working on a wedding dress for one of her customers. She often worked late into the night.

"Yes, I'm available now," she said. "What's wrong? I replied to your text earlier, but never heard back."

"Sorry, I haven't had my phone on me, but I needed to hear your voice."

"Oh, sweetie. I'm right here."

Just like that, everything felt a little more manageable. Clarissa had that effect on her. She was the most unemotional of Avery's friends. Every move she made was calculated to achieve her goals and Avery admired that about her. Especially when she knew things about Clarissa's past that no one else did. Things that made everything she'd accomplished seem that much more impressive.

"I need your opinion."

"About Gareth? Whatever you need, I'm here to listen."

"I think..." Avery trailed off, hating how stupid she was about to sound. Particularly since she always counseled her friends not to be silly about men.

"Yes," Clarissa prompted.

"I think I have feelings for Gareth."

"*Oh.*" There was a wealth of meaning in the word. "Oh, *no*. How did it happen?"

She shrugged, then remembered Clarissa couldn't see her. "I can't really explain. But is it such a bad thing?"

"Remember that he left you." Clarissa's voice was tight with anger on Avery's behalf. "He broke his promise and he left you. You were heartbroken. Be strong. Be the independent woman I know you are."

"It gets worse," Avery admitted in a small voice. "I kissed him."

Clarissa sighed. "You're supposed to be the smart one. If he's interested in you, you just gave him a reason to think he might have a chance. Once men get that in their head, they can be the devil to get rid of."

Avery laughed at the irony of the words. Her stubbornly single friend advising her about men. "How would you know that, Riss?"

A beat of silence. She grinned, knowing that Clarissa would be frowning, her lips curled in a scowl of consternation. Sometimes, her friend was patently predictable.

"You know I'm single by choice," she muttered. "You know how I look. I've become adept at steering men away and I can tell you that kissing them is not a good way to start."

While some people might interpret Clarissa's words as being arrogant or self-indulgent, Avery knew she was only stating the truth. She'd been blessed—or cursed, depending on how you looked at it—with an unusually beautiful face and the kind of figure that tempted men to make grand romantic gestures in the hope of winning her heart. All they'd succeeded in doing so far was making her more determined to be alone.

"Yes, I know. I was only winding you up. You're right, of course. Kissing him was a terrible idea and I clearly didn't think it through at the time." Getting lost in the passion and possibility of a moment was something Clarissa, with her cool head, could never understand.

"What are you going to do now?"

Avery pondered the question. "I don't know. I'm stuck with him."

"Please tell me what's going on."

"I can't, but I will as soon as I get the okay. The thing I'm wrapped up in involves other people and I can't let them down."

"People like Gareth." It didn't take a genius to hear her disapproval.

"Yes."

Clarissa exhaled noisily. "I don't understand, but I'll take your word for it. As soon as you can, I want a full report."

"I'll call you."

"Good." Clarissa made a *hmm* noise under her breath, as she did when she was thinking. "In the meantime, no more kissing."

"No more kissing," Avery repeated, her soul suddenly heavy. "I can manage that. Thanks for the pep talk."

"Anytime. Now get some sleep. Sounds like you'll need it. I love you, sweetie."

"Love you, too, Riss."

10

Gareth showered, dried, and slung the towel around his hips. He raked his fingers through the short tips of his hair to tidy it, and brushed his teeth. Then he checked his reflection in the mirror above the vanity. Normally, he didn't think much about how he looked, but after the kiss last night, he found himself aware of the serious set of his face, his hard-edged jaw, and the slight line between his brows that never seemed to leave.

When had he become so grave? If he were a woman, he wouldn't want to kiss the man staring back at him. He tried to ease his mouth into a smile, but it wobbled and the way his lips peeled back over his teeth gave him the appearance of a caricature.

No. Keep the serious face. Smiling makes it worse.

Tearing himself away in disgust, he shoved open the bathroom door, collected his freshly laundered uniform, which housekeeping had dropped off, and climbed the stairs to the loft. The blankets on Avery's bed were pushed back. She must have gone downstairs to make coffee and breakfast. He dressed, opting to wear the uniform, partly to remind himself of his professional duty and partly because they'd be seeing that smug scientist again, and he knew he wore the uniform well.

He went down to the kitchen and stopped dead in his tracks. *Shit.* If he'd been wearing a heart rate monitor, it would have spiked and beeped frantically. Avery was standing on the opposite side of the kitchen, her back to him, wearing a t-shirt, underwear, and nothing else. Her legs were long and lean, a single mole shaped vaguely like Stewart Island on the inside of her knee. Her calves curved gracefully, her thighs were toned and slim, and the t-shirt rested just beneath her butt.

As if sensing him there, she whirled around. He could make out her nipples through the soft fabric of the t-shirt and his mouth went dry. She wasn't wearing a bra.

"I, uh," he muttered, unable to look away though he knew he should. Any other cop would. Any *decent* cop would. He shouldn't be ogling the woman he was supposed to protect.

"My face is up here," she said, waving her hand and snapping him out of the trance.

His gaze shot upward. Luckily, she seemed to find it funny, a half-smile on her lips and exasperation clear in her expression.

"I didn't expect you to leave the bathroom while I was down here," she explained, turning back to pour water into a coffee mug. "You used to spend hours in the shower." She selected a second mug from the cupboard. "You want one?"

"Yes, please."

"Black, one sugar?"

"That's right."

She remembered how he liked his coffee. Was that significant? He remembered how she liked hers, too. Black. No muss, no fuss. The stronger the better. Even now, he could smell the potent brew she was stirring across the room. "I'll, um, go outside and check in with Rata while you shower and dress."

"No need to go outside," she replied, handing him a steaming hot coffee. "Just keep your eyes firmly on the newspaper."

He took the coffee and went outside anyway. The cold air brought him back to his senses. He needed to be sharp, not distracted by Avery and the attraction that grew every time he was near her.

He waited a good long while before he returned inside.

JESSE STONE GREETED them at the entrance to the foyer, and led the two of them down the corridor to his laboratory. Gareth shrugged into a lab coat without being asked, while Avery and Jesse discussed whatever they'd done yesterday, much of it too technical for him to understand. Instead of following the conversation, he watched the play of expressions over Jesse's face. The scientist's voice was full of enthusiasm, his eyes bright, cheeks flushed with excitement…or was it more than that? Whatever the case, the way he lit up like a high-beam flashlight every time Avery paid him attention left no doubt in Gareth's mind that Jesse wanted her the same way he did.

Too bad.

Last night had made him more certain than ever that she would be his again. He had to hold his tongue until the case was finished, but as soon as Dwayne Broderick was in cuffs, he'd talk to her about their future. Given the explosive kiss they'd shared last night, he knew she was attracted to him too, but she'd also broken it off and fled, locking herself away to call Clarissa. He grimaced. That deceptively sweet-looking woman wouldn't hesitate to slap him for any perceived slight to her best friend, and frankly, she intimidated the hell out of him. It wasn't as if he could hit her back, and she had Avery's ear. If she took it into her head to talk shit about him, she could wield a lot of influence.

He took up a stance at the entrance to the clean room, hooked one of his thumbs into his belt and glared at Jesse in a way that said he'd better not try any funny business with Gareth's woman. The other man shrank in on himself.

"When will you be out, A-Bee?"

"Quit it with that nickname," she muttered, and Jesse's spine seemed to straighten. "Not too sure. Could be any time from late morning to late afternoon. Depends how efficiently we work together."

He found himself in the awkward position of wanting her to finish quickly, but not wanting any proof that she and Jesse partnered well. He jerked his chin up to acknowledge her answer and stewed in silence as the two of them passed through the entrance to the other room. The one he couldn't enter. Where they'd be alone, potentially for hours, with unlimited opportunity for Jesse to make a play.

Please let her be smart enough to consider things other than IQ in a partner.

He rotated so he could watch the two scientists through the circular portal in his peripheral vision. Jesse was adding drops of liquid to small glass vials while Avery added the vials to a box-shaped instrument the size of a standard wall safe.

They were careful not to touch one another, passing vials between them by holding opposite ends. He recalled Avery mentioning something about needing to avoid human contact while in the room. *Good.* But muffled noises indicated they were chatting between themselves. His brows drooped and his lips pressed together. Were they talking business, or something else? *Business*, he assured himself. She wasn't the type to flirt on the job. She was a career woman. She took herself seriously.

Regardless of this belief, his blood continued to simmer

as the morning passed, rising to a near-boil by the time they emerged and stepped out of their bunny suits. He opened his mouth to make a wisecrack but then he spotted Avery's excited smile and the pink flush on her cheeks. He closed his mouth, anger ebbing away. She was happy, and he wouldn't be the one to bring her down.

"Looks like good news," he said.

"All the tests are running," she told him, her grin widening. "All that's left to do is wait for results. We won't have them until late tonight or tomorrow morning. I've rigged it so that they'll get sent to my email automatically, but Jesse will forward them through and save them to a hard drive and to a secure cloud network, just in case. We won't be losing them this time."

Gareth high-fived her and their palms made a satisfying smack. Their fingers intertwined and he grasped her hand in his, entranced by the way she whooped and held his gaze, like she'd done hundreds of times in the past. When Jesse cleared his throat, she leapt back, but Gareth took his sweet time disengaging from her. He wasn't ashamed. And if the good doctor thought there was more between them than a professional relationship, so much the better.

"Let's head back," she suggested. "I'll need to borrow a laptop from somewhere. Will there be one at the station? Otherwise we might need to head to the Meridian Mall so I can pick one up for cheap."

"There'll be one at the station," Gareth said, at the same time as Jesse said, "You can borrow one of mine, it will give me a reason to visit."

Avery glanced from one of them to the other, then busted out in raucous laughter. "Oh, this is too good. It's not often I have men clamoring to attend to my every need." She clapped Jesse on the shoulder and said, "Thanks for the offer, but I'll grab one from G's work. That way I'm not inconveniencing anyone, and it's more likely to be secure."

"No inconvenience," he replied, but didn't argue her other point.

She started out of the room and the men followed, keeping up with her purposeful strides simply by virtue of having longer legs. In the parking lot, Gareth got into his car and watched while she hugged Jesse goodbye. He breathed in and out slowly, reminding himself that it didn't matter who she hugged because she was going back to Itirangi with him. He wiped the scowl off his face and greeted her with a smile as she climbed into the passenger seat.

"Let's get the hell out of Dodge," she exclaimed, buckling up.

He couldn't agree more.

AVERY WAS ON A ROLL. The moment Gareth had handed her a laptop, a police hard drive with a copy of her mapping program saved onto it, and a mobile Wi-Fi device they'd collected from the Timaru Police Department on the way home, she'd pushed back her seat in the car and set to work. To start, she entered the analysis details she and Jesse had recorded into a worksheet. She made notes for each test and the results they'd collected so far. Most were still to come, but she'd tested for carbon content yesterday and noted the results this morning, along with the concentrations of a number of other nutrients. Hopefully she'd receive the output of the tests for major ions and isotopes overnight so she could spend tomorrow working.

The car stopped. She glanced up to see they'd reached Itirangi and were parked outside the shopping center and motel owned by Aria's wealthy fiancé, Eli.

"We'll stay here," Gareth said, before she could ask. "It's better suited to your work. I know we've been lucky so far, but I'd still rather not take you to any of your friends' homes, or to mine."

She nodded. "Makes sense. I'll keep working for now. Come and get me once you've booked a room."

"Nuh-uh." He took her laptop from her, along with the hard drive, and tucked them under his arm. "You come with me. I'm not leaving you alone."

She wanted to argue, but after what he'd revealed last night, she didn't have the heart, so she followed him docilely into the building's office. As soon as they were safely in a suite on the ground floor, she buried herself in data, downloading her program from the hard drive onto the laptop and preparing to enter what information she could into the soil profile. Her fingers danced across the keyboard so quickly that the tapping of keys formed a kind of beat.

Yeah. This was more like it. Time to regain control.

11

very's foot tapped a rapid tattoo on the floor. She stared at the list of emails in her inbox and willed one to appear from the university computer. But apparently, she couldn't speed up technology by the power of will alone. She growled in frustration, placed the laptop on the sofa beside her and stood, pacing from one end of the living area to the other. Gareth sat at a small table beside the glass doors that overlooked the lake, eating buttered toast—he'd refused to use the Marmite his mother had bought.

"It's not coming," she said, squeezing her hands into fists. He glanced over, but didn't reply. The computer pinged. Hurrying over, she checked the screen. An email from Jesse lit the display. She clicked onto it and read eagerly.

Checked the instruments. There's been a delay. Results will most likely be arriving tomorrow afternoon.

She threw her hands up in the air. "I won't get the results until tomorrow." Striding to the door, she yanked it open and hauled in a breath of fresh air. "I'm going to go crazy," she murmured to herself.

"Going to?" he asked, overhearing her. Looking over her

shoulder, she saw that he wore a mischievous smile, dimples in his cheeks.

"Shut your smart mouth, unless you're offering to take me out of here. I'm getting cabin fever again."

His hands dropped to rest on the edge of the table and the smile faded. "No can do, sorry."

"Come on, G. At least take me around to my place to see what's left."

The slight curve of his lips inverted. "I can't, sweetheart. I wish I could, for your sake, but what if the person who set the fire is there watching and waiting for you to come back? I'd be taking you right to them."

She appealed to his ego. "But you'd be there to protect me."

He raised one eyebrow. She should have known he wouldn't buy into her bullshit.

"Well, where *can* we go?" she asked, desperation creeping over her. She wasn't prone to being overdramatic—although she was known for being impatient—but she was going to crawl out of her skin if she didn't get out of this motel in the next half hour.

"What about out into the bush?" she suggested. "We could go hiking. Way out in the middle of nowhere where we won't run into anyone." She went to him and took a hold of his hand. "Pleeeease, G. It's winter. No one is going to be out on the trails. It's too cold and mucky. We'll be completely safe."

"It's also isolated, so no one could hear if you screamed," he said, eyes sliding sideways to look out over the lake rather than up at her face.

He was weakening, she could sense it.

"I'll do whatever you want," she promised. "Wear a whistle, a high-vis jacket, stay within eyesight at all times. I'll even verbally check in every thirty seconds if it'll make you agree."

He sighed. "I guess that would be all right."

"Yes!" She threw her arms around him, then backed off

and ruffled his hair. Or at least, tried to. It was too short to muss. "Let's go," she said. "I'll just change into some more appropriate clothing." Then, feeling magnanimous, she added, "We should bring Snookie. She must be getting bored at Justin's place, and I'm sure you miss her."

"Did you just…" he stared at her like he'd never seen her before, "invite my dog on our outing?"

She laughed, too excited to regret it. "I suppose I did."

His brows lowered and he watched her warily. "But you don't like dogs."

"Eh. She's not so bad. And I really, *really* want to get out of here."

"Okay." His eyes were narrowed as though he suspected she'd pull the rug out from beneath him at any moment. She didn't say anything. "Five minutes," he said. "Make sure you've saved all your work somewhere separate from the laptop, and then lock it away in the safe box and hide it."

"Everything has been emailed to me and Rata, and saved to the secure cloud server Jesse set up."

He was being overly cautious, but she wouldn't argue. Contrary to popular opinion, she knew when to pick her fights. Choosing a pair of yoga pants from the bag Caroline had loaned her, she paired it with a sports bra and Merino undershirt, then layered a tank top and sports jacket over the long-sleeved wool shirt.

They drove the police car to his place, where he swapped it for his personal vehicle, then stopped off at Justin's house outside of town, set back amongst the bush, to pick up Snookie. Even the press of the dog's cold, wet nose into the back of Avery's neck when she bounced into the car didn't dampen her mood.

She was busting out. Out of the hotel, out of town, out of the prison she'd been locked inside for her own safety. She felt like she could sing for joy. Except she wouldn't, because Gareth was doing her a favor and subjecting him to her tone deafness would hardly be a kind way of repaying him.

They passed through the tunnel formed by the forest for a while. Eventually, they pulled into a picnic area. She surveyed their surroundings, struck by recognition. This was the track where they had often hiked together during summer. It led to a number of boulders and small cliffs that could be climbed on a nice day.

Her skin prickled with goosebumps and the crisp morning breeze ruffled her hair, but her spirits buoyed and warm contentment diffused through her body. She'd been happy here.

No.

She couldn't let herself be carried away by fond memories and forget how that relationship had ended. With pain, loneliness, and a great many unasked, and thus unanswered, questions. She tried to summon the bitterness and confusion that had festered in the days and weeks following their breakup, but they kept slipping out of reach, her brain replacing those unpleasant emotions with memories of feeling completely secure and at peace. She pinched the back of her hand, the twinge drawing her back to the present.

The trunk shut and the sound jarred her. The mutt at her side flinched but stayed silent, as though waiting for her to gather her scattered wits.

"This way," she said, striding toward the waist-high sign at the start of the track.

"Hold on," Gareth called.

She turned and saw he'd made no move to follow her, and was instead busying himself packing items into a backpack. A length of rope. A harness. A clip. Her heart galloped. He'd packed climbing gear. It wasn't exactly the season for it, but considering the fine weather, there was no reason they couldn't climb. They'd just need to be careful and methodical, two things she excelled at.

"When was the last time you climbed?" she asked. From the glimpse she'd gotten, the equipment looked dusty and unused.

"A while ago," he admitted. "I'm hoping it's like riding a bike and all comes back to me quickly."

Avery rolled her eyes. Climbing wasn't at all like riding a bike, and he knew it. At least he'd retained a good level of fitness so he had a decent base to start from. "Shall we practice on the boulders first?"

"That's a fantastic idea." His eyes lit with relief and she chuckled. Men and their pride. Couldn't admit he needed to start out slow.

"Come on, then."

After thirty minutes of walking—and bush exploration on Snookie's part—they reached the boulders. Avery stood, hands on hips, studying the rock face that rose before her. She brushed a loose strand of hair behind her ear and raised her eyes to the sky, where the sun was arcing upward in the east, bathing the clearing in cool light. A bird chirped in the trees and some kind of critter rustled softly in the undergrowth.

The forest was a haven of walking tracks and she'd scouted out pretty much all of the ones on the fringes, though she knew there would be more to discover if she ventured further in. She'd climbed these particular boulders so many times she'd secured bolts and rope up the side so she could use quickdraws, two carabiners connected by a semi-rigid material, to slide freely up the rope, rather than setting up an anchor at the top each time she visited.

"Looks exactly the same as last time I was here," Gareth mused.

She tilted her head from one side to the other, sizing up the massive boulder. "You think? I'd say it's growing a little more moss and lichen than when we were younger."

He shook his head and his gaze locked on hers, deep and intense. "I don't see it."

Were they talking about more than a boulder here?

Ignoring the undercurrent of the conversation, she sat on a rock while he emptied his backpack. She grabbed the harness and fastened it around her waist and thighs. Next, she put on the helmet and withdrew an extension pole.

"Me first?" she asked, since he hadn't moved to join her.

"Like I could stop you."

Using the extension pole, she put the first quickdraw in place, then checked the rope, and took the pouch of chalk from Gareth to rub a little on her palms. She started up the rock face, one hand in front of the other, her feet moving confidently into nooks and crannies. When she reached the next bolt, she attached another quickdraw and moved up again.

After a few minutes, her arm muscles were burning, but years of climbing and squeezing dirt through sieves had built them up so that—though she may not look it—she was strong. Her strength served her well as she scooted upward while Gareth urged her on from below, and she reached the top within a short time.

A sense of accomplishment washed over her and she grinned. There was nothing like scaling a near-vertical rock wall to boost a person's confidence. She anchored herself to the top and leaned backward off the edge, abseiling back to the ground, legs dangling beneath her. When her feet hit the dirt, she stumbled as her weight transferred onto them, and a large pair of hands caught her hips, steadying her.

"You all right there?" Gareth asked, his breath disturbing both the fine hairs next to her ear and her mental fortitude. The line of his torso pressed against her back and attraction sparked in her veins, her pulse going mad. So many times he'd held her like this as he kissed the side of her neck or reached around and cupped her breasts. Her nipples pebbled and she thanked her lucky stars she'd worn a thick sports bra that masked the effect he had on her.

Swallowing, she stepped forward so his hands dropped from her hips. "Your turn," she said, her voice barely shaking at all.

❧

GARETH FLOPPED to the ground and mopped the sweat off his brow. Snookie leaned over him, trying to lick his face, and he waved her away. His arms were leaden and his fingers cramped from gripping onto ledges. He didn't think he'd be able to lift a coffee cup to his lips, let along hoist his backpack to carry it back to the car. His left knee throbbed and he'd probably be hobbling like a cripple for a week. Damn it, he shouldn't have let his need to impress Avery drive him to follow her up the boulder. What if he couldn't protect her now because he'd aggravated his old rugby injury?

Though the cop part of his brain was beating him up, the caveman part argued that every ache and sore muscle was worth it because Avery was lying next to him, her breathing even and steady while he puffed and tried desperately to catch his breath. She turned to him, an almost-smile lifting the corners of her mouth, her gray eyes flashing with humor. He could nearly pretend it was nine years earlier, if not for the laughter lines around her eyes and the cheekbones that were more prominent now, their youthful plumpness gone.

"You've lost your touch," she teased, her breath tickling his cheek. "Dare I say you've gotten soft?"

"Have not," he protested, still gasping for air. "You've just gotten fitter. Nothing to do with me at all."

"Of course not. We all know you're a perfect male specimen."

He snorted at her sarcasm, even as he wished it were true. "Cheeky girl."

117

"I think we'd better stop," she told him. "I don't want you keeling over on me while you're on guard duty."

His spine stiffened. "I'd never—"

"Relax, G," she said, rising up on her elbow and patting his shoulder. "I didn't mean anything by it.

Perhaps not, but her offhand comment was right on point. He shouldn't be lounging about, laughing with her and reminiscing about their youth while she was in danger, no matter how unlikely it was that they'd been followed out here. He got to his feet and slung the bag over his shoulder, but pain spiked through his knee and it gave way. He teetered on the spot, and Avery grabbed him until he righted himself.

With a pointed look, she tugged the backpack from him and shouldered it. "Don't be so macho that you do more harm than good," she chided, starting along the track ahead of him.

He watched her retreating figure, and the dog trotting along at her heels. He'd expected to see pity in her expression, or perhaps contempt—after all, she'd proved today she was both smarter *and* fitter than him—but he saw nothing other than annoyance at his pig-headedness.

He smiled. God, he'd missed this woman.

12

"No. Absolutely not."

"But G—"

His jaw clicked as he chewed furiously. "You're not going to the pub. Not when someone could be after you."

Avery looked like she might punch him in the gut. "It's *tradition*. Every Friday is drinks at Davy's Bar. I'll be letting the girls down if I'm not there. They need me and my sensible head to level them out. I bring the logic to the girl talk."

He crossed his arms. "It's not happening. I forbid it."

Oh, he should *not* have said that. He knew it even before he saw her eyes flash and harden.

"I'm sorry," he said, hurrying to catch her off balance before she decided to drug his coffee and go out on her own while he was down for the count.

"You…what?"

"I shouldn't have phrased it that way," he said. "What I mean is, you'll make it very difficult for me to do my job and keep you safe if you go to Davy's, and both of those things are important to me."

Some of the tension seeped out of her and she nodded. "I

get that. I can hardly say I don't when I've spent the past few days harassing you to let me do *my* job."

Well, that was very reasonable. Very Avery. But he suspected she hadn't ceded to his argument completely yet.

"I'm trying to keep you in one piece," he reminded her.

"I know," she murmured. "And I appreciate that. How about if the girls come here? They can sneak in," she continued. "With them here, I can decompress so I'm less of a pain in your ass. Go on, say yes."

This screamed of being a bad idea, but she'd offered a compromise and he was loath to shoot her down outright. Especially when she had that pleading expression etched in every line of her face, and reflected in her pale blue-gray eyes.

"All right," he relented. "But only one of them. Don't make me regret this."

The frown returned. "I can't invite one and not the other."

"Well, they can't both come over. It's too risky."

She went silent, and he could practically hear the cogs in her brain turning. "What if we picked them up and brought them back here? We could drive a different car back, borrow Eli's keys and sneak in via the rear entrance, which has its own parking area, so no one can see us."

"I don't like it." A vision flickered in his mind. Broken limbs, bloody face, vacant stare. "The more often we leave the hotel, the more likely it is that someone will spot us."

She touched his arm. "We'll be really careful, Gareth. I promise. Please."

He sighed. He couldn't deny Avery anything. "Okay, but for the record, I think this is a bad idea."

~

"Hey, stranger. Hey, Gaz."

Avery smiled as Aria darted through the door wearing a

beanie to cover her curls, head ducked low, and squished into the car beside her. She was carrying a bag that rustled as she stuffed it into the space beside her feet. "Hi, cutie-pie."

Aria leaned over to hug her as Gareth started the vehicle —one of Eli's—and headed to Cooper's house to pick up Sophie.

"You're holding up well. So tell me, what's going on?"

Of course, Aria would have to try her luck.

"Like I said on the phone, I can't tell you yet. You'll just have to accept that."

Aria scowled, her natural curiosity warring with her desire to spend some time with her friend. Finally, the scowl faded and she said, "You're awfully chirpy, considering."

"What? Can't I be in a good mood?"

Her friend considered that, one side of her mouth tugging up slightly. Then she shook her head. "After the week you've had, that does not compute."

The words startled a laugh from Avery. "I thought you were meant to be the sweet one."

Aria shrugged one shoulder, then hitched the strap of her tank top up as it threatened to expose more of her cleavage than anyone needed to see. Pregnancy had enhanced her already well-endowed chest. Avery imagined that men ogled her everywhere she went.

"I can be sassy, too," Aria said

"How's the wedding planning going?" Avery asked. "Have you decided what kind of dress you want yet?"

"Rissa is designing one for me," she replied. "With a waist-band I can let out as much as I need to. I'm not sure what it'll look like though, it's a surprise."

"How can you handle that?" Surely the curiosity would eat away at her. Aria wasn't known for being patient.

"It's not easy, but I trust Clarissa's judgment. She's the best, especially with unconventional brides."

Avery's eyebrows shot up toward her hairline. If she'd

expected any of her friends to go for a conventional wedding gown, it was Aria, despite her somewhat unique fashion sense. She was a romantic. "Unconventional?"

Aria gestured to her belly. "Pregnant."

"Ah, right." They stopped outside Cooper's place and waited while the front door opened and Sophie clattered quickly down the path—a remarkable feat in four-inch stiletto heels—and climbed in on the other side of Avery. She propped a pair of sunglasses atop her head, perching them on her strawberry blonde topknot.

"Have you decided on a name for the baby?" Avery asked.

Aria tapped a finger to the side of her nose. "That's a secret."

"From your oldest friends?" Sophie asked, slotting into the conversation. "And by oldest, I mean Avery. I *am* the youngest, after all." She smiled smugly.

"It was Eli's idea to keep it quiet," Aria admitted. "But I agreed. So no matter what you do, you can't pry it from me."

And that was that. Although sweet-natured, Aria possessed a streak of stubbornness to rival anyone.

"Avery," Sophie said as they began moving once again, "you've been smiling since I got in. What's got you in such a good mood?"

Avery fought the urge to bury her face in her palms to hide the offending smile. Trust her friends to tag-team each other.

Aria turned to Sophie with a sly smile. "She won't say. She's being evasive."

"I'm not being evasive. I'm just trying to see the best in the situation."

Her friends exchanged glances but didn't say any anything else until they'd parked around the rear of Eli's motel, entered through the staff door, and locked themselves in their unit. Gareth excused himself to the bedroom to give the girls their space. Aria opened her bag and extracted potato chips, dip, and a selection of crackers.

"Do you think it's spending time with Gareth?" Sophie asked in a low voice, picking up as though they'd never paused the conversation.

"Could be," Aria mused, helping herself to a cracker. "I hope so. It's been so long since she let anyone in, it would be great if she finally gave Gaz another chance."

"I'm not—"

"High school sweethearts reunited!" Sophie exclaimed, giggling. "What's the bet they'll couple up a month down the track? I'd be so happy for you." She scooted across the distance between them and threw her arms around Avery's neck. "Please say you'll be brave enough to put yourself out there again."

Avery felt her cheeks heating, probably beet-red. "*You guys,*" she hissed, "*he's right through there.*"

Neither of them seemed repentant. Not much for hugging, Avery patted Sophie gingerly on the back and extricated herself. It was strange, being on the receiving end of jibes about her romantic life. Typically, it was her role to deliver those jibes as well as the encouraging pep talks. She'd never considered that perhaps she needed support from time to time too, and that her friends were eager to return the favor.

"I love you guys."

"Aww." Aria kissed her cheek. "You really are turning into a big marshmallow."

"Don't get too carried away."

～

WHILE GARETH WAITED in the bedroom, reading the update Inspector Rata had sent through, his phone buzzed. The caller ID read "Mum."

123

He answered. "Hello Mum, how you doing?"

"I'm good," she said, her voice high-pitched. "Just calling to see how you and Avery are, and, you know, whether anything has *happened*."

From the tone of her voice, he couldn't tell whether she meant something criminal or something sexual. "Something like what?"

"Something between you and Avery, darling. You know I love her. I want you to know you have my support if you decide to go after her. Actually, you have *our* support. Your father and I both support you in this."

His face flamed. It seemed like every man and their dog wanted to offer him advice. To be honest, it was a little embarrassing that people seemed to be able to tell how badly he wanted Avery.

"It's been a long time since you two were together," Sharon continued.

"Where are you going with this?" he asked warily.

"What I mean," she explained, "is that you need to remind her of why you fell in love in the first place."

He recalled weekends outside, long walks in the forest and around the lake, the sun shining off her dark hair when she danced along in front of him. Evenings spent lying in each other's arms, watching movies or just being together. Summer afternoons climbing at the pinnacles, then collapsing in an exhausted, satisfied heap. He'd taken those simple pleasures for granted, and then he'd lost them. Now, she'd made a life without him. She had big dreams, and he wasn't sure if he could fit into them.

"What makes you think she'd take me back?" he asked. "Even if I could remind her. She's done nothing to show she might be interested."

Other than kiss him. Once. Maybe twice, tops.

"Oh, she is," his mum replied. "A woman can recognize interest in another woman. Avery has a lot of pride, though."

She had a point. Avery might mask her true feelings to avoid rejection. "Maybe."

"You should put yourself out there," Sharon said. "Remember, there's nothing a woman loves more than having a man make a fool of himself for her."

"Fantastic. Just what I wanted to hear."

"All I'm saying is, don't be afraid to look silly if you really want her. Don't try to be subtle, either. You're like your father: as subtle as a blind bull in a china shop."

"Have some faith in me, Mum."

"Oh, honey. I do have faith in you. Now go and win over my favorite future daughter-in-law."

13

"So," Sophie said, when Gareth, who'd come to check in on them, left the room to shower and they got down to the business at hand. "What color are you thinking, Ri?"

Using the laptop on her knee, Aria opened an online bridesmaid boutique website. "Since you've all got such different skin tones, I thought you could each pick your own color and design. I'm going for a rainbow theme, so if they're different from each other, that will fit nicely."

Avery raised an eyebrow. "Does Eli's family know about this rainbow theme?"

The Lockwoods were snobbish and conventional.

"No," Aria admitted. "And except for Teri, they're not going to. It's none of their business."

Aria still hadn't gotten over Eli's parents trying to come between them, but she would in time. She didn't know how to hold a grudge.

"Good call." Avery wouldn't judge her for it. Unlike Aria, she was perfectly capable of holding a grudge. "So, why are we group shopping if there's no need for us to coordinate?"

"Because it's more fun."

Sophie nodded. "Can't argue with that."

"True." Avery would never have the patience to shop on her own. "What color do you want, Soph?"

Sophie pursed her lips in thought. "Perhaps a pale green or blue. I can't have red, pink or orange because it'd clash with my hair. Yellow makes me look sallow and dark shades wash me out. What about you?"

"Deep blue or purple," Avery answered quickly. She knew what suited her. While she may not be vain, she took care to wear flattering shades on special occasions.

"What do you think Evie and Clarissa will go for?" Aria asked.

"Evie will want something flashy," Sophie said. "Maybe gold or dark red."

"Rissa will go for pink or baby blue," Avery added. "Like usual."

"So…" Aria typed notes in an empty document. "Not much overlap. That's good."

The bathroom door opened and Gareth emerged in a cloud of steam, his hair damp, smelling of a musky cologne. His t-shirt clung to his torso, which he'd apparently failed to dry properly. Either that, or he'd purchased a size too small. Avery swallowed.

"Good lord," Sophie murmured, sounding as though she'd like to eat him up.

Aria smacked her arm. "Remember your boyfriend? My brother?"

Sophie swatted her, but didn't take her eyes away. "No shame in looking."

"Quit it," Avery muttered, gratified when he didn't seem to notice their shameless ogling. Aria had the good grace to blush. Sophie didn't. To be fair, Avery couldn't blame her. She knew what it felt like to be held against that body. Or at least, she once had. But he'd developed a lot since then and she shivered, wondering what he'd feel like now. He looked like he could pick her up with one arm, and Avery was no pixie.

Dresses. Think of the dresses.

"How's the dress shopping going?" he asked, looking sheepish.

Sophie glanced from him to Avery and back, then grinned delightedly. "Improving every moment. Why don't you come over here and give us a man's opinion on these dresses we're looking at?" She patted the arm of the chair.

Next thing, Avery was sandwiched between Aria's side and Gareth's muscular thigh. Biting her lip, she wished he weren't quite so hot. The heat radiating off him practically singed her body where they touched. If he were smaller, less imposing, she could ignore him. As it was, awareness of him overwhelmed her.

"Personally," Sophie confided to the room, "I want to knock Coop's socks off. What about you, Avery? Any special man you want to impress?"

Avery ground her teeth. "No. There's no one for me to impress." Belatedly, she wondered if Gareth would be there. Considering his friendship with Aria, it seemed likely. "Besides, I don't want to detract any attention from Aria."

Aria laughed and leaned her head on Avery's shoulder. "Oh, you're so sweet to worry. In the nicest possible way, I have no concern about any of you upstaging me. At least, not in Eli's eyes, and that's all that matters to me."

Sophie clapped her hands. "Good attitude! Now, what I really want to know is, do you care if you're the most beautiful woman in your brother's eyes?"

"Ick, no. You can have him. And please, keep the details to yourself."

"That's what I like to hear."

Avery chuckled and murmured to Gareth, "They're ridiculous, aren't they?"

"They're fun girls," he replied, his caramel-colored irises twinkling with humor.

"The best," she agreed. "But that doesn't stop them being a little crazy, too."

"Hey," Sophie interjected. "Are you talking about us?"

"Nothing but nice things," he promised, a dimple popping in his cheek as he smiled. That smile warmed Avery's insides, making her feel light, buoyant, as though she could walk on air. Without conscious thought, she smiled back at him, and something frighteningly like butterflies swarmed in her stomach.

Gareth used to unsettle her entire being, just by being near her. Her nerve endings would come alive, every one of her senses hyperaware of him. Now, some of those old nerves fired, as if they'd never gone away, just gone dormant. Her body had never stopped wanting him, even if her brain knew that falling for him would only lead to heartache.

"Here you go."

She flinched. Aria may as well have yelled for the impact her voice had near Avery's ear. She jolted to her senses, breaking eye contact with Gareth and ignoring her friends' snickers.

Aria turned the laptop and they all stretched over to look at the dress she'd chosen, which was a hideously ugly olive color with ruffles around the sleeves and the kind of sack-like form that flattered no one. Gareth, being an unassuming male, cleared his throat and murmured something vaguely approving.

"I like it," Sophie exclaimed, her eyes bright with mischief. "That color suits everyone, but I think it may need a little more." She took over control of the laptop and brought up another dress, very similar, but the ruffles extended down the entire bodice.

"Ooh, you're right," Aria said. "Definitely better. I'm not sure about the olive though, how about something more like this." She reached over, clicked something, and the dress changed from olive to muddy brown.

"Hmm." Sophie appeared to consider it, tilting her head one way and then the other. Avery smothered a chuckle at the bemused expression on Gareth's face.

"Yes," Sophie agreed finally. "But it needs to be longer." Another click of the mouse and the skirt changed from knee-length to ankle-length.

Everyone stared at the awful creation, Aria and Sophie with expressions of glee, and Gareth with horror.

Avery couldn't help but laugh at the poor man. "They're messing with you," she told him.

His eyes narrowed as if he wasn't sure whether to believe her, but something in her friends' twin expressions of false sincerity must have alerted him to the truth.

"Thank god," he said, sighing with relief. "You're all attractive women, but I'm not sure anyone could look good in that dress."

Avery smirked, latching onto the pertinent part of his statement. "Oh, we're attractive, are we?"

He rolled his eyes. "Don't fish for compliments, A-Bee. You know you're stunning."

His matter-of-fact tone was good for her ego. "It's always nice to hear it from a handsome man."

Good god, was she flirting with him?

She *was*.

She heard Gareth's sharp intake of breath as he realized it, too. Neither of them acknowledged it, both fixing their attention on the screen. Awareness hummed between them —awareness, and if she were honest with herself, more than a little attraction.

"Let's get serious," she suggested, drawing in a shuddering breath as she tried to collect herself. "Sophie, you wanted something green, right?" She opened a new screen and brought up a mint green sheath dress with spaghetti straps. "How about this?"

"Hmmm." Sophie nibbled on her lower lip, thinking. "I like the dress, but I'd prefer it to be a shade lighter." Avery made an adjustment. "A little lighter." She adjusted again. "Perfect!" Sophie clapped her hands excitedly. "What do you guys think?"

"If you like it, I love it," Aria declared.

Avery examined it critically. "I think it will suit you. It'll go well with your pale complexion and show off your figure. Coop won't be able to keep his hands off of you."

"What do you think, Gaz?" Sophie asked.

Gareth cleared his throat. "It's a damned sight better than that brown monstrosity."

"Great." Sophie nodded. "Let's lock it in. Can you help me take my measurements, Ri?"

"Sure."

They shuffled away together into the bedroom, no doubt a strategic move to leave Avery alone with Gareth. She laughed low. "Do you get the feeling they're up to something?"

"I do." His voice rumbled through her. Even though the others had left, she was still pressed against his side. "But I'm not complaining," he continued, "because it's working out well for me."

His comment made her feel edgy, restless. Not necessarily uncomfortable though. "You sure about that?"

"I guess we'll find out," he replied easily. "So, what kind of dress do you want, A-Bee?"

For some reason, shopping for clothes together seemed far more intimate than it had when the girls were present. A lump lodged in her throat. When she spoke, her voice was huskier than usual. "Something long and flowing. Purple, I think."

"Still your favorite color, huh?"

"It's a nice color. No need to mess with a good thing."

He shook his head. "You're so predictable."

Her stomach plummeted. *Predictable.* One of the few words she'd agonized over. She wondered whether being less predictable, more exciting, would have kept him around for longer.

Predictable. She used to interpret it as meaning the same thing as boring. Safe. Only now, with the benefit of hindsight, age and experience, she'd learned to accept that being predictable wasn't necessarily a bad thing. She knew what she liked, and she stuck with it. She may not be a wild, impulsive bombshell but she wouldn't let anyone make her feel ashamed of that. At heart, she was a creature of habit, and that was okay.

"I am," she said lightly. "No denying that. Just like you're still too serious."

"You're calling *me* out for being serious?"

She smirked at him. "You know it's true. You were always such a worrier."

"You always told me to lighten up."

"With good reason." She studied his face. Now that the girls were gone, she finally allowed herself to drink in the sight of him. His eyes, that lovely shade of brown, stared back into her, as if trying to see her soul. The dimple was absent from his cheek, but his lips rested in a half-smile, as though at any time it could make itself known. Despite his golden skin tone, his complexion seemed too pale, and violet half-circles rested beneath his eyes.

The past week had been hard on him, as it had been for her.

"Tell me what's wrong," she said. "Is it just the case, or is it something else?"

"What makes you think anything is wrong?"

The side of his mouth quirked up and the dimple appeared, but Avery wouldn't be distracted. "You're an open book, G. At least, you are to me. What's worrying you?"

He frowned, the dimple disappearing again. "It's the case, but something else, too." He paused, then continued in a quieter voice, "I don't understand you like I used to, Avery." She noticed he'd used her proper name and for some reason, disappointment lanced through her. "You're more self-possessed than you used to be. Or maybe you always were, but I never noticed. It makes me wonder what else I might have missed when I was young and stupid."

He took her hand and stroked his thumb over the back of it. "I feel like I don't know you half the time and it's killing me because I want to." His voice thickened with emotion. "Tell me that after all of this is over, there's a chance we can get to know each other the way we used to. If there's not, if you'd rather be with that brainiac Jesse, be upfront with me."

He fell silent, waiting for her reply. Avery's tongue suddenly felt three times heavier than usual. She'd never expected this from him and sensed her answer would be one of the most important ones she ever gave. While it would be easy to lie about her feelings, she couldn't bring herself to voice anything other than the truth.

"I don't care about Jesse the way I care about you." She spoke quietly, but her voice was calm, belying the tremble in her hands, which she thrust between her knees to hide from view. "I never have. I—"

"We're back!" Aria announced, as she and Sophie emerged from the bedroom.

Avery closed her eyes, relieved for the interruption, but also sad that the intense moment between them had ended prematurely. She'd never know what she'd been about to say, because for once, she'd opened her heart and the words had been flowing from somewhere deep within her. They would have been as much a surprise to herself as to him. He stared at her as if trying to discern what she'd been about to say.

If he figured it out, she'd damn well like to know too.

He straightened his left knee, lifted his foot off the floor and flexed it a couple of times before standing, keeping most of his weight on the right leg. Before she knew what she was doing, Avery's hand shot out to feel around the knee joint.

"Is it bothering you?"

His expression became wary, defensive. "Nothing to worry about."

"Of course not," she murmured. The injury clearly pained him, although he didn't seem prepared to admit it. Sophie glanced between them, obviously itching to ask what had happened while they'd been gone. They ignored her.

"Will you be able to come to my hen's party in Christchurch this weekend?" Aria asked, breaking through the tension.

"I'll be there," Avery said, releasing his leg, grateful for the question. Anything to distract her from the jumbled emotions twisting together like a knot she couldn't unravel. "For sure."

"Don't get too ahead of yourself," Gareth cautioned, wearing that same blank mask. "I'll do everything I can to get her there," he said to Aria, "but we can't make any promises."

She harrumphed and pressed her lips together. "I guess that'll have to do. I don't suppose I need to tell you how much I don't like being kept in the dark."

"You don't," he replied. "But I promise you that I'll keep Avery safe, whatever it takes."

Her friends' eyes widened, as though the tone of his voice had given away how serious the danger facing her may be, and they wanted to demand answers. In their place, she would too, but they didn't. Instead, they wrapped her in a hug while she tried not to cry—because damned if she didn't have the most amazing friends in the world.

14

Avery and Gareth spent Saturday morning sprawled on the sofa, watching re-runs of *Criminal Minds*, which she preferred to *CSI* because it didn't try so hard to venture into forensic science in a way that inevitably resulted in inaccuracies. Halfway through the show, which featured a serial killer who sewed his victims' mouths shut, a low snuffle sounded to her right.

Gareth snored again, his mouth slack, eyes closed, cheek resting on the arm of the sofa. Something stuck in her chest. In sleep, he looked younger, and it brought back memories of seeing him like this after they'd passed out together watching a string of ridiculous horror movies one winter night. Then she'd leaned over and woken him with a kiss.

Her eyes dropped to his lips. No, she wouldn't do that.

She needed space, air, and distance, all at once. Easing away from the sofa so as not to disturb his well-earned sleep, she hesitated for a minute before inching the door open and slipping outside. She wouldn't stay out for long. A minute. Two, tops. Just enough to clear her head. He wouldn't even know she'd been gone. She paced along the path that led to the parking lot, stretching her legs. In the open paved area, she paused, taking a moment to look around.

An engine started and she listened to it purr. Seconds later, a dark sedan shot forward, racing at her so fast that all she could do was throw up her hands and wait for the impact.

~

Gareth awoke as the door clicked shut. Immediately, his heart rate leapt from sixty to one-hundred-and-sixty. He'd fallen asleep on the job.

Fuck. Avery had left the building.

Where was she going? He rushed out of the door after her, fumbling in his pocket for the keys so no one could sneak inside while they were gone. He jogged toward the parking lot because he couldn't see her in any other direction, and arrived at the edge just in time to see a sedan hurtle toward her. Without thinking, he threw himself at her, knocking her out of the way. His foot hit the front of the car with a thud and his body spun from the impact. Pain rocketed up his leg, but he clambered to his feet, then reached down and yanked her up, shoving the key into her palm.

"Run back to the room. Lock yourself inside. Go!"

Brakes squealed as the car came to a halt. Was it coming back for a second shot? He focused on the license plate and memorized the digits. EXE816. Instead of coming back around, the car flew toward the exit. He sprinted behind it, hoping to get a glimpse of the driver, but it was going too fast and, with his injured foot, he couldn't keep up. Cursing, he swung around and limped back to their room, grabbing his radio from his belt and calling in for help.

Someone had tried to hurt Avery. Hell, someone had tried to *kill* her. Had he not woken up, they would have been successful.

136

His chest ached. *How could he have fallen asleep on the job?*

He was better than that. He'd worked damn hard to make sure that kind of mistake never happened on his watch, but he'd been worn out. Let himself slip because nothing had happened yet.

He should have known better.

What kind of cop couldn't keep one woman safe? He was literally paid to do exactly that. Not that he needed payment. He would protect Avery no matter what, but the fact was, he'd fucked up, and she'd nearly paid the price.

His head wasn't screwed on straight when it came to this case. She needed someone else. Someone better. This couldn't happen again. He couldn't live with himself if she ended up like that poor woman he'd found on the hotel floor all those years ago. He envisioned what he would have discovered had he been five seconds slower. Avery, bleeding on the pavement, the light fading from her eyes. He cursed again.

She was waiting by the door and opened it for him, throwing her arms around him. He nearly tripped backward, his bruised foot unprepared for the force of her body hitting his. His arms automatically went around her and he held her tight, burying his face in her hair and breathing in the scent of her, reveling in her warmth and vitality.

She was *alive.* Everything was okay. For now.

"I'm so sorry," she said. "I thought it would be fine. I was going to come straight back inside. But I should never have gone out. This is all my fault. Are you all right? I heard…I mean, it sounded like the car…h-hit you."

He rocked her gently from side to side, her tears seeping through his shirt and soaking his shoulder, warm and wet.

"Hey there," he murmured. "I'm okay. It just caught the end of my foot. A bit of bruising, that's all."

"You could have been killed," she cried, drawing back and

wiping her eyes on the sleeve of her sweater. "And it would have been my fault."

"*You* could have been killed," he echoed, "and it would have been *my* fault for sleeping on the job. But we're both okay and the perp is gone, so let's get you a hot drink and wait for the cavalry to arrive."

"I don't need a drink," she said, but her hands were trembling.

He didn't bother to reply. Her white skin, combined with the trembling, told him she was going into shock. He needed to warm her up. He guided her to the couch then hobbled into the kitchen and fixed her a cup of tea, dumping two spoonfuls of sugar into it.

When he approached, she eyed the cup suspiciously, sniffing it when he handed it to her, turning her nose up. "That's not coffee."

"Coffee is the last thing you need, trust me." Her chin lifted stubbornly. "Come on," he encouraged. "Drink up."

"Oh, all right." She accepted the cup gracelessly and sipped. He winced. She'd always been able to drink water straight from the kettle. It was a wonder she hadn't burned all her taste buds off by now. After her second sip, she sputtered and glared at him in outrage. "What did you do to this? It's sweet. Tea shouldn't be sweet!"

At least she didn't look so despondent. "You need the sugar. It'll help."

Sugar, warmth, and sleep. He planned to make sure she got all three. Her eyes narrowed, like she didn't quite believe him, but she drank again, making an expression of disgust. He laughed. He couldn't help himself. Even with her spirits dampened and energy low, she managed to give him attitude.

"All of it. Good girl."

Sirens blared outside. His colleagues had arrived. Rather than heading out to meet them, he sat beside Avery and radioed them the room number. He wasn't leaving her side, not even for a moment, until the person who'd tried to hurt her was behind bars. He wouldn't give anyone the opportunity to do as much as mess up one hair on her head.

Two uniformed officers knocked on the door. Both were men, one in his twenties, short and stocky, the other older and wiry with thinning hair. Brandon and Sim.

Gareth opened the door. "That was fast."

"We were nearby," Sim, the older of the two, explained. "What happened here?"

"Attempted hit and run," Gareth replied, stepping aside to let them in. He gestured to Avery on the sofa. "This is Dr. Brown. She's doing some confidential work for us, and it's made her a target. Someone in a dark sedan, license plate EXE816, tried to run her down."

"You get a look at the driver?" Brandon asked, his attention fixed firmly on Avery. Was that a flicker of interest in his eyes? Professional, or personal? *Get a grip, it doesn't matter.* What mattered was that they were here to keep her safe.

"I didn't," Gareth said. "Tried to chase him down but he clipped my ankle on the way past and I couldn't keep up."

"How about you, Doc?" Sim asked. "You see anything?"

Her brow furrowed in concentration as she searched her memory for answers. "Maybe it was a man, but I couldn't say for sure. I panicked. I know that's not very useful, sorry."

"That's perfectly all right," Brandon said in a low, soothing tone. "You've had a shock. Don't pressure yourself to remember. It will come back to you naturally over the next day or so."

"I'll run the plates," Sim said, backtracking out of the door.

Gareth nodded. Brandon perched on the arm of the chair, knees apart, and withdrew a notepad from his pocket. "Are you up to answering a few questions?" he asked gently.

"Yes," she said, clasping the teacup even though it was empty now. As Brandon started his list of standard questions, Gareth went to the kitchen and made her another cup of tea, which she accepted without complaint, sipping distractedly while she answered. Her eyes didn't remain on either Brandon or himself, but wandered around the room like she'd lost the ability to focus on any particular person or thing.

Sim returned, shuffled over to Gareth, and let him know that the car had been reported stolen. Though unsurprising, the news disappointed him.

"You mind stepping outside with me for a minute?" Gareth asked, confident that Brandon would be occupied with Avery for a while longer.

Sim followed him outside and closed the door behind them. "What is it?"

Stuffing his hands in his pockets, he studied the pavement. "I need one of you to stay and watch over Avery for a while. I'm too tired. I fell asleep earlier and put her in danger. I can't be trusted to do my job properly right now."

"I can stay here while you go home for some shut-eye," Sim told him. "No worries, mate."

"No." Gareth shook his head. "I'll sleep here. A few hours should do the trick."

"You'd get a better sleep in your own bed."

He met Sim's gaze and held it. "I'm not leaving her," he said, hoping the other man could read the emotions he didn't want to voice.

"I see," Sim replied slowly, and Gareth thought he did. "I'll send Brandon back to the office with a report. You take your girl and get some sleep. It looks like the both of you need it."

"Thank you." He clapped the other man on the shoulder.

"Don't let this get too murky," Sim warned. "Things can go wrong real quick if you're not careful."

"I know." He looked in through the window, where Brandon had finished questioning Avery and was tucking his notepad away. A moment later, Sim pulled Brandon aside and explained the situation to him. Meanwhile, Gareth settled beside Avery, wrapped an arm around her and drew her close. She seemed to collapse in on herself, finally giving in to exhaustion. Or perhaps she was simply too overwhelmed to stay strong when someone offered comfort. Whatever the case, he rocked her gently and kissed her temple, murmuring meaningless words of support in her ear.

"Let me tuck you into bed," he said.

"But it's still early," she protested. "I might have an email from Jesse with more results in it. I can't sleep."

"You need to." His tone brooked no argument. "If not for yourself, then do it for me. I need to sleep, and I won't be able to unless I know you are, too. Thinking of the trouble you could get yourself into without me would keep me awake."

She nodded. "Okay, you have a point."

"Come on, then. Don't deprive a poor law enforcement official of his sleep."

She laughed, though it sounded watery and weak. "I said I would. Don't beat a dead horse."

Taking her hand, he led her to her bedroom and offered her an old flannel shirt to wear. She took it without a word, swaying as though she might keel over if he gave her the slightest push. Instead, he slid an arm around her shoulders, steadying her.

"Turn on the electric blanket," he ordered. "I'll be right next door, and Officer Sim will be in the lounge."

He released her and turned to go, but hesitated in the doorway, his hand on the frame, and watched as she sat on the edge of the bed, deflated.

"Thank you," she murmured. "For saving me."

"I always will," he vowed. "I've always got your back." The promise came easily because he'd said it dozens of times before, so she'd always known that even when no one else was, he'd be there for her. As the door swung shut behind him, he could have sworn he heard a soft noise.

"Did you say something?" he asked, catching the door.

"Don't go." She hadn't lifted her gaze from the floor, but her words were clear as day. "Will you stay with me, Gareth? Hold me for a while?"

He suppressed a groan, knowing he didn't have the heart to deny her.

"Give me a moment to change." Retreating to the other bedroom, he pulled on a pair of track pants and a t-shirt, wondering how this day had gone so far off track. Whatever deity had it out for him, they wanted nothing less than his complete annihilation at the hands of the only woman he'd ever loved.

No matter. Gareth could, and would, put aside his reservations and get through tonight. He marched back into the bedroom. She lay huddled beneath the covers. She patted the spot next to herself and smiled tentatively. He drew back the blankets to lie next to her, slipping an arm under her shoulders and holding her close. She rolled toward him, resting her cheek on his chest, over his heart.

She must hear how loudly it pounded for her. He missed this. Just being near her, sharing intimacy with someone who accepted him. Although the circumstances weren't what he'd hoped for, some part of his foolish heart came alive anyway.

They lay together in silence for long minutes before he noticed her wet cheeks. She was crying again. His innards lurched and he hugged her tighter. The realization that she was shedding tears while in his arms ripped him apart.

"It's okay," he said softly, stroking her hair. It was strange, having her here, sharing this stolen moment with her. Gave his imagination funny ideas about her being his girl again. He shut it down, hard.

She's not my girl. At least, not yet.

"Shh. It's all right."

"It's not all right," she whispered. "Someone truly wants me out of the way, and they nearly got what they wanted."

His arms tightened reflexively around her. "But they didn't," he murmured. "You're safe. You're okay. I'm right here with you."

Slowly, her sniffles eased. After a while, he realized she'd fallen asleep.

15

───────

Something buzzed on the edge of Avery's consciousness, like a fly or a bee. She tried to put it to the back of her mind but the droning wouldn't stop. Her eyes fluttered open, but that didn't shed any light on the situation. The room was dark. She focused on the droning. Not a fly or a bee, she realized now, but a man snoring. *Gareth.*

Memories from the last few hours slammed into her. She cringed, remembering how she'd begged him to stay, and he had. He'd taken care of her. There was a lot to admire about the man he'd become. The boy who'd broken her heart, however unintentionally, had grown into a man who could be relied on. Or so it seemed.

Pushing that thought aside, she took stock of her situation, and noticed for the first time that not only was Gareth in her bed, but he was wrapped around her like a big spoon, shielding her from the world. A big spoon sporting a sizable erection, which was pressed against her ass.

Oh, *wow.*

She'd forgotten what it felt like to wake up with a horny male. His proximity set her pulse skipping happily toward Lust Lane without passing Go. Her breath ratcheted up a notch, coming out in pants, like she'd been running, or thoroughly kissed. She forced herself to take long, quiet breaths.

Get yourself under control, girl.

She waited to see if he'd notice, but he didn't stir, except to tuck her closer, his arm draping possessively over her waist as if to hold her there in case she tried to escape.

Why on earth would she want to?

She basked in the feeling of safety that came from having Gareth at her back and all around her. She inhaled his natural masculine scent and sighed, remembering the many nights she'd spent with him like this. That part of their relationship had been blissful. Perfect.

Could it be like that again?

He shifted, drawing her attention to his sheer size. He'd grown since high school, in the most delicious way. Though she'd endeavored not to notice the broad span of his shoulders or the solid muscularity of his thighs, there was only so much a girl could lie to herself. When he was this close, there was no denying it: he was hot, and she wanted him.

Despite the emotional upheaval she'd experienced today —or perhaps because of it—in the span of ten seconds, she'd had three different fantasies that involved Gareth rolling over, kissing her senseless, stripping off her clothes, and touching her. Her heartbeat accelerated as another image popped into her mind. Him, in his uniform. Her, naked. Limbs entwined.

Get a grip. He's not even wearing his uniform.

No, from the feel of him, and the few things she could see now that her eyes were adjusting to the dimness, she could tell that he was wearing soft track pants and one of the t-shirts that displayed his firm torso to absolute perfection. *Dayum.*

She wriggled, trying to relieve the ache between her thighs. Gareth's hard-on pulsed and his breath puffed against the back of her neck, sending a shiver of desire down her spine. God, he was as turned on as she was.

He's asleep. He doesn't know what's happening.

She started to pull away, but he tugged her back into the hollow of his body. So she did what she'd been longing to: rolled over and set her lips to his.

Her body pressed against the bulk of his, she kissed one corner of his mouth, then the other corner, then his nose. She could just see enough that she noticed his lips curve upward. She kissed his smile, feeling playful. The playfulness ended the moment he let out a low moan, clasped her to him and deepened the kiss. When his velvety tongue tangled with hers, heat pooled between her legs and she rocked into him. His hands came to her hips and she gasped, reveling in the sensation of being surrounded by him, excited by the knowledge that he wanted her.

He groaned and rubbed himself over her. Then he drew back. She tried to follow, but he held her off.

"Much as I'd love to give us what we both want, you've had a hard week and you're vulnerable right now. I don't want to take advantage of that."

Her free hand skated over his shoulders and down his rib cage, around to grip his butt and anchor him more firmly to her. She wasn't about to let him leave. Even if she could hardly string together a coherent sentence.

"G, I appreciate the sentiment, but I need you. Just once, can you not overthink this?"

He exhaled shakily and his fingers trembled at her hips. He gave the impression of a barely leashed beast restrained by a civilized veneer but desperate to break free. She'd never seen him like this. Yes, they'd had good sex back in the day, but he'd been softer around the edges. More boyish. This Gareth was all man. She yearned for him. She wanted to unleash the beast.

Holding his gaze, she writhed sinuously against him. If

she'd had room, she'd have slipped her hand into his pants, but the space separating them from the hips down was nonexistent. Instead, she delighted in amplifying the friction between them, watching his pupils dilate. His thumbs edged beneath her shirt and started drawing tiny circles on the skin of her hips. Her entire body hummed with desire.

"You really want this?" His voice was rough, gravelly.

Her eyes fluttered closed as his thumbs quested upward, traversing the underside of her ribs. Mm, yes. The man had a way with his hands.

"Open your eyes," he growled. She did. "No regrets. Promise me."

"I promise." The words were oddly solemn, for the occasion.

He heaved in a great breath, as though he'd been holding it while he waited for her answer. "I want you so much. God, I want you. But we shouldn't do this. Not until we've cleared up this case. I can't afford to be distracted by you."

He was so good. So determined to do the right thing. It turned her on so much.

"No regrets," she whispered. "I promise I'll let you get on with your job later. Just touch me now, okay?"

It was like she'd given the beast inside him the green light.

GARETH COULDN'T HEAR anything over the thundering of his heart. He couldn't feel anything but the warmth of Avery's palms on his chest, slowly sliding up over his shoulders. He shivered, skin prickling with pleasure at her ministrations, even through a layer of fabric. He wanted to be skin to skin with her, but he'd have to back off in order to strip off his clothes and he wasn't prepared to do that. So he kissed her again, thrilled when she sighed with pleasure and her hands came up to cup his cheeks, all of her attention now on the kisses they exchanged. Slow, drugging, wet kisses.

Then she wriggled out of his grasp. He could barely see her in the dim light, but the glint of her eyes in the dark captivated him.

He moistened his lips. "What are you doing?"

"Undressing," came the reply. "I thought that would be obvious."

It was becoming more and more obvious. She stripped off the shirt, kneeling before him in a pair of panties and nothing else. He traced the edge of them. While her under-things weren't the stuff of male fantasy, because they were on her, he couldn't have asked for anything better. His mouth filled with saliva and he swallowed.

He could only make out her outline, but that was enough to know that her body had changed during the time they'd been apart. Her limbs were lean and strong, with shapely muscles curving her thighs and upper arms. A groove indented the center of her stomach.

"Take them off." His voice was rough, but he didn't have the presence of mind for smooth words when faced with her nearly nude body. "I want you naked."

Avery shimmied out of her panties. He stroked her high breasts. They'd grown fuller since he'd last seen them. He reached for her hips, drew her near and kissed the tip of one breast.

"You're so unbelievably sexy," he murmured, his hands scooting around to caress the naked globes of her ass. He lathed the other breast with his tongue and hummed his approval. "And you taste so good."

She shuffled forward, straddling his lap, her knees on either side of his hips, and ground down on him, purring her pleasure. His body flexed in response.

He tore his mouth away from hers, panting. "I need to get these clothes off."

"God, yes."

He lifted her off his lap, then without any finesse, tugged his t-shirt over his head and yanked his pants down to kick them off, his ankle twinging as he did. He lifted his head and froze. Avery was staring at him like a starving woman before a buffet. She trailed a single finger down his chest and abdominal muscles, stopping just above the place he ached for her to touch. He shivered and his muscles twitched.

"It's like you're a living fantasy," she said appreciatively. "Except I can touch you." She did so, stroking her palms across his abdomen, then tracking upward, flicking the nub of his nipples with her thumbs. If it was possible, he hardened further, making him genuinely concerned that if he didn't get inside her soon, he'd bust prematurely. Such a thing hadn't happened since he was a green boy. With Avery, as a matter of fact.

"Please." He didn't know what he was asking, but that didn't seem to bother her. She held his gaze while she lowered herself, took the base of his cock in her hand and licked her way along the shaft. His knees went weak. She pumped her hand and he clenched his fists at his side to stop from taking hold of her head and thrusting into her mouth. He wanted no regrets—on her side, anyway. He was bound to have a few given their perilous working relationship.

She sucked him, and he groaned. "Ah, yes, feels good, baby."

"Shh," she admonished. "Your buddy is outside."

Damn, he'd forgotten about Sim. No doubt the other cop had gotten an earful. Maybe they should stop. Maybe—

"Stop thinking." Her hands came around to clasp his buttocks and she worked him with her mouth. All thoughts of Officer Sim fled.

After a few moments of bliss, Gareth snagged her hair. "No more. I can't take it."

She released him and his erection thumped his lower

stomach. He tucked her to his chest and rolled, turning the tables so he was on top, then fixed his mouth between her legs. He licked luscious strips down the center of her folds, then eased off, grinning when she made a sound of disapproval.

"You want more, sweetheart?"

"Yes."

He rewarded her directness. She bucked against him, her breath coming in ragged gasps.

"I want you inside me." Her hips lifted toward him as he teased her without mercy.

"You do?"

"Yes."

He pressed kisses to the soft insides of her thighs and they trembled. "Are you sure?"

"Yes, I'm sure!"

Sitting, she tried to haul him up her body. Unfortunately for her, he was somewhat larger, heavier and stronger, and he didn't move an inch. Her honest desire warmed his heart and sent happiness unfurling outward from it. For a second, just a second, he wanted to confess the feelings growing within him, but he held back. Now wasn't the time. Instead, he looked about and grunted in disgust.

"No condom," he muttered. "You got one?"

"No," she said, and he felt like he could cry frustrated tears, but then she added, "I'm on the injection. Clean bill of health a month ago."

Yes. Trust her not to leave anything to chance.

"I'm clean too," he said. "Do you trust me?"

"I do."

"Thank god." He sagged with relief. Then, crisis averted, he leisurely studied what he could see of her body. He positioned himself above her, and eased into her body. Breath hissed between her lips as he sank to the hilt. She wrapped her legs around his waist, heels digging into his lower back as she urged him on. He braced a forearm on either side of her head and started pumping into her, slowly at first, gliding in and out like he had forever to make love to her.

Avery met him thrust for thrust. His balls tightened and he knew if he didn't take it easy, he wouldn't last more than two minutes. He stopped moving, lavishing kisses on her while he regained control of himself.

"Why did you stop?" she asked, shifting restlessly beneath him, driving him crazy.

"Baby, it's been a while for me," he admitted. "If you keep that up, I'm gonna come too soon."

She stilled, then whispered in her sexy, husky voice, "I'm close, too. Go wild. Take me with you."

He closed his eyes and thanked the lord. "You are perfect, Avery Brown."

He lifted her legs to get even deeper and set loose the beast within him, which wanted nothing more than to sate itself in her body. She cried out encouragement and her nails scraped down his back, sending bolts of lust through him, one after another. His balls slapped against her ass and he felt her shudder and clench around him as she came. Her whimpers sent him over the edge and he jerked against her once more, then collapsed to the side and pulled her close.

One thing was for sure: Officer Sim would look at them differently come morning.

16

*A*very woke gradually, the weight of Gareth's arm over her waist, and his chest at her back, cocooning her in a warm, sleepy bubble. She wriggled backward, fitting the curve of her backside into the hollow formed between his torso and his thighs, and hummed contentedly. His hold tightened, dragging her closer, his fingers splayed across her belly. Her heart felt light, her limbs weightless.

She took one of his hands from her waist and raised it to her mouth, pressing a kiss to the palm. What a perfect way to start the day. He came fully awake and tried to caress her cheek, except his face was buried in her hair and he couldn't see a thing. Instead, he poked her nose. She giggled. He uttered a disgruntled noise. She giggled harder. Suddenly, his hands were at her sides, tickling.

"You think that's funny, do you?" he asked, his voice thick with sleep. She tried to wiggle away and found herself stuck. His fingers tickled up and down her rib cage, dangerously close to her armpits.

She gasped for breath. "Not funny," she wheezed. "Have mercy."

The tickling ceased. They resumed cuddling, her heart

still pounding from adrenaline. She grinned. She'd have to remember that he knew her weaknesses and had no qualms exploiting them. She was about to tell him how evil he was when something long and hard pulsed against her butt. *Oh, my.*

"Get your mind out of the gutter," she said, chuckling. "I can't believe you're ready to go another round." They'd had sex twice last night, and while she had no idea what they were doing together or where it was going, she'd never been so well satisfied in her life.

"It's all you," he said helplessly. "Everything about you makes me want more."

Well, she'd heard far worse than that she inspired lust in a sexy man. "Unfortunately, we can't indulge your dirty mind. I need to get up and check my emails, and you need to send your colleague home. God only knows what the poor man heard last night."

His palm curved around her breast. "Can't you talk to him for me?"

"No, and don't be such a prude. He's a married man in his fifties. I'm sure he knows all about sex."

"I'll make it worth your while." His thumb rubbed back and forth across the tender skin beneath her breast and her head flopped onto the pillow.

"Stop." She didn't even convince herself she wanted him to stop.

Lifting himself up on one elbow, he kissed her lips. "Before we get out of bed, we should talk."

Uh-oh. She rolled away and sat, yanking the duvet up around her waist. "Okay, so talk."

He gestured between them. "What are we doing, A-Bee?"

Her lips twitched with mirth. "I should think it's obvious. I can draw a diagram if you want, though."

He snorted. "Enough, smart-ass. Be serious for a minute. I

want to know if this means we're dating, and if so, are we exclusive? Because I don't share with others."

Studying his face, she realized he was dead serious. Shit. How had she gotten herself into this situation?

"We're not dating," she said. "And saying that sounds so old-fashioned. Do we really need to label this?"

She'd been enjoying herself, but she wasn't ready to offer up her heart and hope he wouldn't discard it later. He'd broken his promises and made her feel less than perfect once before, and that was enough for her. She was a woman who learned from her mistakes, especially the painful ones.

She considered suggesting that they end this—whatever it was—before it went any further, but she couldn't bring herself to say the words. Not just yet, anyway. "How about we take this one day at a time and agree not to see anyone else?"

"All right," he agreed. "But for the record, I plan on asking you out for an official date as soon as Mr. Broderick is behind bars."

She cleared her throat, uncomfortable with this proclamation. She didn't want his promises, or his pretty words. She already knew how much they were worth, and she wouldn't hang her hopes on them.

"Let's not go too far too fast." He flinched, almost imperceptibly, but she felt like a bitch. "I'm sorry." She truly was. "But I'm not ready to dive into the deep end with you."

He shuffled up in the bed, his arms coming around her as he nuzzled the side of her neck. She tilted her head to give him better access. Yeah, they had chemistry. She wasn't denying that. But wanting anything more than sex would only cause trouble.

"That's okay." His breath whispered across her cheek. "I'll convince you."

"I look forward to it." Provided his method of "convincing" involved more naked grinding, and less talking. "But let's keep this quiet for the moment." She sensed him stiffen and hastened to add, "There are a lot of people who'd love to hear we're giving it another shot, but I want us to be able to enjoy each other without that pressure."

And she wanted to be able to bow out without causing a scene if she needed to.

"Not indefinitely." It wasn't a question.

"Just while we get to know each other again." Until she decided what to do about the hole she was digging herself into. She needed time and space away from him to think, and that wouldn't happen for a while. "Your parents would ask a million questions if they knew."

His body relaxed again. "Yeah, they would. Avoiding their harassment for a while probably isn't a bad idea. We can focus on each other."

She nodded, pleased they'd reached an accord. Her hand journeyed across his chest and she drew him in for a deep kiss, breaking apart breathlessly when her alarm blared.

He laughed and ran a hand through his hair. "Does that mean we have to get out of bed?"

"Hell, no." She planted a kiss on him.

He dimpled. "I love that smile."

The grin lessened. She hadn't heard the "L" word from Gareth in years and it didn't sit well with her, whatever the context. Believing that word was what had gotten her blindsided back in high school.

"You okay, A-Bee?"

"Fine," she said, brushing aside his concern. "Just kiss me."

He did, running his hands along the outline of her body. "You've changed since we were teenagers."

Shoving him back, she rolled her eyes. "Of course I have. If you were hoping everything would be the same now as it was back then, sorry to disappoint you." Strangely, it felt like she was talking about more than her body.

"Disappoint me?" he asked, disbelief in his voice. "I love the way you are now."

She shivered. That word again. A cold tendril of fear wrapped around her chest and squeezed. She forced herself to breathe evenly. He hadn't declared his undying devotion, just expressed appreciation for her physical being. Nothing to worry about. Nevertheless, it felt like she'd boarded a train that was hurtling toward the edge of a cliff and the brakes had malfunctioned.

"What's going on in that head of yours?" he murmured, tilting her chin back to look into her eyes. "I can see the cogs in your clever brain spinning round."

It was too much. Add in the way the line between his eyes softened as he smiled at her, and it was way too much. He was tender, concerned. She had to get away. If he kept looking at her like that, she'd fall for him again, and she couldn't afford to do that.

She slid off the edge of the bed, searching the floor for her clothes, then tugged on her panties and a pair of jeans, sprayed on deodorant, and slipped into a t-shirt that read "I make bad chemistry puns but only periodically" without checking to see if he'd followed her lead. She beelined for the exit, opening the door just enough to leave and no more, in case he hadn't dressed. Officer Sim was sitting on the sofa, sipping a steaming mug of coffee and reading the newspaper.

"Morning," she said as she bustled past him to make herself a cup.

"Morning, Doc. Feeling better today?" He didn't give any hint of knowing what had happened between her and Gareth. The consummate professional.

"Much," she called over her shoulder. "Thanks for staying. Sorry I wasn't a lot of help."

"It's difficult to remember details in stressful situations," he replied, and his matter-of-fact tone eased her guilt over not being a better witness.

While the kettle boiled, she switched her laptop on and waited for the emails to load.

"Yes!" she cried, elated to see Jesse's name at the top of her inbox.

"Did the last of the test results finally come through?" Gareth asked from the doorway.

She nodded, glued to the screen as the files began downloading to her hard drive. Coffee forgotten, she got to work compiling the data into something meaningful. Something she could use to get revenge on whoever it was that thought they could murder a young girl, burn Avery's house down, trash her lab, and run her over in public without facing the consequences.

WHILE AVERY TAPPED MADLY at her keyboard, Gareth walked to the kitchen, favoring his sore leg, but only a little. It was healing fast. He poured hot water from the recently boiled kettle into a coffee cup and stirred in coffee and a sugar. He wished briefly that Sim wasn't there, so he could interrogate her about the reason she'd left the bed. He wanted to know what he'd said to send her running, so he could avoid doing it again. But he forced himself to smile at his colleague, who'd gone out of his way to help, and tip his head in greeting.

"No news?" he asked.

Sim shook his head. "No luck tracking down the stolen car. A bunch of little old ladies called in to report suspicious men skulking in their backyards, but none of those claims were verified. Probably they've got possums in the bushes that gave them a fright."

"Wouldn't be the first time." On a number of occasions, Gareth had been called to deal with an intruder, only to encounter a furry tree-dweller instead.

"You okay here if I head home and catch up on some sleep myself?" Sim asked. "I can send Brandon over if you want a second pair of eyes on the doc."

Gareth glanced at Avery, who was bent low over the screen, fingers hovering above the number pad. He didn't think she'd move anytime soon. "You go," he said. "If I need backup, I'll call for it myself. I appreciate you staying. You did me a solid. I owe you." He reached out and clapped hands with Sim.

The cop ducked his head. "You'd have done the same if it were my Beth who was in trouble."

"I never said—"

"Man, it's as plain as the eyebrows on your face how you feel about that woman," Sim told him with a little smile.

Gareth shot him a look that warned him not to continue if he valued his silver-fox good looks. *She's right over there*, he mouthed.

Sim downed his coffee and followed Gareth's line of sight to watch Avery at her computer. "That girl ain't hearing anything," he said, then rose to his feet and rolled his shoulders back. "I'd best be off. Take care of her, Gaz. Holler if you need help."

"Will do."

Gareth watched his colleague collect his jacket and leave, locking the door behind him. Then he lifted his legs onto the sofa and stretched out, leaning on the arm, so he could see the door and Avery at the same time. She was completely absorbed in her work. He got the impression he could dress in his full police uniform and perform a striptease with a brass band behind him and she wouldn't notice.

He'd always admired her focus. Her brain was a thing of beauty. Constantly turning over new ideas, weighing up likelihoods, assimilating new information. Always learning and improving. She was brilliant.

There had been a time when that intimidated him, though

he'd never let it show. He could admit that her career path still intimidated him, and he felt a little inadequate by comparison, but her mind… Her mind fascinated him. He wished he could close his eyes and step inside her stream of consciousness to see the mechanics of her thought process. But for as long as she was withdrawn into her own world, he couldn't follow. Perhaps that was for the best.

He wondered about Sim's offer to send Brandon to join them. Had that been merely a friendly suggestion, or did he think Gareth was emotionally compromised? Because the truth was, Avery had him tied in knots and he couldn't be objective about her. Should he stand down? Ask Rata to assign another policeman to protect her?

No fucking way.

Denial roared inside his ears, as though his heart was screaming at his brain for even contemplating the possibility. The force of it startled him and he peered at Avery, half-expecting her to be staring at him, but she carried on as though he hadn't made a sound.

He drew in a deep breath. The voice in his head was right. He may be emotionally screwed when it came to Avery, but no one else would defend her the way he would. He would put himself on the line for her, over and over, and he couldn't ask any of his colleagues to do the same.

So for now, he had her back. And he wouldn't let her down.

The next two days were torture. Avery was completely absorbed in her work, leaving Gareth with nothing to do except wonder what came next for them. He didn't get the chance to raise the subject, since she woke before him each morning, went to bed after he did each evening—while a duty officer kept guard—and worked constantly in between. She didn't even pause to eat. If he hadn't brought her meals, which she shoved distractedly into her mouth while she typed with the other hand, he doubted she would have remembered to eat at all.

Obviously, the status of their relationship wasn't high on her list of priorities at the moment. Still, he couldn't help wondering, had he messed things up by sleeping with her? Was hot sex all she'd wanted from him? For her, had it only been a distraction from the shittiness of the past few days? Because for him, it had been much more. The start of something shiny and new and promising. Then she'd made those cryptic statements, and run.

Now, it seemed like she was channeling everything she had into work. He tried to do the same. He was hypervigilant, standing inside the entrance to the hotel room, primed to fight if needed, his hand hovering over his hip where he wore his taser on a belt. He reminded himself, as he watched the top of her sable head over her laptop screen, that it was probably for the best that she focused on work right now. Probably best that they *both* focus on it. But it would have been nice if they'd at least discussed it. Even if she'd taken thirty seconds to raise her head and let him know it wasn't all over between them, he'd have been happy.

Okay, maybe not happy, but less goddamned anxious. He wasn't used to feeling this way. To needing reassurance from someone else. Alas, her neck stayed bent, and they didn't talk about it. In fact, they hardly spoke at all.

Had she realized that he hadn't kept her safe? That he'd let her down? His jaw clenched. He couldn't slip up again. Taking care of her was the most important thing. Another reason not to disrupt their new status quo. He'd gone too far too fast, anyway. His impulse control had been lowered because of the gamut of emotions he'd run, from the moment he'd seen that car racing toward her to the moment he held her in his arms and accepted she was truly safe. He should slow down, reassess, and give her time.

But he desperately wanted to know whether her reluctance on Sunday morning had been because she knew he wasn't good enough for her. That he wasn't as smart or ambitious as her. Was she having second thoughts? Did she want to shut him out of her life without actually having to say the words? His heart squeezed uncomfortably. God, he hoped not.

No, he told himself. *She's obsessive about work, that's all.*

He'd certainly seen enough of her single-mindedness both when they'd been together and during the past week. It was sexy, how she could give something her undivided attention. Sexy, and a little frustrating.

Her work comes first for her. Always has. Always will. You're just a distraction. A chain around her ankle. That's why you let her go, remember?

To dispel the morbid thought, Gareth stood, went to the kitchen and made two coffees. His foot had healed now, except for a nasty bruise, and he barely noticed it. He added a spoonful of sugar to his and left the other black, dropping it on the table beside her. She didn't so much as twitch. He tried to look over her shoulder to see what she was working on, but he couldn't make heads or tails of the numbers and charts on the screen. With a sigh, he returned to his post by the door. He flicked the light on, because it was late afternoon and the sun had begun to set. Surely peering through the growing dark at an electronically-lit screen couldn't be good for her eyes.

Damn, but she was beautiful. Even scruffy and unshowered, her eyes were bright with intelligence, her hair was glossy, and her chin was set in a stubborn point. A weight settled in his chest and he rubbed a palm over his heart. He wanted her so much. He *longed* for her. He *ached* for her. But he couldn't verbalize his feelings because he couldn't take her attention away from her work.

Yeah, sure, that's the only reason. It has nothing to do with the fact that you're terrified she doesn't feel the same way.

He ignored the little voice in the back of his mind, but unfortunately, that didn't make it go away.

AVERY HAD HIT PAY DIRT. She'd spent nearly every waking minute on her computer since Sunday morning and now, just before noon on Tuesday, she'd finally managed to narrow the potential burial site to a two-kilometer radius near the pine plantations north of Christchurch city.

"G, get over here!" she called.

Gareth, who was sitting near the door, raised his head. "What is it? Are you okay?"

The microwave pinged and the smell of sweet and sour pork wafted toward them. Avery's mouth watered and her stomach growled. She hadn't eaten since yesterday evening, too absorbed in her work to take a break for breakfast.

"I've got it," she exclaimed, fizzing with excitement. "Get Rata on the phone, ASAP. I know where Millie Grant is buried."

His eyes widened and he caught his breath. "Yeah?"

"Damn right," she confirmed.

"That's the best news I've heard all week. Where?"

She rotated the laptop to face him and pointed at the circular purple blob superimposed over a map of Canterbury. "Right here. It's a reasonably large area, but it's searchable."

"Especially if they bring in cadaver dogs," he said, tracing the outside of the blob with his finger. "You're a genius! I'm so proud of you."

He strode into the kitchen and returned with his phone held to his ear.

"Inspector," he said urgently. "Avery has found the approximate location of the burial site. Start searching in a two-kilometer radius around these coordinates." He hovered at her shoulder and read numbers from the screen, then was silent for a moment. He added, "I'd like to know as soon as you find anything, and also if you make an arrest. Thank you, sir." He hung up. "Can you screenshot that map and send it to Inspector Rata? She's mobilizing a search party as we speak. This is the breakthrough we've been waiting for."

Avery stood and high-fived him, ridiculously pleased to be the cause of his excitement, and even more ecstatic that her program had performed as promised. Now, she just had to wait and see whether it worked on the ground. If they found a body, it was all go. The police could launch nationwide. Sure, she'd have to collect many of the samples again and recalibrate the system, but what mattered was that murderers, rapists and thieves could be apprehended, thanks to her work.

"It's amazing." She shook her head, not truly believing that she'd done it. The thankless, tireless work she'd done over the past years had finally paid off and the past few weeks from hell might be about to end.

"*You're* amazing," Gareth corrected, and yanked her into an embrace.

Her cheek landed on his chest and she wrapped her arms around his waist, clinging to him. Relief made her knees weak and they would have given out if not for his support.

"I've got you," he said.

Despite his words, which struck a little too close to a sensitive spot, she smiled. This hell was over. She could leave the hotel room, visit her friends, return to work, and decide where she was going to live.

It was overwhelming. Good and terrifying, at the same time.

Whether or not they found the body, she'd done all she could. There was no reason for anyone to come after her because the police had full access to everything. The tests were complete, and could be used as hard evidence. There was no need to rely on any information contained only within her mind, and subsequently, nothing to be gained by hurting her.

Still, she thought as she listened to the rhythmic beating of Gareth's heart, *I'll stay here for the rest of the day. Just to be safe.*

To be honest, she couldn't remember why she'd been panicking the other day. She could think of nowhere she'd rather be than in his arms.

~

THE MOMENT of truth had arrived. Gareth had been waiting impatiently, his phone rarely leaving his hand. They'd ordered celebratory room service, eaten a bowl of pretzels and shared a beer, but his stomach had been tied in knots waiting to hear from his boss. To tell the truth, his work-related nerves were a welcome relief from the anxiety over Avery's increasingly distant behavior the past few days.

"Wayland," he answered, the instant the phone rang.

"Sergeant, this is Rata."

"Did they find her?" he asked without any preamble.

A silence, then, "The search team found a body that may be Millie Grant. Hard to tell at this stage given the state of decomposition, but the coroner's initial report is that age and gender match, and based on where she was found, near the center of Dr. Brown's search radius, I'd say we have her."

"And Broderick?"

"The shovel in his car led to a girl's body." He could hear satisfaction in Rata's voice. "Regardless of who the girl is, that's damning. A team have been dispatched to pick him up."

With his tongue, Gareth pushed his wad of gum into his cheek, then exhaled slowly. "So, it's over. Avery is safe. We can go home."

"You can." He fancied her voice warmed a fraction. "Go and see your family, Sergeant. Take care that Avery gets the rest she needs."

"I will, sir. Thank you."

He pocketed his phone and grinned as a pair of arms came around him from behind. He relaxed into the hug.

"Is it done?" Avery asked, her cheek resting on his back. His pulse picked up, and it had nothing to do with the phone call.

His hands came up to cover her forearms. "It is. You got him, A-Bee. Want to get out of here?"

"Hell, yeah."

﹏

AVERY CAME to a stop outside her house. Or rather, she stopped outside the burnt-out wooden shell that used to be her house. This was the first place she'd come after showering off the filth of the past two days at Gareth's home. She'd left him at the police station. She needed to be alone for a while.

As she stepped over the yellow crime-scene tape and padded through the blackened remnants of her hallway, tears burned in the backs of her eyes. Sinking to her knees, she let them fall. She'd cried more in the past ten days than she had in the preceding ten years.

The tears cleansed her soul, washing away the last stains left on it by the man who'd attacked her. The man who was now locked firmly in a cell at Timaru Police Station, having been picked up after using a credit card at McDonald's an hour earlier and charged with murder in the first degree. The man she'd have to testify against at his trial, whenever that may be. As far as she was concerned, it couldn't come soon enough.

She watched as her tears dropped into the ash. One, two, three. She wiped the rest away and collected herself.

The entire building would have to be demolished. There was no repairing it. She'd call the contractors tomorrow. They could knock it down, cart away anything worth salvaging, and she'd load the rest on a trailer and dump it. Perhaps she'd rebuild in this spot, or maybe she'd sell the land and buy another place.

She could move. The opportunities were limitless. She didn't have to stay in Itirangi. But at the thought of leaving, something twinged inside her. She may not *need* to stay, but where else would she find friends, a lab, space for a garden, and rocks to climb all within a few minutes' drive?

Itirangi was home for her. She'd traveled enough for a lifetime. She had roots here, and those roots mattered.

She kicked the ground, then paced around the interior of the house, stepping over the remains of furniture as she pondered what to do next. Her phone had been ringing all afternoon, but she'd ignored every call. Now, she walked outside and called Sophie.

"Hey, Soph," she said when her friend answered. "You mind if I stay at your place tonight? I've sorted out everything I need to and I don't have anywhere to go."

"Of course you can," Sophie exclaimed. "You're always welcome at my place, babe. Mum is still at the treatment center so the Big House is empty. You can either sleep there or on my couch, whichever you prefer."

"That sounds fantastic." Hearing Sophie's voice, Avery almost cried all over again. *Toughen up, woman. You're better than this.* "Is it okay if I walk over there now?"

"Don't go anywhere," Sophie said. "I'll come and get you. Where are you?"

"My place."

"Oh, hon…" She trailed off. "I'm so sorry."

"It's a disaster zone. Everything was destroyed."

"But not you. You came back stronger than ever, and I'll be there in two minutes to get you." She hesitated. "Actually, do you mind if we pick up Aria, too? We can have a slumber party in the Big House, like old times. She's been going out of her mind worrying about you, and you did promise her the big scoop."

"I did." Now that the initial hype had worn off, she didn't particularly feel like talking, but she needed to spread the word so people knew they were safe in their homes. Plus, a little good publicity for her work wouldn't hurt. "Bring her. Saves me telling the story twice."

"See you real soon."

They hung up and she sat cross-legged on the front lawn,

eternally grateful for having been blessed with wonderful friends who'd drop everything for her in her hour of need. Not everyone had that, and while she didn't always tell them, those girls meant the world to her.

A smile flitted around her lips when Sophie pulled up with a screech and tumbled out of the car to envelop her in a hug. Avery linked arms with her and walked forward, toward the future, leaving the burned-out past behind her.

18

Gareth sat in a chair in the principal's office of his old high school, across the desk from his old principal, doing his best to pay attention. The man was mid-rant about a kid who smoked a lot of weed—but twenty seconds into the rant, his phone had vibrated in his pocket and now he was growing impatient to check it. Avery had been on his mind nonstop since they parted ways yesterday. He didn't know how things stood between them, and it was driving him crazy. For some reason, he'd expected her to stay with him. Hadn't actually considered that it might go any other way. But then he'd gotten home and she hadn't come back. He'd wanted to give her space because she hadn't had any since this whole debacle began, but when it started to grow dark outside, he texted her and she let him know she was staying with Sophie.

To say he'd been bothered would be putting it mildly. He missed her, and he had this awful feeling that she was slipping through his fingers and there was nothing he could do about it. The logical part of his brain was telling him to be patient and not push her too hard, but his instincts were screaming at him to seize her with all his might and not let go.

"Excuse me, Sergeant. Are you listening?" Principal Hotene scowled, coming around his desk to get up in Gareth's face. "I don't think you're taking this seriously."

He wanted to fall back a step, purely because Mr. Hotene had been his principal and part of him found it difficult to have a conversation with the man on a level footing. Be that as it may, he'd been an adult for years, and a sergeant for a fair while, too.

He gave Mr. Hotene the look. The one he reserved for lawbreakers who questioned his authority. "I promise you, John," he forced the man's first name out with difficulty, "I take the future of our town very seriously. If you're having problems with this young man—" he tried to remember the kid's name, came up empty "—and you're concerned he'll corrupt others, then we need to act quickly."

"Yes, we do." Mr. Hotene backed off, appeased. "So you'll speak to Lewis's parents?"

"I will. You're making the right call here, John. I could take Lewis down to the station, but I doubt it would be as effective as exchanging a few words with his parents. If you don't see any change in his behavior, give me another call and we can discuss taking it to the next level."

"Thanks, Gareth." Mr. Hotene shook his hand. "I appreciate it." As Gareth made his way toward the exit, Mr. Hotene called after him. "I always knew you'd turn out right."

Gareth looked around, surprised.

Mr. Hotene shrugged. "Sometimes you just get a feeling."

Gareth fidgeted with his belt buckle and chewed furiously, unsure how to respond. Eventually, he tipped his head toward his old principal and headed out the door. Some things were better left unsaid.

He called the kid's parents before checking his personal phone. Work before play. It went about as well as expected, but finally, he was free to take a moment for himself. He slouched into the driver's seat of his cruiser and retrieved his phone. As he'd hoped, the text was from Avery.

I'm cleaning up the mess in my lab. It's depressing as hell. I need a distraction. Think you can help with that?

He straightened. His heart hammered wildly. Even this tiny bit of contact from her exhilarated him. He reread the message. A distraction? That, he could manage.

Tell me what you're wearing.

The response barely took thirty seconds to arrive. *A lab coat. Obviously.*

Smart-ass. *What about beneath the lab coat?*

He closed his eyes and leaned against the headrest, overcome by relief that she'd reached out to him. The phone vibrated and his hands shook as he raised it to read the screen.

Sorry, big boy. I'm not that *kind of scientist. There's a whole two layers of clothes beneath the lab coat.*

Layers he would happily peel off. *Huh.* Sexy scientist. Not a fantasy he'd had before, but all of a sudden he wanted nothing more than to strip a lab coat from her body and bury himself between her legs atop one of those chemistry benches. He went hard.

You're driving me crazy.

Me and all my clothes are driving you crazy?

He could imagine her expression—part smirk, part disbelief. *Yes,* he replied. *You'd drive me crazy in a cardboard box.*

Oh, really. A moment later, she added, *If you were here, what would you like to do to me?*

He licked his lips, no less than a dozen ideas springing to mind. He picked one at random. *I'd want to screw you in your office, so whenever you're there, all you can think about is me. On the desk, under it. Up against the wall.*

He held his breath, aroused beyond belief, and waited an eternity.

I'm in my office now...

He envisioned her at her desk, legs clamped tightly together to relieve the ache at the juncture of her thighs. Perhaps she was even going further. She'd never been shy about her sexuality. *Tell me you're touching yourself, you naughty girl.*

You'd like that, wouldn't you?

Damn right, he would. His phone vibrated again.

Sorry, you're out of luck. But I am a little turned on, thinking about you in your uniform. Your hands on me. Fucking me on the desk. Thanks for the distraction.

Gareth swore. His dick twitched, as if seeking refuge in her body. Only she wasn't here. Hell, what was she doing to him? He couldn't think straight. He needed to get off, but he could hardly take care of himself here, practically in public.

Shit, I want you so much.

Can you wait until five?

He sighed, his breath coming raggedly. *Guess I'll have to. But I'm going to make you scream for me.*

God, yes, G. I'm planning to screw you until we're both exhausted and can't think of anything else.

He swallowed, not sure that he liked the thought of being used for sex, but willing to give her whatever she needed. If that meant sex, so be it.

GARETH'S POLICE car was idling in the parking lot when Avery exited work. He wound down the window and leaned out. "Hop in."

She chuckled and stooped to talk to him, but didn't open the door. "Are you arresting me, Sergeant Sexy?"

"Do I need to?" he asked with a raised brow. "Or will you come willingly into custody?"

She snorted. It was like a line from a bad police drama. Or a porno.

"I need to get my car."

"Then you leave me no choice." He reached over, taking hold of her wrist. Before she realized what he was doing, she found herself handcuffed to him.

"Really?" she asked, torn between exasperation and amusement. "You're actually doing this?"

His eyes flashed then he sucked one of her fingers into his mouth, warm and wet and oddly erotic. He pulled it out and murmured, "You've got me wound so tight I can't think straight, A-Bee."

She experienced both a pang of guilt and a wave of triumph. While she didn't believe in messing with men's heads, she couldn't deny she'd been toying with him like a cowboy waving a red flag at a bull all day, partly because it took her mind off the devastation in her laboratory, and partly just for the fun of seeing how he reacted.

"Good." She grinned. "You can unlock me. I'll come willingly. Where are we going?"

He reached over to free her. "To my place."

"You'll bring me back for my car later? Or drop me off at work tomorrow?"

"Yes." The reply was terse, like there were other things he'd rather be doing than having this conversation. Too bad. She didn't plan to follow him anywhere without an exit strategy.

"Okay, then." She tried the handle, but it didn't budge.

"Only opens from the inside." He shoved the door open. "Get in."

"Bossy." But she did as he said.

He shot away from the curb, pulling onto the road toward Itirangi. She was about to make a smart-ass comment about policemen speeding, or being a little too quick out of the gate, when he exhaled slowly and looked at her like she was a slice of cake he'd been forbidden to eat.

"You're all I've been able to think about, all day. Picturing you in your lab coat and nothing else, wishing I could be there with you." His grip on the wheel tightened, his knuckles turning white. "Do you know how inappropriate it is for a cop to walk around with a stiffy? But I couldn't help it, because of you. I hope you're pleased with yourself."

Her underwear became damp. She thrilled at the power she held over him. "Very pleased," she admitted. Then, feeling audacious, she reached over to stroke his crotch. He was, indeed, sporting a massive hard-on beneath the uniform. She traced the outline of it.

"Jeez," he hissed from between gritted teeth. "Don't do that."

She smiled mischievously. "Why not?"

"B-because," he sputtered, "I'm driving. It's not safe."

She tutted, rubbing the length of him, cupping him intimately. "Guess you better keep your mind on the road, then."

She squeezed, drawing a long, low groan from him. They'd left Timaru now and were flying between fields of crops and sheep, which she could barely make out in the dying light of the day. She massaged gentle circles around his crotch. He was so tense it was like touching a marble statue. Except he was very, very hot.

With a muffled oath, he swerved off the main highway and pulled onto a gravel farm road. Two hundred meters from the highway, he parked behind a copse of trees and unbuckled, swinging to look at her with fire in his eyes. She swallowed, even while she celebrated inside.

Now she was in for it.

He fisted her sweater and fused his mouth to hers. Their tongues tangled but she shoved his chest before getting too caught up in the heat.

"Let's move to the back seat," she suggested.

She thought he might refuse—too much the good cop—but a slow smile spread across his face. "Why not? You've already got me feeling like a high school kid."

They exchanged a flirtatious glance and hurried around to the rear of the car. He climbed into the driver's side and Avery into the opposite. He slid the seat back to give them as much room as possible and hauled her onto his lap. She settled down, the press of his erection firm beneath her thigh, then shifted so that the soft flesh of her ass hovered over it and rotated in circles, gratified to hear his sharp intake of breath.

He turned her so his chest was flattened against her back, and banded his arms around her waist. Heat pulsed at her core and she melted into him. God, she loved his arms. Muscled, strong, holding her secure as though he'd never let her go. If only that were true.

She maintained the slow brush of her ass over his lap, wishing she could see his face. His uneven breaths tickled her ear and she leaned her head to the side to give him access to her neck. He sucked the tender skin at the juncture of her neck and shoulder. Hard enough to leave a hickey.

"What are you doing?" she demanded. No one had given her a hickey since…well, since him.

"Now everyone will know you're taken," he rasped, sounding smug.

She tried to be annoyed—he never used to be possessive—but it only excited her more. Then, to top things off, he clamped his hand around her damp core. She whimpered.

"Not such a tease now, are you?"

She ground into his hand. She'd had so many different fantasies about him today—allowing herself, for once, to be carried away from reality. Having his rough man-hands all over her was setting fire to her nerve endings. But if only he'd unzip her jeans and give her what she really wanted.

Sadly, his strong fingers stayed on the outside of the denim. She squirmed.

"I want your fingers on me," she said, cringing at the whiny tone of her voice.

He huffed in amusement, but didn't move his hands. "Such a demanding girl. Say please."

"Don't be a dick."

His touch became firmer, shooting pleasure through her lower half.

"You've been playing with me all day," he said darkly. "Now it's my turn. Say please, Avery."

Though she considered refusing on principle, she wanted the orgasm she knew he could give her. "Please, Gareth, fuck me with your fingers."

With a low groan, he did as she asked, maneuvering her zipper open and lowering the jeans down over her hips. She raised herself to make it easier for him.

"I never knew you had such a dirty mouth." It didn't sound like he minded.

Her head flopped back, resting on his shoulder as the blunt tip of his finger stroked through her folds and pushed inside her.

"Mm." She rolled her hips into the thrusts of his finger. "Feels so much better than when I do it."

Turning her face, she found him watching her, eyes dark with intent. She kissed him, wet, open-mouthed kisses which he returned, his erection pulsing beneath her. Pleasure built within and she grew needy, limbs languid, desperate for release. With all the strength she could muster, she shoved his arm away and took a great, shuddering breath.

"Too close," she panted. "I want to come with you inside me."

She shimmied from his lap and he fumbled with his fly, yanking his trousers down to his knees, then encircling himself with his thumb and forefinger, aiming upward.

Agonizingly slowly, she descended onto him. They both sighed in pleasure.

His hands splayed across her lower belly, holding her in place. Once again, he was surrounding her on every side, overwhelming her with his maleness, and she found she didn't mind at all. She leaned back onto his chest, her legs working to lift her up and down, building the exquisite friction between them. One of his hands ventured lower, pressing against the pulsing point that seemed to have become the center of her nervous system. Sensation shot through her.

"Oh, fuck," she gasped, her legs trembling, chin dipping as she bit her lip.

"That's it," he murmured. "Take what you need."

She did, riding him, spurred on by his sighs and groans. A wave of ecstasy was growing inside her, carrying her higher and higher, until everything she knew coalesced in a dazzling moment of euphoria. Beneath her, Gareth's powerful body shuddered as he peaked, her name spilling from his lips. Her legs could hold her no longer and she collapsed on top of him in a sweaty, sated heap.

They didn't speak as they struggled to catch their breath.

Eventually, he stirred. "So, back to my place for a repeat?"

Behind the curtain of hair he'd loosened during their lovemaking, she smiled. "You sure you can keep up with me?"

His arms squeezed her from behind, holding her tight. "You bet your sweet ass I can."

Turning into his embrace, she nipped at his jaw. "Prove it."

"With pleasure."

19

—————

*L*ying sweaty and content in Gareth's bed, her body aligned with his, the sheets tangled around their knees, Avery smiled widely up at the ceiling.

"Wow," she said. Understatement of the year.

Gareth's chest rose and fell as he panted. "Wow is right." His hand snaked down from where it rested on his stomach to entwine with hers. "You know, we still got it."

No argument there. She squeezed his hand to show she agreed. "I think we've actually gotten better."

"We improved with age," he agreed. "Like cheese."

She laughed. "I'm not sure how I feel about that comparison."

"Well, I think it's brilliant." He turned to smile at her, his eyes dark with emotion. "I'm glad you texted today. After yesterday, I was a bit worried I might not hear from you. But this is nice. Better than nice."

"It is, isn't it?"

"I really think we could make a go of this," he continued, and she closed her eyes, wishing they could have continued to ignore the elephant in the room. She wasn't ready to trust him with her heart again, but he seemed determined to push her boundaries.

He inhaled sharply, as though about to say something, but then released the breath in a huff.

"What is it?" she asked, with extreme reluctance. "You're doing that thing you do when you want to say something, but you're not a hundred percent sure you *really* want to say it."

Please don't ask for more than I can give, she begged him silently. *Please don't ruin this.*

He lifted her hand and secured it against his chest. Beneath her palm, she could feel his heart beating a rapid tattoo. "Things have been going really well between us," he said. "I mean, they have been when no one's trying to kill you, right?" He didn't wait for a reply. "We have great chemistry. We know everything there is to know about each other, and we're good friends."

A sense of impending doom weighed down on Avery. *Don't do* it, she pleaded with him in her head. *Don't make me push you away.*

"I think you should move in with me," he finished.

Every deliciously lax muscle in her body went rigid. She pulled her hand from his, then sat up, her blood pounding so loudly in her ears that she wondered if she'd misheard. *"What?"*

He swallowed, but his jaw firmed. "I know it's fast, but think about it. We're getting on well, you don't have a home at the moment, and I have more than enough room. If you don't want to share a room with me right away, you can move into the spare bedroom. It's logical."

Raising a finger, she gestured for him to shut up. "Don't you try and use logic with me, buster. I'm the Queen of Logic."

He lifted himself up on one elbow. Though his gaze was

shuttered, she got the impression he was taking this very seriously. "You must see it makes sense."

"No." The denial leapt from her mouth before she realized she'd opened it. "Not true. We may be getting on well now, but the past couple of weeks is hardly an accurate representation of how living together would be. It's been a tense situation, and emotions have been high. As a result of that, we feel strongly toward each other. But we're not even in a relationship, and those adrenaline-fueled emotions will fade." He started to interrupt. "No, let me finish. I stayed in the Big House at Sophie's last night. Her mum won't be back for a while, so there's an entire house standing empty that I can use until I figure out where to go next. *That* is the logical choice. *That* is what makes sense."

"Or you could move in with me and save yourself the trouble of figuring anything out. It's a permanent solution. Let me do this for you." His eyes begged her to agree with him, but she couldn't. She studied the determined thrust of his chin and the groove between his eyebrows, but didn't look lower. She refused to be distracted by his glorious body. She yanked the sheet up to cover herself, needing to put a physical barrier between them.

She couldn't believe they were actually having this conversation. Hadn't they only just talked about taking it day by day and not labeling anything? Nothing said labels and commitment like sharing a house and a dog in a small town where half the population would know before nightfall.

"The answer is no. I didn't realize you were thinking long-term yet. It's too soon. I'm not in the right head space, and the truth is, when it comes to you, I might never be."

He winced at her bluntness, and confusion filled those amber eyes. "I don't get it. I know we haven't talked about anything serious, but I planned to do that as soon as the case was over."

"Then why didn't you? I could have cleared up any misunderstandings."

He shrugged. "You left, and then today we… well, suffice it to say, I didn't think I needed to. I want to go all-in with you, A-Bee."

She ignored the last part of his statement. She couldn't afford to listen to proclamations like that. "It doesn't pay to make assumptions, G."

Irritation flickered across his face. "I know that, *Dr. Brown*. I may not be as clever as you, but I get by."

He climbed off the bed and stood, dragging the sheet with him, which ripped it from Avery and left her exposed. Her arms came up to cover her breasts and she drew her knees to her chest. She hated herself for hiding, wished she had the balls to lie there like she didn't give a damn, but her biological defense mechanisms overpowered her conscious mind, and told her that he was a threat she needed to defend herself against.

"So, you're telling me this was all about sex?" he demanded, planting his legs wide, his eyes becoming flinty. "What, were you trying to work me out of your system or something?"

Much as she wanted to say yes, that wasn't strictly the truth, and she wouldn't lie about something like this. "No, it wasn't just sex. That part was good, yeah, but I've enjoyed spending time with you. I just don't want to rush into a relationship, and no matter how much I like being around you, I'm not sure I can do long-term again, after how it ended last time."

His nostrils flared and his grip on the sheet tightened, his knuckles turning pink then white. Avery watched this display of emotion, both disturbed and fascinated.

"Explain it to me," he spat. "Because I sure as hell don't understand. How does our high school break up affect us now? It was mutual. We were both moving away. It was the best thing for everyone. And fuck, I always thought we'd find our way back to each other." He scanned her, from her bed hair to her unpainted toes, and made a sound of disgust. "I just never figured it would be like this."

Avery's world shifted out from beneath her. She felt like she was scrambling to find purchase, and to align his words with the belief she'd harbored for years. The belief that something about her hadn't been good enough for Gareth. He'd alluded to the truth over the past days, but she'd intentionally ignored him, choosing to deceive herself. The truth was, he hadn't cast her aside and forgotten about her as she'd always assumed he had. She'd wasted years keeping him at an emotional distance so he didn't hurt her again. She'd spent years being cynical about love and suspicious of her friends' partners to save them from the fate that had befallen her.

Doesn't pay to make assumptions, girl.

"I...I..." she stammered. "I didn't know."

"That's all you've got to say?" He laughed scornfully. "You didn't know? We agreed at the time that we'd re-evaluate down the track."

She'd thought he was just saying that to spare her feelings. A version of, "it's not you, it's me." Or, "let's be friends." How had she been so wrong? Had she been too prideful to take the time to really listen to him? What a massive level of conceit.

"I didn't know you meant it," she said, barely loud enough to be heard. "I thought you broke your promise."

What was wrong with her? Why wasn't she saying more? Doing more? Anything to stop him from looking at her the way he was, as though he couldn't stand the sight of her. If any of her friends were in this situation, she'd advise them to talk through the misunderstanding, or to throw their shoulders back and give him a piece of their mind, but it was like the will to fight had deserted her.

She needed him to be quiet, to give her time to think.

Important conversations like this had to be weighed care-fully, and he wasn't giving her space to breathe.

"What promise?" he demanded.

"That you'd always have my back. It didn't seem like you had my back when you left me, G."

His gaze softened ever so slightly, and only for a moment. Then he shook his head, turned away, and collected his clothes from the floor. "I've always had your back," he told her, his voice flat and emotionless. "Even when it's been to my own detriment." He tugged his shirt over his head. "I don't like what it says about either of us that you don't believe that." He stepped into his pants. "I'm taking Snookie for a walk. If you don't want to stay with me, then do me a favor and be gone before I get back."

It was what she'd wanted: time alone to think.

Then why did she feel like he'd taken a part of her with him out that door?

THE OAR SLICED through the water. Arms aching, Gareth lifted it, dipped the other end into the lake, and stroked. Only another couple hundred meters and he'd be back at shore, where Snookie was tied to a post, wagging her tail furiously.

His arms kept up their steady rhythm. Dip and pull, dip and pull. The cold wind bit into his exposed skin. Thankfully he'd worn gloves, or he'd have no feeling in his fingers. In contrast, the muscles in his shoulders burned as he glided over the water.

The wooden frame of Ram's cabin was barely visible from this angle. The small clearing it inhabited gave the impression of isolation, despite the road that passed not far behind it, hidden by centuries-old trees. With a bump, the kayak met the shore. Using the oar to push himself securely onto dry land, he leapt out. Snookie jumped toward him only to be pulled up short by the rope. She barked.

"Hey, girl," he crooned, setting her free. She bounded in excited circles, as if he'd been gone for days rather than an hour. He waited for her to settle and scratched behind her ear. "What a good girl."

She nudged his thigh with her nose, and he petted the top of her head. Then, with Snookie close on his heel, he dragged the kayak over to the cabin and turned it upside down to prevent rain or debris from entering.

A rush of warm air greeted him when he opened the door. Snookie padded inside and curled up at the hearth, in front of the smoldering fire. He joined her, his legs sprawled out before him. His track pants were damp, but they should dry before nightfall. It could get cold in these parts, and he'd only brought one change of clothes because he didn't plan to stay long. He just needed a break to screw his head on straight.

Avery had walked out on him. Damn, it hurt how she'd done that. He'd thrown down the gauntlet, but he'd hoped more than anything she'd still be there when he returned, having realized how much she loved him.

Yeah, right.

Snookie stretched out, exposing her belly to the fire, and he reached over and rubbed it. She sighed contentedly. If only all women were so easy to please. His thoughts returned to Avery. Remarkable, intelligent Avery. Capable of searing his soul with a word.

It was true that he hadn't been completely up front with her about how seriously he viewed their relationship, but he hadn't wanted to scare her away. Then, after she jumped into his bed, he'd believed everything was golden. He should have rocked the boat more to begin with, so she knew what his intentions were.

Rolling onto his back, he winced when a hard board dug

into his hip. He struggled upright and shifted to the bed, staring at the roof and wondering where she was now. How she felt. Whether she'd been as blindsided by their misunderstanding as he had. He hated the panic he'd seen in her eyes after he asked her to move in with him. He wasn't that bad, was he? Yeah, it was fast, but they'd been sharing a wonderfully intimate moment and it had seemed like the perfect time to ask. Things had been a bit off between them, and he'd had this insane urge to push his case while he had an advantage, but he'd made a poor judgment call.

"Shit," he said out loud, realizing exactly how much he'd screwed up. He should have had an honest conversation with her about how much he wanted her in his life. Should have slowed down and let her adjust to the idea of them being a couple again rather than rushing her. Hell, he should have gone after her years ago, as soon as she came back to town, rather than letting so much time pass.

So many "should haves".

"Aw, hell." He rubbed his temples. *Women.* Damned if he could understand them. She'd made some comment about being surprised he thought they'd get back together, but he'd said as much when they went their separate ways. How could she possibly have misinterpreted that? She was a smart woman and it didn't take a PhD to see he was crazy for her.

And what was that business about breaking his promise? He'd only ever acted in her best interests, even when it meant letting her go. It grated that she didn't seem to recognize or appreciate that.

But he couldn't wallow all afternoon. He needed to do something. He sat up so fast his head spun. He waited for it to stop, then reached for Snookie's lead. He'd run off his frustration, since his session on the lake hadn't done the job.

20

"Drink, drink, drink!" the girls chanted as Sophie tipped her head back and drained a glass of cider in a few long gulps, slamming it back to the table when it was empty.

"Piece of cake," she said. "Bring on the next."

It was Aria's bachelorette party, and they were in a bar situated beneath the Christchurch hotel they'd checked into earlier in the day. The evening had started rather benignly, with a few games and a wearable arts competition, then somehow ended up here, most of them the worse for wear, except Aria, who was limited to soda. Avery had only had a couple of beers, but Sophie had no such inhibitions. She wobbled as she stood and wrapped an arm around Avery's waist for balance.

"Let's go to the casino," Sophie suggested.

One of the girls cheered at the idea and they headed as a group toward the exit. Avery's gaze skimmed over the girls, one at a time.

Aria and Sophie were two of her dearest friends. Sophie had made her very happy when she'd dumped her cheating boyfriend Evan to take up with Cooper Simons a couple of

186

months ago. Aria was the sweetest girl in town, with the possible exception of Emily Parker, a pretty redhead who could've had any man but chose Aria's cranky brother Justin.

She met Emily's eyes and smiled. They were completely different people, but she liked Emily because of her unconventional choice of men. Justin was a great guy, just a little cynical after a bad experience with an ex. She could relate.

Next, her gaze settled on Evie, the free-spirited one who never stayed anywhere for longer than a few months. They'd gotten on well during high school, but recently Avery had been feeling a disconnect. Evie was everything Avery wasn't —flighty, unreliable, impulsive.

Next was Clarissa. Her best friend in the world. No distance could come between their friendship, forged as it had been through heartbreak and abandonment. They'd been two rafts tossed on a wild sea, but they'd found a safe harbor in each other. Clarissa glanced over and smiled. Avery blew her a kiss. Clarissa caught it and blew one back.

The other girls present were colleagues of Aria's. Her fiancé's sister had wanted to come, but being only sixteen, she was too young. Aria would probably do something special with her later. The two of them were close.

Avery tried not to think about how her friends were choosing men to spend their lives with, while she was charting out a solo future.

It's all good, she reminded herself. *You don't need a man to make your life worthwhile.*

While it was one hundred percent true, that didn't stop her from picturing Gareth's handsome face, strong chin, and cheeky dimples. When he grinned, it was all a girl could do not to swoon.

Don't think about him.

Soon, they reached the casino, a strange building with a domed glass roof and two square wings. The girls strolled up to the entrance and handed their IDs to the bouncer, a solidly built guy in his twenties whose eyes twinkled in the streetlight.

"Congratulations," he said to Aria, nodding at the bridal sash that hung off her shoulder and to the kid-sized tiara on her head. "You ladies have fun."

"We will," she replied.

Sophie fanned herself as they moved inside. "What a hottie, with a capital H."

"Soph!" Aria swatted her arm. "Aren't you forgetting someone?"

Sophie rolled her eyes. "As if I'd ever forget Coop. I'm just saying."

"Totally agree," Evie said, so close to Avery's ear that she winced. "And you married ladies can step aside because I'm still on the market."

Avery gritted her teeth. They didn't need Evie's theatrics tonight, but nor did they need Avery making scathing remarks and ruining the mood. She took a deep breath and ignored the anger bubbling through her veins, recognizing it for what it was: a disproportionate reaction because she was stressed and overwrought. And okay, perhaps seeing her flirty, feminine friend in action brought home her own shortcomings in being so tomboy-ish and practical.

They entered a cavernous space dotted with gaming tables, many of which were at the center of small crowds. They headed directly to the counter to buy tokens, though they were pathetically small gamblers by anyone's standards.

"What shall we do?" asked one of Aria's colleagues, gesturing widely around the room.

As always, Avery's attention was drawn to the slot machines in the corner. Having grown up spending a lot of time at the pub with her father, the slots were familiar. Comfortable. Not so for everyone else. Aria pointed toward the blackjack table and began waddling toward it, the other girls trailing behind. Avery followed, too. She was more adept at cards than most, even games with an element of luck. With her mathematical brain, she almost always left a card game with more money than she had going in.

The blackjack dealer, a Japanese woman with glittering eyelids, glanced up as they approached. "We've got room for three more."

The girls looked at each other. Someone pushed Aria into a chair. Evie happily took the spot next to her, and Aria's colleague took the final seat. Avery stood behind Aria, ready to murmur advice in her ear.

Two hours and a tidy profit later, the girls stood by the bar, cocktails in hand. Sophie had talked Avery into buying a coconut-flavored drink, insisting she'd like it. She took another sip of the sickeningly sweet concoction and scowled, contemplating ditching it in the nearest rubbish bin.

"You look like you need a pick-me-up."

She looked up to find a man standing at her elbow, showing off his blinding white teeth. "Excuse me?"

"You need something to make you smile," he continued, oblivious to the "piss off" vibes she was sending in his direction, his eyes crinkling at the corners and one side of his mouth lifting. He had no dimples, was too short, and she couldn't have been less interested. "Come and join roulette with me."

"No thanks," she said, searching for an escape route.

"Are you sure?" he asked, touching her shoulder. "I promise you'll have fun."

She shrugged away from his hand, aware of several pairs of eyes on them, and said, "Yes, I'm sure. Try your luck somewhere else."

No one said anything as the man left.

Sophie sidled over. "What was that about?" she

demanded, drawing herself up to her full height, which scarcely reached Avery's nose.

"He was interested. I'm not." Really, was it too much to ask to pass a week without having some man foisted on her?

"He was totally cute," Evie said, peering at her closely. "What's up with you? You should have given him a chance."

"I'm not in the mood." And she shouldn't have to defend her choices to her friends.

Sophie and Evie exchanged glances, then they each grasped one of her shoulders and marched her to a barstool.

"This is an intervention," Evie announced, with flair. "You've ignored every man who's looked at you today."

"What's going on?" Sophie asked. "Is something wrong? I know we pushed you to give Gareth another chance. Did something happen? Did he hurt you?"

Oh, how she hated their concern. She'd managed to avoid discussing Gareth since she'd moved into Sophie's mother's house, but she'd known it couldn't last forever. She sighed. Why didn't she have no-nonsense friends who'd slap the silly out of her and leave her alone?

"Nothing's wrong."

"*Is* there someone else? Gareth?" Evie asked. Avery hesitated. It was slight, but Evie caught it and pounced. "There is! Tell us."

"There's not." At least, not anymore.

"I almost believed that, but not quite. How about you, Soph?"

Sophie shook her head. "Not for a moment. Come on, 'fess up."

"I said it's nothing," Avery snapped.

They fell silent, each watching her with the kind of caution typically reserved for poisonous spiders.

Avery huffed out a heavy breath. "I'm sorry for growling at you. He asked me to move in with him the other day." She ran a hand through her hair, tugging it so that her scalp prickled. "I don't know what got into him. We had sex a few times. It was fun. Then he went and ruined it." She took a deep breath and tried to grin, hoping they'd be satisfied and drop the subject. Based on their expressions, it looked more like she was baring her teeth.

"Forget about it. We're not here for me, we're here for Aria. We're meant to be having fun, so let's have fun. I don't need a man for that."

Sophie leaned over and took her hand. Usually, Avery would have pulled back, but today she didn't. "Babe, Gareth is a good guy. Perhaps you should give him a shot."

So says Sophie, the queen of second and third chances.

She bit back the sharp retort. After all, Sophie had found a man who adored her. Sophie, for all that she was a flirt, was brave. Avery preferred not to take unquantifiable risks.

"I can't," she whispered.

"Let go for once," Evie urged. "You wouldn't have jumped him if there was nothing between you. You're not that kind of girl." One side of her mouth quirked up. "Not that there's anything wrong with being that kind of girl."

Avery shook her head, dismissing the topic. "Let's get back to the group. They'll be wondering where we are."

WHEN THEY'D GAMBLED themselves to exhaustion, Avery and Clarissa returned to the hotel room they were sharing. Avery sprawled on the sofa and Clarissa headed to the bench and switched on the kettle.

"I was so stupid," Avery groaned. There was no response, but a minute later, the smell of hot chocolate wafted toward her and she came upright to accept the mug Clarissa offered.

"This is not your fault," Clarissa said. "You slipped up. You're human."

"Do you think he was telling the truth about how he'd

always planned to get back together one day?" Avery asked, having explained the situation during the walk to the room.

"I think—"

"No, don't worry." She waved a hand in the air. "Forget I asked. It's pointless to wonder."

She couldn't help it, though. He'd seemed sincere, and it felt like there had been something real between them. But no. Mooning over a man who'd hurt her once before wouldn't lead anywhere good.

"I think," Clarissa began again, "that it doesn't matter what he intended. It matters what happened. You stayed apart for a reason."

She had a point, and true to form, she said exactly what she thought and didn't pull any punches. Avery loved her for it.

"You're right, but you already know that."

"Of course. You know that men do what they want, and we pay the price." Scorn tinged her voice. They'd always shared a mistrust of relationships—at least since senior year of high school—but listening to Clarissa now, she wondered exactly when her friend had become so bitter. At least Avery was open to the possibility of having a man in her life. Clarissa sounded like she'd rather bathe in acid.

No one could go through what her friend had and emerge unscathed, but it seemed as if the intervening years had served to amplify her resentment rather than diffuse it.

"Not all men are like that," Avery said quietly, barely believing the words coming from her mouth. Avery Brown, the defender of mankind. Who'd have thought it? "Look at Eli. He adores Aria, and Cooper is crazy for Sophie."

Clarissa inclined her head. "Eli seems to be one of the good ones, I grant you. I hope for Aria's sake it stays that way."

Avery frowned, noticing what she hadn't said. "You don't think Coop loves Sophie?"

She shrugged and shifted into a cross-legged position. "Maybe he does, but how many hearts did he break before he found his way to her?"

Fair point. Although the PTSD he'd suffered from gave him a reason for his behavior, if not an excuse.

"You were right to leave," Clarissa told her.

"Technically, he left," Avery said. "I just ran away after he'd already gone."

"That was a smart decision," she reiterated. "You know, if you need to get away for a while, you're welcome to come and stay with me."

"Thanks." Avery rested her head against the cushions, closing her eyes. God, she was tired. Bone-deep weary, with gritty eyes, yet her mind remained awake. She tried to slow the flickering of her eyes beneath the eyelids.

A warm weight pressed against her side, then Clarissa's head settled next to her own. They'd sat like this often when they lived together, but back then, Avery had been the one offering comfort. Unobtrusive, but present. She slipped her hand between them and clasped Clarissa's, their fingers intertwining.

"I got you, Riss."

"I got you, too."

They echoed the words they'd spoken to each other every night for one traumatic summer. If Avery trusted anyone to have her best interests at heart, it was Clarissa.

She slept, knowing that she was safe in the company of the sister of her heart.

21

By the time Sunday came and Gareth was still at the cabin, he was beginning to look like a wild man, with unshaven cheeks, unkempt hair, and clothes that had been dipped in the lake and hung up to dry instead of being properly washed. Even Snookie seemed wary of the transformation, approaching him with less than her typical enthusiasm when he called.

That must have been why, when his friend Davy arrived, the first thing he said was, "You look like hell. What rabbit hole have you been hiding down?"

"Give off," Gareth replied. "I get enough of that from Mum, I don't need it from you, too."

"Seriously, Gaz," Davy said, taking the ax from his hand and carrying it to the woodshed, "do you need an intervention? 'Cause I can arrange one of those. But personally, I'd rather see you get your act cleaned up without inviting half the nosy beggars in town to stick their beaks in."

"I'm good," Gareth told him, mopping the sweat off his brow with the back of his hand. "No intervention needed. I'll even be back at work tomorrow." Rata had messaged to let him know the trial date for Dwayne Broderick had been set, and he was determined to make sure the asshole got the prison time his crime warranted. "Just been a big couple of weeks, you know."

"Come on, man, don't try to sell me that crock of shite." Davy rolled his eyes, then picked up a stick and threw it for Snookie. Gareth noticed his dog had no problem bringing the stick to Davy. Traitorous mutt. "You're not crying yourself a river out here because of work. It's about Avery. Best I can figure, you made a move on her, and she shot you down. That about sum it up?"

"It's a bit more complicated than that."

"Complicated." Davy sighed and tossed the stick again. Snookie splashed into the water behind it. "Did you think it wouldn't be? You know I love her, but she's pricklier than a hedgehog, and about as trusting as a feral cat."

Gareth didn't say anything. Couldn't argue with the truth.

"Now, I didn't come out here to lecture you, but my point is, she's stubborn. So are you. When you set your mind to something, you're the most pig-headed sonofabitch I know. Are you really going to give up without a fight?"

Was that what he was doing? Lying down and playing dead?

For what reason? Because he was afraid that if he went after what he wanted, he'd find out that his fears were true, that he really wasn't good enough for her?

He was being a chicken shit, and it had to end. He'd spent the past nine years keeping his distance. Davy was right. It was time for action. When Gareth wanted something, he made it happen, and he wanted Avery Brown in his life.

"No," he announced, nodding decisively. "I'm going to fight for her."

"Good man!"

Gareth strode toward the hut and called Snookie to heel. He kicked his boots off and crammed gear into his bag while Davy waited by the door. Then, finally, he dared to turn on his phone. Ten missed phone calls appeared from his Mum, Caro, Aria and Davy. None from Avery. He cringed and decided to deal with them later.

"What now?" he asked.

Davy shrugged. "I'm just here for the pep talk. That's as far as my planning went. The rest of it is up to you."

"Some help you are."

Davy laughed and shook his head. "You're lucky I like you enough to bother coming at all. You had your head well and truly up your ass."

"Yeah, yeah. Unless you've got something useful to say, shut your big Irish mouth."

They fell silent, walking to the cars side by side.

"Did she say why she shot you down?" Davy asked.

"Something about not being able to be with me after how things ended last time."

"Huh." Davy wore a puzzled frown. "I thought it was mutual last time."

"So did I." He tried to recall exactly how their breakup had gone down. "I suppose it was my idea, but she seemed to agree, and it was mostly for her benefit."

Davy snapped his fingers. "Do you know who'll be able to tell you exactly what you missed?"

Dread unfurled in the pit of Gareth's belly. "Don't say it."

"Clarissa," he declared. "The best friend always knows everything."

Burying his face in his palms, Gareth groaned. *Clarissa.* Could his luck get any worse?

GARETH STOPPED at Aria's house on the way home and cajoled Clarissa's number out of her. Not that it took much cajoling—she was ecstatic he was "finally" making a move on Avery. When he got home, he slumped on his living room sofa and called Clarissa with the same trepidation he'd experience facing down a six-foot-two, one-hundred-kilogram rugby player who'd drunk too many beers and decided it would be a laugh to challenge a cop to a fight. His nerves were frayed. Hell, they were rubbed raw. Clarissa was staunch in defense of her friends. While he appreciated her loyalty to Avery, she might take it into her head to drive up here and kick him in the nuts, poison his coffee, or stab him through the heart with a pair of her enormous fabric shears.

The phone call started sending and his stomach lurched. To say Clarissa didn't like him would be equivalent to saying Napoleon hadn't gotten along with the French monarchs. She *despised* him, though he'd never quite known why.

"Clarissa Mitchell speaking."

Swallowing the lump in his throat, he said, "Hi, Clarissa. It's Gareth here."

A silence, then, "I have nothing to say to you. Goodbye."

The line went dead. He dialed again. He'd expected hostility, and he could handle it.

"I don't wish to speak to you," she snapped, upon answering for the second time.

Closing his eyes, he clung to a shred of courage. "I get that you don't like me, but I need to know: why did you slap me when Avery and I broke up? Why won't she give me another chance?"

Her breath hitched as though she were about to reply, but then she asked, "How is it possible that you don't know?"

"Don't know what?" he asked, desperate. "Have pity on me. I'm a clueless man."

She huffed, and he pictured her stretching out her hand, ready to deliver a slap if required. "Avery was heartbroken when you dumped her. She thought you'd have a long-distance relationship while you studied, then move into a house together as soon as you were done. She was planning a future with you, only you didn't want her."

"But…" He grasped for words. "That's not true. The decision was mutual. We both agreed—"

"She agreed for the sake of her pride. Not because it was what she wanted. You wanted to end it, and she wanted to save face. If you hadn't said anything, she would have tried to make it work. When you talked about splitting up, she thought you were sick of her and wanted an easy out."

"Fuck." The ugly truth struck Gareth with the force of a taser, nearly knocking him onto his backside. He'd thought they'd been on the same page, but she'd completely misunderstood, and because of her ridiculous pride, she hadn't asked him to clarify.

He'd *hurt* her.

She'd believed that he hadn't wanted her, when nothing could be further from the truth. He'd wanted that silly, prideful woman every day of his life. He remembered the message he'd been hearing on repeat lately. From Aria, Sophie, even his mum…*Hold onto her this time.* Like an idiot, he'd repeated over and over again that it had been mutual. Amicable. But that wasn't how it had been at all.

"*Excuse me?*" Clarissa demanded, not partial to swearing.

"I never meant for her to feel like that," he said. "You've got to believe me. How do I convince her? You're her best friend. What do I do?"

An excruciating moment of quiet followed his question, and he thought she'd hung up again, but then she asked, "What's her favorite color?"

His jaw ground down on the gum between his back teeth. Every second she delayed kept him from making things right. "Purple. Always has been, always will be. What's that got to do with anything?"

She fired another question. "Favorite food?"

"I don't know," he admitted. This was a test. To see whether he deserved her. "But she loves pretzels and salted popcorn. Takes her coffee black, no sugar. Likes hot chocolate, but only when she needs comfort. Hates pets, but I'm hoping she'll warm up to my dog." Clarissa scoffed at that, but he pushed on regardless. "She likes people to think she's tough, but inside she's a marshmallow. That's what all of her attitude is about. She's trying to keep the marshmallow part of herself safe. I want that, too." He took a breath. "Do I pass your test?"

She sighed softly. "I don't know how you can make anything right, but starting with an explanation may help. I doubt she'll listen to you if you call or visit. Your best chance is to find her at Davy's this Friday. There's a masquerade dance she's going to." She paused, then added, "Good luck, and you'd better pray I don't regret talking to you."

"You won't," he promised.

"Yeah. Well. We'll see."

AVERY SQUEEZED herself into the slinkiest black dress she owned—the *only* dress she now owned, thanks to a shopping session with Sophie when she'd first come to stay with her—and tugged the hem down until it covered her bum and a few inches of thigh. She didn't dress up—or rather, down—often and she couldn't believe she'd let Sophie talk her into buying this outfit. She'd wanted to look sexy, and it had seemed like a daring purchase that could shake her out of a funk a few days ago, but it was hardly practical now that the temperature outside had dropped and she was shivering.

She frowned at the mirror on the bathroom wall and changed angles. Was it too short? She didn't want to be indecent. She fussed with the hem again. Definitely not too short. But was it too "out there" for her? Probably. She could head over to Sophie's cottage and ask to borrow a different dress, but she doubted anything in her friend's wardrobe would fit her any better. She had a good few inches on Sophie. Dresses that were conservative on her would be outrageous on Avery.

Don't be stupid. Who cares if this dress is a little much? You look hot.

She gave her reflection the thumbs-up. Damn right she did. Searching for another option would be pointless. Instead, she applied a neutral layer of makeup—she'd bought some with her savings, which had taken a thrashing lately and would continue to do so until the insurance pay-out for her house and belongings cleared—and eyed herself critically. *Boring.* Borrowing from Sophie's style, she darkened the makeup around her eyes and went for a brighter shade of pink on her lips. A pair of sparkly earrings gifted by Sophie earlier in the day completed the look. She smiled at herself. She looked different. More alive. Perfect.

Shrugging into a warm jacket, she drew it closed and slipped on a pair of boots with low, chunky heels. A car engine hummed to a stop in the distance. Aria, Eli, and Cooper, arrived to pick up her and Sophie. She checked to make sure her purse contained her cell phone, lipstick, ID, and credit card then strolled out to greet them, collecting Sophie as she passed through the cottage.

At Davy's bar, cars were packed into the parking lot bumper-to-bumper. Cooper circled around and parked a block away—the nearest they could find—and they walked to the bar, the girls donning simple black eye masks before joining the line to enter. Itirangi had limited nightlife and it seemed like everyone had turned up. Many wore half-masks similar to theirs, but others' entire faces were dwarfed by elaborate creations.

As they reached the doorman, Avery rustled in her purse for her ID, waved it, and he ushered them through. They reached the coat rack and she discarded her coat. Whether it was the heating system or the crowd of bodies, the temperature in the bar was enough that she didn't need it.

"Let's dance," Sophie said, dragging Cooper into the throng of bodies. Aria and Eli followed suit, although Eli looked somewhat less than enthusiastic—both about being surrounded by so many people and about having his pregnant fiancée in the middle of a rowdy crowd.

Aria turned back. "You okay?"

Avery nodded. "I'm fine. I'll join you in a minute."

She surveyed the room and noticed a booth in the corner where she could have a little breathing room. Before she could move toward it, a hand landed on her elbow. She turned to smile at whichever girl had returned to check on her, but an unfamiliar man smiled back. Classically handsome, with unruly dark hair, even features, and twinkling brown eyes, he equaled her height in heels.

"Not who you were expecting?" he asked good-naturedly.

"No."

"That's all right." His smile turned boyishly cheeky. "I'm frequently not." He extended a hand. "Mark Talbot, a pleasure to meet you."

"Avery Brown," she replied, searching for the girls over his shoulder. Seeing them busy with their men, she looked back to Mark. "Are you visiting town?"

"Ah, so you're a local." He nodded knowingly. "My friend Eli has explained to me that all locals know all other locals, so if you think I'm visiting, you must be a local. Otherwise how would you know I wasn't one?"

Strangely, she followed his logic. "You're a friend of Eli's?"

She found it hard to believe. Eli was reserved and coolheaded. This guy radiated charisma and confidence.

"I am. He invited me tonight. Do you know him?" He shook his head. "Wait, don't bother to answer. Of course you do."

"His fiancée is a good friend of mine."

"Would you believe I helped him woo the lucky lady?"

"That would explain why it took so long." She couldn't

resist the barbed reply, but rather than be taken aback as she'd expected, his smile took on an appreciative slant.

"You're a sassy one. I like that in a woman."

Against her better judgment, she found herself grinning back. There was something so unflappable about him that she couldn't help but like him. She sensed he'd be fun to be around.

"You're bad news," she informed him.

He winked. "But you like me anyway." He'd read her mind. "Tell me, Miss Avery Brown, which of these men is the one you're here with tonight?"

She turned up her nose. "Actually, it's *Dr.* Brown. And what makes you think I'm here with a man?"

"Touché. Clever women are even better than sassy ones, and clever, sassy, single women are my favorite."

She rolled her eyes. "You're ridiculous."

Before he could reply, a pair of broad shoulders appeared between the two of them.

"Is this guy bothering you, A-Bee?" Gareth asked, voice rough as he shoved Mark further away with one shoulder and insinuated his way into her space, wrapping an arm around her. Where had he come from? He hadn't been here when they arrived, or she would have noticed.

"Not at all," she replied, shocked by the territorial display, especially given the way they'd parted and the radio silence since.

Gareth had never been possessive of her in high school, but now, if he'd been a dog, his hackles would be raised and he'd be growling, ready to rip the throat out of the opposition. His hand rested on her hip, fingers splayed over her midsection. The gesture lacked subtlety. He'd all but publicly claimed her.

Mark blew her a kiss, already stepping back. "See you later, doc."

She raised an eyebrow, unsure what to make of him, or whether she actually had anything to thank him for.

Gareth's lip curled like he had a bad taste in his mouth. "Who the hell was that? Do you know him?"

"Never met him before. He's a friend of Eli's, apparently."

He frowned. "I wouldn't have thought he'd have anything in common with Eli."

"A sense of self-entitlement, perhaps."

She could tell Gareth didn't agree—but then, he wasn't privy to the backstory of Aria and Eli's relationship.

"You weren't…interested…in that guy, were you?"

Did he actually just ask that? "What if I was?"

"He doesn't seem right for you. A bit too slick, if you ask me."

"I didn't." His eyes narrowed and shifted away from hers. Her mouth dropped open. "Are you *jealous*?"

It hardly seemed plausible, and yet color rose on his cheeks. Part of her wanted to laugh at him for being stupid, but part of her was thrilled that he felt so strongly about her.

Strange. Since when had she wanted his affection?

He cleared his throat. Looked away. And then she realized. Despite the proprietary way he held her and the determined set of his jaw, he was a man in desperate need of reassurance. She shouldn't give it to him, shouldn't encourage him, but the way he'd defended his turf inflamed her. She laid one hand over his heart and pulled his head down with the other, fusing her lips to his. As if she'd told him everything he needed to hear with that kiss, he slid his hands under her bottom and lifted her clean off the floor, his long strides eating up the distance between them and the booth in the corner. Her back hit the wall and she was sandwiched between cool wallpaper and hot man.

His lips trailed down the side of her neck. She shivered as his breath whispered over the sensitive skin where her neck met her shoulder. His grip tightened. He'd noticed her response. He blew softly across the skin, sending jitters down her spine. His lips curved and he pressed a kiss to the delicate spot. Yep, his confidence had returned in full force. The pad of his thumb rubbed up and down the length of her neck, generating spectacular friction. Heat shot downward. She'd never been so aroused without having a man's hands on places a whole lot less PG than her neck.

"What are you doing to me?" she murmured, not really expecting an answer.

"Seducing you," he replied, a hopeful note in his voice. Then he stilled, lowered her to the ground, put a foot of space between them and scraped a hand down his face. "In public, no less. I'm sorry, A-Bee. I don't know what I was thinking."

She shrugged, not quite sure why he was apologizing. "I liked it. In fact, you can kiss me like that again if you want."

He reddened. "I got carried away. Sorry. Just didn't like the way that guy was looking at you."

"Neanderthal," she teased, wrapping her arms around him and resting her head on his chest. It felt good to be close to him. *Right*. "As if I'd go for a man like that. Cavemen are far more my style."

"I'm glad to hear that." His hand lingered on the small of her back and the gesture blared as loudly as a trumpet to anyone who glanced their way that they'd reconnected and he wouldn't let her deny it this time. Wouldn't let her push him away again.

She ought to tell him to back off. Remind him that she wasn't ready for anything serious, but she couldn't bring herself to do it. Belonging to him again was a wonderful feeling, even if it was only for a while.

"Shall we dance?" he asked.

A club song had started playing, the bass rattling the dim lights hanging overhead. He took her hand and tugged. She tripped forward into him—no doubt as he'd intended. His arms looped around her waist, resting on the small of her back He swayed from side to side, rocking her with him as if they were waltzing.

"This isn't a slow dance," she hissed in his ear.

"Shh," he chastened her. "I'm enjoying it."

She gave an Olympic-worthy eye roll and humored him. The bass vibrated through her toes, shook her core and caused a tremble in her chest. Closing her eyes, she let him guide their movements, simply along for the ride. She breathed in deeply, welcoming the comforting scent of mint that swirled around her and warmed her on the inside. Was it from his soap, or the gum he chewed?

Another tune started. She pushed away from him and bopped on the spot, amused when he followed suit. She raised her arms above her head and shimmied to the beat. He shuffled closer and traced the lines of her body with his hands, dipping into the curve of her waist, over the slight flare of her hips, caressing the skin where the bottom of her dress met her thigh. Her breath caught in her throat, both because of the soft touch and the casual possessiveness it spoke of.

It should rile her, but instead, it excited her. She was tired of always doing and feeling what she *should*. Tired of being sensible. She wanted to be in the moment for once. Little pinpricks of awareness fired at each place his fingers brushed and she wondered what he'd do if anyone challenged him. His every movement screamed of intent. To what? Seduce her, as he'd said?

Mission accomplished, Sergeant.

They danced for another three songs, getting handsier with each one until her front was plastered to his, her arms draped around his neck. The music stopped, the DJ announcing a brief break, and she nipped at his strong jaw. He groaned and adjusted his stance.

She chuckled. "It's like high school all over again."

"But better," he murmured. "I love the way you feel in my arms"

Reveling in the sensation of the solid planes of his chest and abdomen rubbing against her breasts, she couldn't help but agree. "Wanna get out of here?"

He groaned. "We can't. I need to talk to you, and it won't be happening if we go somewhere private."

She stiffened, not sure that she wanted to talk. "Gareth…"

"Easy," he said. "No pressure. How's this? We'll play a game of pool. If I win, you hear me out. If you win, you can have your wicked way with me, no strings attached."

"You mean it?"

"I don't know." He sighed. "We have so much history, there might always be strings between us. But if that's all you can give me, I'll take it."

She considered the proposition. Nothing to lose, really. She'd win. She always did. Even if she didn't, she could tune him out if she didn't like what he had to say.

"Game on, G."

2 2

---

*A*very set up the pool table with a few brisk movements and handed Gareth a cue. He ran his fingertips along the smooth wooden surface.

"Do you want to break, or shall I?" she asked.

"I will," he said, rising to the challenge. Hopefully, pool was a skill that stayed with a person. He played on occasion, but nothing compared to Avery and her friends, with their standing Friday night date at the bar.

He thwacked the ball and it flew into the others, breaking them apart quite tidily for someone who ought to be rusty. He stood back, pleased with himself. There was a lot riding on this game, and not for the first time he wondered whether this had been a smart approach.

Avery's first shot sank a colored ball, then she tossed a glance over her shoulder, lips curved in a taunting smile. *Well, hell.* She'd remembered his superstition about the colored balls being luckier than the stripes and beat him to them. He focused on the positive. She remembered, and that meant she cared. He might have a chance here.

She made her next move, and he sized up his options. Opting for boldness, he did the obvious, hoping he wasn't

207

playing into some scheme she'd devised. Back and forth they went, Avery clearly the better of the two, but Gareth hanging on like a Chihuahua clamped onto a paperboy's ankle. With every turn, the rosiness of her cheeks became deeper, and the sparkle in her eye grew more luminous.

She was beautiful in her desire to destroy him.

Finally, there was one colored ball left and three stripes. She succeeded in pocketing the colored ball, as he knew she would, but when she whacked the white ball into the eight-ball, it bounced harmlessly off the side of the table and missed the pocket. Her eyes narrowed.

"Poor shot, A-Bee," he goaded.

She rested one hand on the cue, the other on her hip. "Back off. Don't be a sore loser."

He took his turn and missed. She arranged the cue across the table, hands shaking. He held his breath as, with a gentle bump, the white ball tapped into the eight-ball and rolled it into the pocket.

"Yes!" She pumped her fist, then turned and pointed at him. "You lose, I win. Game over."

His shoulders slumped and his heart dropped to his shoes. She'd beat him. He sighed and laid the pool cue down. His throat felt dry and he swallowed—the only visible sign of discomfort that he allowed—then he shoved his hands into his pockets.

He didn't know if he could do this.

Didn't know if he could touch her and pretend to feel nothing more than attraction. He adored every part of her. Longed to make her his own, forever.

But he'd promised, and he was a man of his word.

"Should we head to my place then, or Sophie's?"

Avery's brows lowered. "Are you okay?"

He didn't look up. "I'll be fine."

Something touched his hand. Her palm, pressing to his. She smiled at him, just a little, and led him to the bar where she requested two bottles of Heineken and sat on a bar stool. What was she doing? Why wasn't she gloating, or dragging him out of here already?

"You want to talk?" she asked, resting her chin on steepled fingers. "Talk."

〜

"No." Gareth swigged the beer and thunked it down onto the bar. "You won, so you get what you want. Naked time, no strings. That's what I agreed to, and I don't say things if I'm not willing to go through with them."

She was beginning to realize he placed a great deal of stock in keeping his word. It was a trait to be admired, but clearly, he needed to get something off his chest and he deserved to be heard out.

"Go on," she said. "I'm listening."

He reached for her hand and held it between both of his. "If you really want to know the truth, I'll tell you. Are you sure you want to hear it?"

She nodded mutely.

"I talked to Clarissa. She explained a few things to me."

"You talked to Clarissa?" Her eyebrows shot up. "That must be the first time in, what, eight or nine years?"

"Something like that. The point is, when we were kids, I said we should think about getting together some day down the road, and I meant it. Clarissa told me you thought that was a line I fed you to let you down easy. It wasn't. I always thought you were the one for me. I'm so sorry I hurt you. That was never my intention." He paused, searching her eyes for permission to continue, and found it. "The truth is, I was afraid that if we stayed together, I'd hold you back. I wanted you to be free to do whatever you liked without worrying about me. I didn't want to weigh you down."

"You never weighed me down!" she exclaimed, horrified

209

that he'd ever think such a thing. Had she given him that impression? Made him feel like a lead ball around her ankle? Nothing could be further from the truth. He'd been her rock. The person she came back to, whatever else was going on in her life. How had they misunderstood each other so completely?

He shrugged. "That's how I felt. You had big dreams, I had modest ones. The least I could do was make sure I didn't stop you from achieving them."

She'd gotten everything wrong. *Everything*. She'd thought he ended their relationship because she wasn't good enough for him, but instead he'd been totally selfless—if a little high-handed—and she'd wasted months, if not years, hurting inside and hating him for it.

"So you spent years being miserable because you wanted me to go after my dreams?"

"It wasn't all miserable," he muttered defensively. "I won't lie, I had my share of fun after we broke up. Dated other girls. But I didn't care for a single one of them as much as I cared about your little finger, let alone the rest of you."

He brought her hand to his lips, pressing a kiss to the back of it. Tingles diffused from the place where his lips lingered on her skin. She didn't shake him off. Hearing him talk about dating other girls had caused a painful cramp in her chest, but she hung on his every word. With his intense expression and reverent touch, he'd woven a net around them, keeping the world out.

"Then I saw you during one of your holidays, and you were beautiful. I swear, you got more stunning every year. I kept an eye on you, and the gossips updated me about what you were doing, but you never even looked at me." His mouth took on a wry slant. "You were too busy visiting exciting countries, earning your PhD, doing things I'd never be able to. That's when I knew I'd done the right thing, but I wanted you back so badly. I was going to take you out when you moved here, but you never gave me any indication you were interested, so I stayed away. I guess I worried that I wasn't enough for you anymore."

"What a pair we are," she murmured, leaning over to wipe away a tear that streaked down his cheek with her thumb. "I thought *I* wasn't good enough for *you*."

"That couldn't be further from the truth." He turned his face into her palm and exhaled roughly, his shoulders shuddering. God, he was so huge and hot and he'd come undone by emotion because of her. Somehow, that made him sexier. The last wisps of her earlier anger ebbed away.

"I noticed you these last years," she admitted, closing her eyes when he kissed her palm, the stubble on his cheeks abrading her, but the caress so tender it stole her breath. "I told myself I was over you, but every time I saw you, it was like someone twisted a knife in my chest."

"I'm sorry." His lips tickled her palm. Pulling back, he sucked in a deep breath and squared his shoulders. "Here's my proposition: you leave with me right now and give me this entire weekend to convince you we're good together. No holding back or pushing me away. Just the two of us spending time together without the pressure of a criminal case getting in the way, and without all of our baggage coming between us. Just you and me. Say yes."

Her hand tightened involuntarily and a tennis ball lodged in her throat. She coughed, clearing it out, but the airway still felt restricted.

"Um," she croaked. *Great, Avery. Real articulate.* She searched for the right answer. Her heart was pumping so furiously she was surprised she hadn't passed out from high blood pressure. Could she really do this? Start over with a blank slate? She'd like to, she realized. "Okay, yes."

A wide grin split his face. "Really?"

"Really."

"*Thank you.*" He leaned forward and brushed a kiss over

her lips. "Now, don't panic, but if you enjoy the weekend, I'd like you to consider a relationship with me. I won't push for anything you're not ready to give, but I'm totally committed to this."

The room spun dizzyingly. Everything was moving so quickly, she felt pulled by a current, speeding out of control. The most surprising thing? She liked it.

"I'll keep it in mind."

If possible, his grin widened. The dimples deepened, and she closed the distance between them to kiss one. He turned, so her lips landed on his mouth instead. She chuckled, but he swallowed the sound and licked the seam of her lips. She accepted his tongue into her mouth. The kiss grew frantic, heated.

"I love kissing you," he murmured against her lips.

"Same here. Let's take this somewhere else," she whispered.

He groaned, but in frustration rather than desire. "Where?"

Smiling against his lips, she suggested, "Your place."

He kissed her nose. "I love the way your brain works. Have I told you that?"

She smirked. "Come on, Romeo, get me out of here."

"With pleasure."

They stood, and she gasped when he swept her off her feet. "Are you going caveman on me?"

"If I say yes, will you let me drag you back to my cave and have my wicked way with you?"

"As long as you promise not to club me over the head."

"Cheeky," he remarked. "I make no promises."

She snuggled into the shelter of his chest as he carried her to his car, feeling both wonderfully safe and like she'd plunged headfirst into deep water.

Luckily, she knew how to swim.

areth was buzzing. He held Avery tight as they exited the bar.

She shivered. "Forgot my coat."

"You won't need it," he told her. "I'll keep you warm."

After all, he'd warmed her on many a cool night when they were younger. He remembered how she'd clung to him, and he'd been only too happy to share his body heat. Carrying her down the street to his car, he lowered his face to inhale the scent of her.

"Is that a new perfume?"

"It's Sophie's," she said. "I borrowed it for tonight."

Her words landed like a punch in his gut. "Did I interrupt any big plans?" he asked, straining to sound normal, and failing.

She noticed his tone—nothing slipped past his girl. "No big plans. If you want to know the truth, I was feeling a bit sensitive so I wanted to be my best."

He laughed. She scowled.

"Oh, you were serious?" he asked.

"As death."

He sobered. "Sorry." They arrived at the car and he pressed the button to unlock it, then gently set her down in the passenger seat. "Why were you feeling sensitive, A-Bee?"

She squinted at him, as though trying to determine whether he was making fun of her.

"I won't laugh again. Swear to god."

Her lips pursed and she looked like she wanted to bury her face in her hands, but she maintained unflinching eye contact. That was his girl. Tough as nails.

"Ever since we broke up, I guess I've worried about not being pretty enough or girly enough. Most of the time, I'm over that now, but I needed a reminder. I wanted to feel sexy for *myself*, not for the sake of finding a guy to go home with. Does that make sense?"

"It does." Although it gutted him to be the cause of her insecurities. "But I want you to know that I never thought you were anything less than perfect, and if you let me, I'll spend the rest of your life convincing you that I like you exactly the way you are."

"Beer drinking, horror film watching, and all?"

"I don't even mind if you take me down on the rugby field. God knows you've done it enough times before."

She smiled. "Good to know. Now, will you hurry up and get me to bed?"

"Your will is my command." He moved around to the driver's door, got in, and drove to Sophie's place so she could collect whatever she needed for the weekend.

"Once I get you naked, you're not leaving for anything," he said.

She didn't object.

He didn't bother to stop at his house. Caroline had dropped by earlier to pick up his bag and a few other bits and pieces. He wanted this weekend to be perfect for Avery, so he'd enlisted the help of a woman he trusted not to spill the beans to her ahead of time.

"Wait, aren't we going to your place?" she asked as they flew past and started onto the road through the forest.

"Nope." He kept his eyes on the road, afraid to sneak a peek at her in case she was angry at his deception.

"Okay."

"*Okay?*" he repeated incredulously. "What about the questions? Where, what, who, why, how?" This was the most suspicious woman in Itirangi, right here.

"I trust you."

He choked up and tried like crazy not to cry. That might be the sweetest thing he'd ever heard. His eyes watered and he had to sniff.

"Ugh, don't be like that," she grumbled. "This is why I never say nice things."

"I love it when you do." *Love*. He'd been saying that word a lot tonight, and it wasn't by mistake. He was warming her up to it. Getting her used to hearing it. Then, when he laid the big "L" on her, it wouldn't be wholly unexpected.

"I know where we're going," she said. "You're taking me to the cabin."

"Spot on, little lady. Just you and me and nature. But this time, you won't be under house arrest."

"What about Snookie?"

"Caro is minding her."

She laughed sharply. "You really were confident, weren't you?"

"Not at all." He didn't want her to think he'd assumed she'd be a sure thing. "Just optimistic."

A while later, he parked outside the cabin and asked her to wait while he dashed inside. He used his cell phone as a torch and switched on the strings of solar-powered fairy lights Caroline had laid out. The room was cast in a soft orange glow. Then he returned to the car and took her hand.

"You know I can walk without your help," she said.

"You can," he agreed. "But I like touching you."

"Well." She sounded stumped. "Can't argue with that."

When he opened the door, she gasped. "Oh my god! It's beautiful, G. I can't believe you did this for me."

"That's not all." Caroline had promised to leave food, and a cane basket sat on the table. He lifted the lid and saw...not what he'd expected. "Caro left provisions," he said, "but she might have gotten carried away. Come and look."

She crossed to his side and peered into the basket, then laughed. "I'm taking it Caro approves of us."

"I'd say so."

The basket had been filled with aphrodisiacs. Strawberries, chocolate cherries, instant whipped cream, watermelon, figs, avocado, and wine. He chose a bottle of pink champagne and poured it into two champagne flutes, then offered her one and clinked his against it. They both sipped. Bubbles fizzed on his tongue.

"That's enough champagne," he said, taking her flute and placing it back on the table.

"I barely had a sip."

"I know, but I really need to kiss you now."

So he did. Then she kissed him back. Their clothing seemed to fall away and they stretched out naked on one of the bunk beds, which had been fitted with a silk sheet. Their bodies moved together in the glow of the fairy lights, and when they were sated, they lay together, limbs entwined, and talked deep into the night.

A SLIGHT PRESSURE on Avery's mouth woke her. Her eyes fluttered open, then closed when she saw Gareth's face immediately above hers. He dropped another light, affectionate kiss on her lips, then buried his face in the crook of her neck and nuzzled. His stubble rasped against her skin and she tucked herself closer to him, cocooned in warmth and lit from the inside.

Content. She was *content.* For once, she was happy to luxuriate in bed rather than getting a move on right away.

"Mmm. I could get used to waking up like this."

"That's the plan," he mumbled, his lips tickling her shoulder.

A grown man shouldn't be adorable, especially not one as hot as Gareth, but her heart melted and her insides went gooey when he drew back and smiled at her in his familiar way, dimpled cheeks, hair mussed, almost the same shade as his eyes in the morning light.

There was something soft about him. Vulnerable. He hadn't been like this during their days and nights together previously, and she wondered whether he'd been holding part of himself back. Whatever the case, he was completely in the moment with her now, and she kissed the tip of his nose and hugged him tight.

She was screwed. In every possible way. But maybe that wasn't so bad after all.

"I love seeing your face first thing when I wake up," he said. "It's nice not to have to sneak out of your room like I did in high school."

"You weren't very sneaky," she replied, chuckling. "Dad must have known what we got up to."

"Oh, he did. He had a talk to me about it once or twice, but he knew I was a responsible guy so he didn't see any point making a fuss about it."

"Huh." Yet another thing she hadn't known. She tried to picture her old-school Kiwi father having a man-to-man talk with Gareth and snickered.

"That sounded evil."

She shook her head. "Why did you worry about sneaking out all of those times, if Dad wasn't bothered by you staying?"

His cheeks flushed and he dipped his head to lay a lingering kiss on her throat. "Because it stopped you from being embarrassed."

Aw. Wasn't he just the cutest thing ever?

Suddenly, he sat up. She reached for him. "What's up?"

"I'm going to make you breakfast and a coffee," he told her. "Wait right here."

Wearing nothing but his birthday suit, totally shameless—and most likely freezing—he strutted to the bench and started to heat water. He spooned coffee into a pair of mugs and fetched a few items from the picnic basket, then he sliced avocado and tomato, arranged them on bagels and sprinkled salt and pepper over the top. He poured the coffee, shifted breakfast to a metal tray and carried it to the bed, where he slid in beside her and rested it on his lap.

"That's fantastic." She took a cup and swallowed a mouthful of the burning hot coffee, then helped herself to a bagel. "Tell Caro she rocks."

"You can tell her yourself. At dinner with my family next weekend."

She busied herself with the bagel and the silence between them extended until she finished and licked her fingers clean. "Awfully cocky, aren't you?"

"Optimistic," he corrected. "When it comes to you, always."

She waited to feel the panic that typically followed any declaration of that kind, but instead she realized she was pleased. She *wanted* him to feel the way he did.

She wanted Gareth, full stop. And she was done fighting it.

"What's next, G?"

"Next, we kayak."

~

AFTER GLIDING HALTINGLY over the placid surface of Lake Itirangi, attempting to paddle in tandem, Avery and Gareth collapsed on the shore and dissolved in laughter. Every time Avery got herself under control, she glanced over at his heaving chest, caught his eyes and started all over again. Her abdominals had never hurt so much. She'd have a six-pack after this, for sure.

"Just remember," he panted between gusts of laughter, "that kayaking is not symbolic of our relationship. The fact that we can't paddle in a straight line doesn't mean a thing."

Wiping her eyes on her sleeve, she curled into a ball to relieve her sore muscles. "I bet if we'd coordinated perfectly then you'd be telling me what a good omen it was."

"Hell, yeah. I'm no fool. I'll claim whatever I can."

"No shame."

"None." Rolling to his feet, he sauntered toward the cabin. She watched the delicious muscles in his calves bunch, his tread slightly uneven as he favored his left leg. Being cramped in the kayak must have made his knee stiff. Even with the limp, he was a superb specimen of a man. Broad shoulders, tight glutes. Damn, she wanted to jump him.

"You coming?" he called over his shoulder without looking back.

"What for?"

"Passing a rugby ball around."

She got up and dusted herself off, then looked over just in time to see a rugby ball hurtling her way. She caught it without much grace and threw it back, pleased when it flew in an even arc. Gareth plucked it from the air and, without pausing, swung it under his arm and lobbed it back.

She caught the ball, tucked it under her arm and ran with it. "Come and get me!"

Feet pounded behind her and she dodged right. He stumbled past and she started back in the other direction, but she'd only made it a few yards when he crashed into her and dragged her to the ground.

"No fair," she complained, holding the ball out of his reach. He tickled her ribcage and she reflexively drew her arms to her sides. He snatched the ball.

"I win," he gloated.

"You cheated."

"Did we agree on any rules?"

"That's not the point."

His mouth touched hers. "I think that *is* the point."

"Shut up and kiss me," she muttered, flicking her tongue out to brush his lip. She was about to deepen the kiss when something in his expression made her pause. An emotion was stamped across his face. One so significant that everything else faded into a vague haze of background noise. The warmth in his caramel eyes absorbed all of her concentration. She could sink into them forever. *Wanted* to sink into him forever.

"How do you feel about me, Gareth?" The question leapt unbidden from her mouth.

He didn't hesitate for a moment. "I love you."

Her lips formed a silent "O." She interlocked her fingers at the back of his neck to steady them. He said he loved her like it was obvious, and she finally realized he'd been saying it in a dozen little ways since they met at the bar last night. She hadn't reciprocated, but that didn't mean she didn't feel it. In her scientific heart, she suspected Gareth was the only man she'd ever love. It wasn't quantifiable, but the anecdotal evidence—the fact that no man had stirred her as he did— suggested they'd bonded all those years ago in a way deeper than either of them had known or expected.

"I've shocked you," he said, brushing a lock of hair off the side of her face, his touch feather-light. She longed for more. "It's all right if you don't feel the same yet. Give it time. I meant to wait—"

"You did shock me," she interrupted, for once not knowing what she was going to say before she said it, acting purely on instinct. "But I think I love you too. No, I know it. I don't think I ever really stopped."

A slow smile curved his mouth. "I'm so happy to hear that. I love you," he said again.

"I love you," she whispered, running a hand along his strong jaw and nipping the underside.

He swallowed. "I'm not sure if you're ready to hear this, but you're it for me. Forever. And you should know that even if I'm never as successful or ambitious as you are, no one else will ever love you the way I do."

"I know." She snuggled into the shelter of his chest. "Second time's the charm."

"You've got that right." He stared down at her, his expression achingly tender. "Does this mean I've earned that second chance? Will you be mine, A-Bee?"

She kissed him, chaste and sweet. "I've always been yours, G."

A fierce surge of emotion swelled within her as she finally admitted the truth. She loved this man, with every part of herself. Perhaps they'd argue and vie for dominance every day of their lives, but she'd rather tease him than make goo-goo eyes at anyone else.

"For the record, I'm expecting a lifetime of weekends like this. You've set a precedent. If you don't deliver, I might think you won me under false pretenses."

His brows drew together and his mouth formed a serious line. "We can't have that."

"Glad to hear it." She patted his cheek and grinned. "Shall we go and take advantage of the treats Caro left for us?"

He leapt to his feet and hauled her into his arms. "That's the best idea you've had today. Last one inside is the other's sex slave for the rest of the day." He started to sprint. Laughing, Avery ran after him, grabbing his hand to hold him back.

They reached the door at the same time.

EPILOGUE

CHRISTMAS, LATER THAT YEAR

"Can you believe it?" Avery asked Sophie as they lounged on the deck at Aria's house, beneath flashing lights and red and green tinsel. "This time last year, we were all singletons. Now, Aria has snagged a guy who's rich as bejeesus and has a baby, you've bunked down with her sexy brother, and I've—"

"Finally got over your pride and given your high school sweetheart another chance," Sophie interjected, laughing. "It only took nine years."

Avery rolled her eyes but could hardly object when the past few months had been the happiest of her life. "Yeah, yeah."

"*And,*" Sophie continued, smacking her palm on the arm of the chair for dramatic effect, "you killed it in court and put a murderer in prison for a really long time."

"Broderick deserved it." And thanks to the conviction, she'd been assigned a team to speed up the process of rebuilding her soil library to make sure others like him didn't escape justice. She'd coordinated the team from Timaru while training a pair of research assistants to do the analyses. They'd already collected and tested eighty percent of the necessary samples, with the work on track to be completed before the end of summer.

"Not to mention…" Sophie trailed off as Cooper approached.

"Hey, lover," he said, and a blush spread down her cheeks and neck.

"You're shameless," she replied, not looking like she minded at all.

Cooper turned and winked at Avery. "Can I steal Sophie away from you for a moment? I promise my intentions are anything but honorable."

Avery's lips twisted into a smirk. "Go ahead." She waved her hand. "If anyone deserves a good roll in the hay, it's Soph."

"You'll get no arguments from me."

Sophie offered Cooper her hand and he yanked her to his side. They strolled toward the back of the yard together.

Avery checked her watch and wondered where Gareth had gotten to. They'd spent the morning with his family, unwrapping presents while his nieces shrieked with delight, then indulged in a cooked breakfast and adjourned to his house, where they'd lived for the past five months. She'd had her own place bulldozed and sold the vacant lot for a tidy profit, which she'd squirrelled away and planned to use to take Gareth on a vacation to the tropics.

At *their* home, they'd wished each other a merry Christmas in the most delicious way, and then they'd come here. Aria's place was always the best spot to be on Christmas if you wanted to feel connected.

"Earth to A-Bee. You in there?"

She snapped to attention. Gareth was looming over her, his palm splayed in front of her face.

"Sorry," she said, stretching in the sun, her muscles languid. "I was miles away."

He took the chair Sophie had vacated, and reached over

to hold her hand. She entwined her fingers with his and squeezed. They felt sticky.

She raised an eyebrow. "What have you been eating?"

He ducked his head, sheepish. "Aria's spicy date cake."

"Typical." She chuckled. "One day, all of those cakes she feeds you are going to catch up with you."

"You'll love me anyway, right?" he asked, a dimple appearing in his cheek.

"Maybe," she hedged.

He smiled the smile of a man utterly confident in his woman. "You will."

"If you insist." Her eyes fluttered shut and she basked in the warmth of the high summer sun. Birds chirped in the trees, and the bustle of people in the house behind her blended into a pleasant hum. She couldn't remember enjoying a Christmas more.

"I do."

"Hmm?"

"Insist."

Gareth extricated his hand from hers. Sensing his change in mood, and the underlying tension that had gripped him, she sat up and focused. He slipped his sticky fingers into his pocket and withdrew a small, black box.

"In fact, I insist you love me for the rest of your life. Marry me, A-Bee?"

He flipped the box open to reveal a sparkling solitaire set in a white gold band. Simple, elegant, beautiful. She extracted it from the box and noticed an engraving on the inside of the band.

One love.

It was absolutely perfect. The moment, the man, the ring. A girl couldn't wish for more. She eased the ring onto her finger. When she replied, she'd never felt more certain of anything.

"Yes, Gareth. I'll marry you. After all, someone has to help you with your walking frame when you're ninety."

He kissed her, and she stopped talking.

"Congratulations!"

They both turned, separating reluctantly. Clarissa clacked across the path on heels that would give Avery vertigo, and hurried to embrace her.

"I'm so happy for you," Clarissa exclaimed, kissing her cheek. She shot Gareth a warning glance. "Take care of my girl."

Something about Clarissa seemed…different. Lighter, even. And who was that behind her?

Avery shook her head. It didn't matter right now. What mattered was the man beside her.

"I love you," she whispered.

"Show me how much."

She did.

THE END

DREAMING OF YOU EXCERPT

Clarissa Mitchell lit the bergamot-scented candle beside her bed and settled amongst the covers. She grabbed the bowl of honey soy chicken her assistant had cooked from the bedside cabinet and reached for a glass of wine with her other hand. After taking a sip, she placed it back on the cabinet and switched on her laptop, which sat on the far end of the bed. The screen was tilted at such an angle that she could easily see it while leaning back on a mound of pillows and eating her dinner.

She was glad—not for the first time—that the podcast's livestream connection was one-way, so she could stare at Mark Talbot's gorgeous face while stuffing her own with food, and he was none the wiser. As both the owner and head designer of a bridal boutique, she didn't have the luxury of time, so she couldn't give her full attention to the weekly podcast for small business owners. She had to multitask. Hence, dinner and learning simultaneously.

Her screen flickered and came to life, the image of Mark flashing across it. She sighed around a mouthful of chicken. With unruly brown hair, twinkling eyes the color of milk chocolate, and a ready smile, she was sure he'd broken hearts all over New Zealand. Fortunately, hers would never be among them because she had no desire to feel the effect of those eyes in person. She was perfectly happy admiring him from a safe distance, thank you very much. That said, she did try to catch the livestream each week rather than listening to the later-released podcast. She'd never get enough of seeing his smile and knowing that, at this particular point in time, they were sharing similar thoughts and space, even if it was virtual.

"Hello, everyone," he said with a lopsided grin that caused heat to pool low in her belly. "Welcome to episode two hundred and seventy-four of 'Your Main Hustle.' You're here with me, Mark, and our topic today is the legal aspects of email marketing."

That particular combination of words shouldn't have made her hot, but it did. She had no control as far as her fantasies about him were concerned. He could, and did, frequently speak in legal jargon, which really got her going. She suspected Freud would have a field day with her, especially considering she never gave men the time of day in person, unless it was work related.

He started talking, and Clarissa paid close attention. The sessions typically lasted for forty minutes, with the last ten dedicated to answering questions his listeners had sent in the previous week. When the question segment began, Clarissa clutched her wine and waited with bated breath to see whether he'd get to hers. Sometimes he only had time for one or two, and lately he seemed to prefer answering hers by email. She liked to think it was because he enjoyed interacting with her, but she had no evidence to support that theory.

She had to admit, she looked forward to receiving emails from him and tried to come up with a question each week so she could initiate contact. But no email could conjure up the same level of excitement she experienced when he raised his eyes to the camera, as he did just then, and said, "This one is from Clarissa Mitchell, one of the podcast's regular listeners."

She shivered. Holy moly, she loved his voice. And that velvety brown gaze… Even in the form of pixels on a screen, it could melt her.

"Clarissa asks, 'Would you advise a single opt-in or double opt-in to marketing emails from a legal standpoint?'" He smiled, and bunnies somersaulted in her stomach. "The answer, Clarissa,"—ooh, he said her name again—"is that a double opt-in is always preferable from a legal standpoint, even if it isn't necessarily a legal requirement in all countries. Using a double opt-in is a great way to cover your backside." Said backside tingled at his mention of it. "Of course, I need to remind you that I don't know your exact circumstances and that this doesn't constitute fully informed legal advice."

He always made that disclaimer—yet another thing she liked about him. He was a professional down to his toes. And, yeah, she might like to pretend he was flirting with her sometimes, but he was never anything less than appropriate. He was also cheerful and too handsome for his own good.

As he moved on to another question, she refilled her wine glass. She jotted notes when he was discussing the legal requirement to have unsubscribe options in every email and an address for service if recipients wanted to make contact. Finally, he drew to a close. She reluctantly exited the livestream, brushed her teeth, changed into a silk teddy—she loved the feel of silk against her skin—and imagined Mark Talbot speaking only to her as she drifted off to sleep, all alone in her queen-size bed in the one-person apartment above her boutique.

~

"You'll be a groomsman, of course, and your sisters will be bridesmaids. I won't have a maid of honor because I refuse to choose between Megan and Mikayla."

"You'd never hear the end of it," Mark Talbot agreed, smiling at his mother, Rose, who sat opposite him, at a table in their favorite downtown cafe. "But I don't expect Joe to make me one of his groomsmen. Surely he'd rather have his brother or one of his tennis buddies. But," he added, hoping to erase her frown, "maybe I could give you away?"

"Oh, Mark!" Her hand flew up to her mouth, and her eyes shone. "That's so sweet of you to offer. It hadn't even occurred to me that anyone would want to give me away. Are you sure I'm not too old for that?"

"Psh." He swatted her worry aside. "You're never too old, and it would be my honor."

He knew immediately he'd said the right thing, because she beamed at him and nodded to herself. "Wonderful. And, yes, you're right, Joe probably would like Craig to stand up with him. Are you sure you don't mind?"

"Of course not, Mum. Your wedding is all about you, so don't worry about me or Meg or Mik. We'll be happy if you're happy." Though the twins would no doubt be thrilled by the opportunity to dress up. They'd inherited their mum's interest in fashion.

She leaned toward him. "I truly want you all to enjoy yourselves."

"We will," he promised her. "But it's your day."

She ducked her head, her cheeks pink. He could tell he'd both pleased and embarrassed her.

"What have you got there?" he asked, gesturing at the stack of magazines beside her elbow.

"Oh, these?" She laughed, the sound light and cheerful. "I've been scoping out wedding dresses." She selected a magazine from a pile and showed him the dog-eared pages.

"I've marked my favorites, so I can find something similar or by the same designer."

Mark held out a hand. "May I?"

She passed it to him, and he flipped through the pages, pausing at the ones she'd marked. He scanned the photographs and the names of the designers that produced each of the dresses, noting that she seemed to prefer ones with sleeves and slender forms rather than puffy skirts or extravagant lacework. He was about to look at the fifth one when his subconscious sounded an alarm and his gaze skittered back to the designer's name on dress number four. *Clarissa Mitchell.*

"Hey," he said, as much to himself as to her. "I know her."

He turned the page around, and Rose shuffled closer, reading over his shoulder. "That dress is in my top three." She traced the line of the bodice with her finger. "Isn't it elegant? And I love the color."

"Pale pink?"

"Champagne is what it's called." As if he should have known. "I like that it's clearly not white—I don't want to be wearing white at my age—but it's not far off, and it's very flattering."

"Anything would be flattering on you, Mother."

"You're such a suck-up, darling."

"But you love me."

She pinched his cheek. "Rascal. So, did you say you know Clarissa Mitchell? How did you meet? She's one of the rising stars in the wedding industry, or so I've heard."

He chuckled at her enthusiasm. "I wouldn't know about that, and I suppose it might have been going a bit far to say I *know* her. She's one of my podcast's regular listeners, and we correspond by email sometimes. She seems like an intelligent woman. She certainly asks some good questions, anyway." Questions that occasionally stumped him to the extent he had to hit the books or use Google to find the answer—not that he'd ever admit such a thing.

Rose clapped her hands. "This is a sign!" she declared. "What are the chances I'd find a magazine that just happened to have a dress by a designer you know, and which just happens to be one of my favorites? It's meant to be." She settled back into her chair and crossed her arms over her chest in satisfaction. "I simply must have a dress by Clarissa Mitchell. That's all there is to it."

Mark groaned and buried his face in his palms. "Don't you go getting all 'cosmic force' and 'grand design' on me. It's a coincidence, pure and simple."

"No such thing," she said, setting her chin in such a way that he knew she'd made her mind up. Come hell or high water, she'd get what she wanted. "Now, why don't you be a dear and email your friend to arrange an appointment?"

He tried again to make her see reason. "The article says her boutique is in Dunedin. You'd have to fly to the South Island for an appointment."

"Something I can easily afford to do, as can you."

"But you'd find something you like just as much here in Auckland."

She shook her head. "It wouldn't have the same meaning."

He sighed. "Okay." Never let it be said that he didn't indulge his mother—especially when he'd been arguing only minutes earlier that her wedding was all about her and she should have what she wanted. Reneging now would be the height of hypocrisy. "I'll email Clarissa later today."

"Much appreciated."

For the remainder of lunch, they discussed more mundane topics, like his work, her upcoming jaunt to the Pacific Islands, and the latest stupid thing his sister Megan's boyfriend had done, in an ongoing saga of stupid things. They finished with coffee, then separated outside the cafe, Mark heading toward the Lockwood Holdings offices while his mother made the short walk to her private law firm. He took the elevator up to the top floor of the glass-and-chrome skyscraper, where Lockwood Holdings was based, and used his key card to let himself in, nodding to the receptionist as he passed.

In his office, he stripped off his navy blazer, adjusted his tie, and started his laptop. He opened the email account he used for the podcast and found the latest email from Clarissa. He knew exactly where it was, because he paid more attention to her emails than many of the others he received. Truth be told, she was refreshing—concise and to the point, which was very much not Mark's standard MO. She never engaged in pleasantries or included meaningless small talk. Perhaps others would find that off-putting, but considering the number of women who fawned over him because of the way he looked—not that he minded their fawning, mind you—her businesslike approach was a nice change. He never needed to worry that she might read more into their interactions than he intended. He tapped out a brief email.

Hi Clarissa,

My mother is newly engaged. She found out we know each other and has her heart set on wearing one of your dresses. We're looking at a wedding date about a year from now. Can you fit her in for an appointment sometime in the next month?

Regards,

Mark

He read over it twice. The email seemed too short and unemotional to convey how much this wedding meant to him, how important it was that his mother have the fairy-tale day she deserved. But really, what else was there to say? He hit Send.

ALSO BY ALEXA RIVERS

Little Sky Romance

Accidentally Yours

From Now Until Forever

It Was Always You

Dreaming of You

Little Sky Romance Novellas

Midnight Kisses

Second Chance Christmas

Haven Bay

Then There Was You

Two of a Kind

Safe in his Arms

If Only You Knew

Pretend to Be Yours

Begin Again With You

Let Me Love You

Destiny Falls

Stay With You

Come Back to You

Always Been Yours

ACKNOWLEDGMENTS

Thank you to all of the women I know who wear lab coats, kick ass and take names. You're an inspiration. Thank you to my early beta readers who told me where I was going off the rails and pulled me back in line. Thanks to Kate S and Serena C who helped make this story the best it could be—I couldn't have done it without you. Thanks to Deranged Doctor Design for designing me a gorgeous cover. Last, but certainly not least, thanks to my husband and family for their ongoing support and encouragement.

ABOUT THE AUTHOR

Alexa Rivers writes about genuine characters living messy, imperfect lives and earning hard-won happily ever afters. Most of her books are set in small towns, and she lives in one of these herself. She shares a house with a neurotic dog and a husband who thinks he's hilarious.

When she's not writing, she enjoys traveling, baking, eating too much chocolate, cuddling fluffy animals, drinking excessive amounts of tea, and absorbing herself in fictional worlds.